THE PURPLE BOW

The Purple Bow

Emil Mihelich

iUniverse, Inc.
Bloomington

The Purple Bow

iUniverse books may be ordered through booksellers or by contacting:

iUniverse
1663 Liberty Drive
Bloomington, IN 47403
www.iuniverse.com
1-800-Authors (1-800-288-4677)

ISBN: 978-1-4759-2707-8 (sc)
ISBN: 978-1-4759-2708-5 (ebk)

Printed in the United States of America

iUniverse rev. date: 05/24/2012

To the people of Butte, Montana, and to authentic
Butte people everywhere who have listened to the timeless love
song of the gallus frames and for whom John Keats meant to write:
"Butte is truth, truth Butte."

"It's still the same old story, a fight for love and glory, a case of do or die. The world will always welcome lovers as time goes by."

Herman Hupfeld
'As Time Goes By'

I

❀

$\mathcal{M}$y name is Dan Kristich, and you last encountered me in September of 1949 when I was five years old. I had just run the bases at Butte, Montana's Clark Park—sliding into home plate in a cloud of dust—after my dad, Pete "Snuffy" Kristich, entering the game as a pinch hitter, had just driven in Kenny Sykes with the winning run, clinching the South Side Athletic Club's first Copper League pennant. So, when you last saw me, I was brushing off some of the Clark Park dirt from my freshly-pressed corduroys and walking toward the open left field gate, with my two Copper League heroes. My mother, my sister, my grandparents and my dad's friend, Joe Mandic—Butte's renowned philosopher of the streets—were waiting for us as we walked through the gate, leaving behind, for then, the enchanted world of Clark Park.

But now it's early spring in 1962, and I'm 17 years old, almost 18. I still live in Butte, and I can't stop thinking. I don't know if I should blame William Shakespeare or Brother Kelley, my senior English teacher here at Butte Central Catholic High School, or simply Butte Central as it's known in athletic circles throughout the state or Boys' Central as it's always known in Butte. Boys' Central sits directly across the street from Girls' Central, but those of us who attend either school simply say we go to Central. That's enough.

I like being separate but equal and never have had any desire to attend Butte High, the co-ed public school and our hated athletic rival. To anyone who's part of Central the sight of the purple and white of Butte High inspires a hatred as intense as the love inspired by our own maroon and white. I don't hate the individuals who go to Butte High. I went to grade school with many of them in Butte's public school system and played baseball with them in Little League and Babe Ruth League, and I've been known to fall in love with a Butte High girl more than once. But I hate Butte High and love Butte Central or, as I said, Central.

It's important to admit that love and hatred because I've been thinking about Shakespeare's 'Macbeth' that Brother Kelley's been teaching. I can't help being impressed with Shakespeare and Macbeth and Brother Kelley as well. All three of them make me think. It's scary but adventurous at the same time. Brother Kelley says that if you don't think, you never understand anything. And if you never understand anything, you can't be an interesting person. He says that people who don't think, people who don't want to understand, are boring. He also says that if you don't understand anything, you never have anything of substance to say. He must understand because he has a lot to say.

I don't always understand the substance of what he says, but I want to. Shakespeare must understand as well because he, too, has a lot to say, and I can't help being impressed by how he says it. I like the majesty of his language because it seems to fit the situation he's writing about. Macbeth has some important things on his mind, and his thoughts deserve to be expressed in majestic language. If you think, the language isn't too obscure. Besides, I like majesty. Just think what a football game would be like, for example, without school colors, music, lights and fight songs.

I don't always understand Shakespeare's substance either, but I'm trying because I think he and Brother Kelley have a lot in common. In fact, I'm glad Brother Kelley's teaching 'Macbeth.' It's like Shakespeare really isn't dead, and it's easier to believe someone who's alive. You can tell Brother Kelley's a thinker because he's so passionate. He really teaches. He doesn't just make you memorize lines of poetry that don't mean anything. He's dedicated and his dedication should be returned. Any student in his class should want to listen because Brother Kelley is more than willing to explain what he understands.

Unlike the other Brothers, he tries to teach us how to think more than he does what to think, and I'm not so sure, as a result, that he has any real friends among them. But I can tell he's proud of his identity with the Irish Christian Brothers, or the International Child

Beaters as we sometimes call them, because his black cassock always is neat and clean. It may be covered with white chalk dust at the end of school, but it's always clean when we come back the next day. He reminds me of my dad who died in 1950, less than a year after he drove in Kenny Sykes with South Side's pennant winning run. I was six days away from my sixth birthday then, but I can remember my dad saying that he never would wear a dirty uniform to Clark Park. My mother always kept it clean and pressed and neatly folded and always laid it on the floor at the back of their bedroom closet. As you probably remember, I used to walk into the closet just to touch the uniform and trace with my fingers the SAC emblem, for South Side Athletic Club, that was stitched on the white jersey to the left of the red-trimmed, buttoned-down front.

I had a love affair with baseball then and I still do, even though I'm almost 18. I still haven't recovered from Bill Mazeroski's home run off Ralph Terry in the bottom of the ninth inning in the seventh game of the 1960 World Series, and that was almost two years ago. I never trusted Terry. I've always called him 'Rainbow Ralph' because of the slow curve he likes to throw. He must have hung one to Mazeroski because he hit it out of sight and sunk the Yankees. They humbled the Cincinnati Reds in five games last year, but I don't think I'll ever forget Mazeroski's home run. I you're a Pittsburgh Pirate fan, the memory of it instantly will bring back the rapture. But if you're a New York Yankee fan, its memory instantly will bring back the anguish.

I've had my share of rapture with the Yankees, and I suppose I have to experience my share of anguish as well, just to keep me honest. Still, if Bill Virdon's ground ball hadn't hit Tony Kubek, the Yankee shortstop, in the throat, Mazeroski's home run would have been harmless. But you can't predict baseball, with its built in anguish and rapture. It gets you when you're young and it never lets go. I'll be 18 this summer, and I have to admit that I can feel more alive from April to October than I can from November to March. I endure those months and celebrate the baseball months. Nothing compares to Opening Day.

Earlier this year Brother Kelley taught Geoffrey Chaucer and 'The Canterbury Tales.' I had a hard time understanding Chaucer because Butte's hardly a medieval town. I had never seen anyone in Butte wearing the costumes Chaucer describes, and I haven't spent too much time outside the Mining City, although I have visited Seattle and San Francisco. But then Brother Kelley pointed out that Chaucer's pilgrimage takes place in April, and only under certain conditions do people feel like going on pilgrimages. Then he mentioned that we greet Opening Day of the baseball season with similar enthusiasm. When he made that connection, I began to understand, and like, Chaucer.

I think he would be a great baseball fan. I still don't understand if the pilgrimage he describes is real or made up, but Brother Kelley says it doesn't make any difference. It's still the truth. I have to think about that a little more, but, for now, I'll take Brother Kelley's word for it. You can trust him. I'm beginning to think Shakespeare would be a great baseball fan, too. And I'm interested in Macbeth because I think he could be as well. But it seems to me that he wanted all rapture, and he wanted it all right now. If he could have decided to love baseball, or something equivalent to it, maybe he wouldn't have concluded that "life is a tale told by an idiot full of sound and fury signifying nothing."

Those are the words that have made me think lately. If Macbeth were some kind of a coward, I wouldn't pay any attention to them. But someone who can slit an enemy "from the nave to the chaps" is no coward. From what I've heard in stories about Butte and from what I've seen myself, Macbeth would feel right at home here and would be a match for any barroom veteran—both legendary and real. He wasn't without courage, and in Butte you learn to appreciate that virtue. As a mining town, it's a town of courage. I can't think of any other word that accurately describes what it takes to ride a cage down a mine shaft, day after day for years and years, to work in the depths of the earth. And I can't think of any other word that accurately describes what it takes to face life in a white frame house built in the shadow of a copper mine, a house that may have a black or dull orange slag heap—instead of green grass—for a lawn, a house clustered with others just like it and built on hills naturally formed by ancient volcanic action that never had cars in mind, a house removed from the green-grassed comfort of the country club. Maybe Macbeth isn't real, but courage is. I've seen it in the men who ride those cages, and I've seen it in the women who turn those houses into homes, slag heaps and all. Do those men and women think that "life is a tale told by an idiot full of sound and fury signifying nothing?" I've never received that impression, but then I've never thought about it before, either.

Macbeth's courage catches your attention, and his passion and eloquence make you think. And as Brother Kelley says, you have to think. You're supposed to think. He says the worse thing you can do is to avoid confronting Macbeth's conclusion because, you never know. He just might be right. He says only cowards choose not to confront it. Then he says we're boys from Butte and boys from Butte aren't cowards. They're boys of courage who aren't afraid, and he says we owe it to the men and women who have built Butte to confront the possibility that "life is a tale told by an idiot full of sound and fury signifying nothing."

He says that if you don't confront it, you can't become a man and that it's your duty to become a man and that you don't have to go down a mine shaft to fulfill your duty because if you do, there'll be no more men whenever, or if ever, the mines close down for whatever reason. He says that if you don't confront it, you'll never discover what life does signify, if it signifies anything, and you'll never be happy because you'll never truly enjoy life. He says people who have courage and people who then enjoy life are called heroes and that we should aspire to that heroism and to the accompanying enjoyment of life. He says that we should want to live as heroes or we have nothing noble to live for. I know he means what he says. He speaks with such eloquence and passion that even Shakespeare himself would have to listen.

Brother Kelley won't tell us whether Macbeth is right or wrong because, he says, then we wouldn't have to think and would be at the mercy of his conclusions. He says we should be free, that we should confront Macbeth's conclusion and that he has the job to teach us how to think about it so that we can decide for ourselves whether or not Macbeth's right. He says heroes are courageous and free. You can't help admiring Brother Kelley. He lives what he teaches. That's why I believe him. I don't want to be Brother Kelley because I'm Dan Kristich, but I want to be a hero. I don't know what I want to be beyond hero and myself just yet, but I do know that if I ever become a teacher, I want to be the teacher Brother

Kelley is. And if I ever become a writer, I want to be the writer Shakespeare is.

But right now I'm going to do what Brother Kelley says we should do. He says we shouldn't take anyone's word, one way or the other, for Macbeth's thoughts and leave it at that. He says we can think if we want to. He says we can test Macbeth's conclusion against our own 17 or 18 years of experience we all have accumulated right here amidst the slag heaps of what he calls "the ugliest city in the continental United States" but a city he believes to be "The Richest Hill on Earth"—just as the sign at the Greyhound Bus Depot indicates as it welcomes travelers to Butte. He says that if we test Macbeth's words against our own experience, we can decide for ourselves whether he's right or wrong. He teaches us to value our own experience. We just have to remember and think to interpret and understand. He says you have to have courage and demonstrate a desire to know. I want to have courage and I want to know. I don't want to be afraid. So I'm thinking and remembering. Brother Kelley's my hero now, but he's not my first. I have to think and remember back to 1950 to discover my first hero.

II

❀

*A*s you know, my dad wasn't a big man—he was only five eight and I've made it to five ten—but never has a man stood so tall in my eyes. His name was Pete, and I remember him as Dad. But most people who rode the city buses and who went to the ball games at Clark Park remember him as 'Snuffy.' My mother always called him Pete, as did my grandparents and aunts and uncles, but to everyone else who has ever mentioned him or talked about him with me, he was Snuffy. I've always been proud to be the son of 'Snuffy' Kristich. Not everyone has such a chance.

People who rode the buses knew him as Snuffy because he worked for the Butte City Lines for the last seven years of his life. He came to know Butte from his bus driver's seat, and he came to know its population. I can remember him talking to me about the city and its people with genuine affection that he said didn't really develop until he started to drive buses and began to notice the city he had come to take for granted. My sister, Judy, and I used to ride with him on the bus every now and then, and I can remember sitting on his lap and steering. I was driving a bus when I was four or five years old. I never thought anything was more important.

Only playing baseball could compete with driving buses. I always was impressed with my dad when I saw him dressed in his bus driver's uniform, but that was nothing compared to how I felt when I saw him dressed in his baseball uniform. He wore many uniforms during his 22 year career, but I only remember, first hand, the white and red-trimmed flannels of the South Side Athletic Club. And the walk to the ballpark—two blocks west on Aberdeen Street—with my dad dressed in his South Side uniform and with me carrying his glove and black, steel-spiked shoes, was the highlight of my life. I lived for that walk, and I lived to run the bases at Clark Park after the game was over.

I'm beginning my thinking and remembering in 1950 because, as I've said, that's the year my dad died—six days before my sixth birthday. I didn't know he was going to die. I didn't even know what death was, but my sister did and my mother did. My sister was ten and ten-year-olds know more about sickness and death than do five-year-olds. Judy asked my mother if my dad was going to die because she could tell that he was awfully sick, and my mother had to tell her the truth. She had to tell her he was going to die.

I knew he was sick because he swatted me once and it didn't hurt, and I could tell he couldn't throw a baseball with much speed anymore. Before, he made few concessions for my age. But I don't think I ever consciously thought about my dad dying. I really didn't understand death and its finality then. I do remember that he said he'd be home for my birthday when we took him back to the hospital in Missoula sometime in the spring of 1950—when he should have been in Clark Park playing baseball as he had been for the last 22 years.

I didn't even know that 1949, the year of his pinch-hitting heroics, was to be his last year as a player. He and my mother already had made that decision before he realized he was sick. It has to be hard to give up something after 22 years of devotion to it. I think September of 1949 until July of 1950 had to be hard on us in different ways. It's interesting how unaware you are at the age of five, but sometimes you can find out in a hurry. When you're five, the last thing you think about is whether or not "life is a tale told by an idiot full of sound and fury signifying nothing."

But Brother Kelley says you have to think about it sooner or later or you can't become a man no matter how deep into the shaft you ride the cage and no matter how much copper you mine. He also says that the younger you are the easier it is to confront what Macbeth eloquently expresses. The realization of the finality of death can make you confront the possibility of life signifying nothing as nothing else can. I kissed my dad goodbye in his coffin the day of his funeral, and I knew there was no way something that cold and waxen ever was going to come back to life.

Somehow I must have had Macbeth's thoughts in my mind ever since that day because when I came across his speech in the play and when Brother Kelley started talking about it, something happened to me. As I said, I always listened to Brother Kelley even if I didn't understand what he was talking about, but for some reason I listened more intently when he talked about Macbeth's speech and our need to confront the possibility of life being meaningless. He said we all would be better off for having confronted it, and then he said that maybe some of us already had and didn't even know it.

I don't know how his comment affected my classmates, but I know how it affected me. As soon as he said that some of us may already have confronted it without even knowing it, the image of me kissing my dad in his coffin came back to life. The image always was there. I never had forgotten it because I didn't want to. It represented the last memory of my dad, and I wanted to hold onto it. I don't think Brother Kelley necessarily had me in mind with his comments—he probably was thinking of his own experience—but he couldn't have been more effective if he had hit me with a sledge hammer.

After studying Macbeth's speech with Brother Kelley, I could see how Macbeth could say that life, which included the finality of death that I already had experienced, could be meaningless. But I wasn't immediately convinced it was meant to be, or had to be, meaningless. I thought my 17 years had to have some purpose. I hadn't taken them for granted. They had been exciting and they had been full of sound and fury. But I guess I hadn't thought about that sound and fury signifying anything. Then Brother Kelley said we should want to live as heroes to give our lives a noble purpose. I'd never heard that conclusion before.

I'd always accepted the Baltimore Catechism that said we were to know, love, and serve God in this world and be with Him forever in the next. My dad was in that next world, I was assured, and because I wanted to join him someday, I had tried my best to follow the catechism's direction. But then I started to think. Where was this next world? Just how far up there was it? I was curious, and I began to wonder what astronauts Alan Shepard and John Glenn really saw up there. I could see a lot of sound and fury surrounding us by

1962, and I knew it had to signify something or nothing. But then I thought—what if Alan Shepard and John Glenn, and the other space explorers who surely would follow, didn't find anything out there? I realized that we'd never ventured out into space before to test the answers we'd always accepted. What if the explorers found no proof? What if they found no evidence? What did we do then?

Brother Kelley was almost 40 years old, and he grew up in a different era. When he was 17, nobody was exploring space, making it easier to accept the answers offered in the Baltimore Catechism. I could tell he was thinking, and I began to think. If no next world existed out there, then my dad's death had to be meaningless. And if his death was meaningless, so was death for anyone else. And if death was meaningless, so was life. But if a next world did exist out there someplace, then both death and life were meaningful because you went to someplace better and life went on. But if you journeyed out there and didn't find any next world, you couldn't help confronting the possibility that life in this world was meaningless—with no place to go after it ended.

I have to admit that I'm scared. I almost wish we'd stay out of space. But I like the majesty and the adventure of it all. We have to journey into space, but on the possibility the explorers won't find this next world we've always counted on, I'm going to take a journey, too. I'm going to explore the past right here, and I'm going to start in the dugout in Clark Park in Butte, Montana, in the fall of 1950 after I went to first grade. I want to mine the past to see what I can discover. I don't want to be afraid. I don't want to conclude that "life is a tale told by an idiot full of sound and fury signifying nothing" if Alan Shepard and John Glenn don't find any next world up there. I don't want to give up that easily. I want to have courage because I want to be a man—just like my dad and Brother Kelley and my Uncle Tim Shannon.

III

I shouldn't have been sitting in the dugout. I had disobeyed Miss Healy, my first grade teacher, and I had disobeyed my mother. I had no intention of playing hooky when I left home that morning with my sister, Judy, for the Emerson School, just less than a half mile from our house on Aberdeen Street. We always cut through the grass of Clark Park on our way to school, and I always stared at the gray fence that hid the diamond and the dugouts from me. I've never seen Yankee Stadium, but at the age of 17 I know that I couldn't be more impressed by its majesty than I was at the age of six by that of the old, wood ballpark that sat on the corner of Wall Street and Texas Avenue in Butte, Montana.

I learned early that something special went on behind that fence and behind similar fences across the country. I remember that my dad's friend, Joe Mandic, who owned Joe's Doughnut Shop at the intersection of Park and Main in Uptown Butte and who played baseball for many years at Clark Park, always equated baseball with religion. In fact, he trusted baseball much more than he did church. I don't think I understand his ideas, completely, just yet, but I'm still thinking. Brother Kelley may have inspired me to think with his teaching of 'Macbeth,' but Joe Mandic, I'm sure, helped inspire me to think about the nature of religion and of God long before I encountered Brother Kelley and Shakespeare. The doughnut shop still sits between the Board of Trade and the Rialto Theater, but Joe Mandic no longer owns it. He died in 1960, ten years after my dad. Baseball defined them both, and no one can think of baseball and

Butte without remembering my dad and Joe Mandic. In my case, I can't imagine life without baseball, and, as corny as it may sound, I can't imagine ever not loving it. My friends think I'm crazy, and sometimes I even start to agree with them. But not for long.

I saw my first big league game in the summer of 1960 in San Francisco when I was 16. The Dodgers, led by Don Drysdale, Duke Snider, and Sandy Koufax, played the Giants, led by Willie Mays, Orlando Cepeda, and Willie McCovey. I've experienced many winters in Butte, but I've never been so cold as I was that summer night in Candlestick Park. The wind blew in from left field, and the game had to be stopped for at least a half hour as the fog obscured the outfielders. Finally, the Dodgers, behind Drysdale, beat the Giants, behind Sam 'Toothpick' Jones, 5-3. I remember the wind and the fog, but mainly I remember being disappointed because my big league experience in the concrete majesty of Candlestick Park didn't prove to be any more, or as, satisfying than did my Copper League experience in the wooden majesty of Clark Park. Now, I suppose the experience could have been different if I'd seen the Yankees and Yankee Stadium because I've always hated the National League and the Dodgers especially. I still can't stand the sight of Dodger blue.

In Candlestick Park I hated the Dodgers and felt indifferent toward the Giants. But in Clark Park I loved the South Side Athletic Club and hated whoever they played, whether it was Silver Bow Parks, North Side, Miners' Union, or McQueen Athletic Club. That love attracted me to the wood ballpark that held 6,000 people at the most while the concrete Candlestick Park held 40,000. At the age of 16 I'm not so sure I would have chosen to sit in its concrete grandstand if I had been given the choice of watching the South Side Athletic Club battle the Silver Bow Parks for the Copper League pennant at Clark Park or the San Francisco Giants take on the Los Angeles Dodgers for the National League pennant in Candlestick Park.

There was no Copper League, and there was no Clark Park, by 1960, but given the choice I'm not so sure I would have chosen the concrete grandstand over the since-burned-down wood grandstand. But I should be sure. It sounds like an easy choice to make. Why would anyone ever choose to watch amateurs, who really were miners and bus drivers, play baseball in a wood ballpark with a dirt playing field when he could watch professionals play the same game in a concrete stadium with green grass decorating the infield and outfield? I'm sorry, but it doesn't make any sense unless you consider love. I can't think of any other reason, and I can't think of any other reason for playing hooky and sitting in the dugout at Clark Park in disobedience to Miss Healy and my mother.

Uncle Tim wasn't very happy when he found me. I was sitting in the first base dugout, looking toward left field and watching the snow cover the Clark Park dirt, when I first spotted him. He walked through the same left field gate I had used earlier in the day. For some reason that gate was left open, but then I can't remember a time when it was locked. I walked through it during the summer and then during the winter when the baseball diamond gave way to the ice skating rink. I skated all winter under the shadow of the empty, wood grandstand, but the ice always melted sooner or later. I welcomed the ice, even if it meant the end of baseball because it helped me appreciate baseball's inevitable return all the more. I know I'm telling the truth because I remember Opening Day at Clark Park as being the happiest day of my life.

But I was scared as I watched Uncle Tim limp through the snow toward the first base dugout, dragging his walking cast that reached to his right knee. No one who knows Uncle Tim ever makes the mistake of confusing his name with timid. Tim is an Irish name, a Harp name, as he always says, and he's Irish through and through. I don't know anyone more proud of being a Shannon and an Irishman, and Uncle Tim was one of the few men who approached my dad's stature in my eyes. Of my five uncles he was the one who seemed to take up most of the slack after my dad died, probably because he was married, lived in Butte, and had the time. Still, he didn't hesitate to accept the responsibility, and being with Uncle Tim turned out to be almost as good as being with my dad and carrying his glove and black, steel-spiked baseball shoes to the ballpark. I'm almost 18 now, and I can't wait until I'm finally old enough to drink with Uncle Tim in one of his bars. But twelve years ago I was wishing that somebody other than he was walking through the snow. He took his role of uncle and male authority in my life very seriously. And I had disobeyed my teacher and my mother.

Uncle Tim didn't drive buses or play baseball, but he did build gallus frames—the black, iron head frames, or 'gallows frames,' that identified Butte's copper mines. And be could fight. If you couldn't drive a bus, the best of all occupations, and if you couldn't play baseball, the truest of all sports, then building the gallus frames that stood watch over the mines on the Butte Hill—or simply The Hill—and being able to fight had to be the next best thing as far as I was concerned. He still refers to the gallus frames as 'monuments to eternity,' and he's still proud of them. As long as Butte's around, he says, he can point to the gallus frames and say that he built them. But if they're 'monuments to eternity,' then so is Uncle Tim's nose.

No one ever could accuse it of being straight, and more than one bump rests on its bridge. But it's Uncle Tim's badge and a reflection of his courage, of his commitment to never back away from a fight. You don't have to win, but you have to fight when honor is at stake. He says you don't fight to prove how tough you are. Instead, you fight to defend your honor. Uncle Tim's honor has been challenged many times by the looks of his nose. Brother Kelley has inspired me to think quite a bit about Uncle Tim lately, especially when he told us we were boys from Butte and boys from Butte had courage. I'm thankful for having uncles like Uncle Tim, and I hope I can fight my battles with as much courage as they've fought, and continue to fight, theirs. I never want to forget Uncle Tim's nose. I've yet to see one that can surpass it in character and dignity. But I was thinking more of his belt than I was of his nose, and I was more scared than inspired as I watched him limp through the snow toward the first base dugout.

He was angry. He wore the walking cast on his right leg because he had fallen from a gallus frame a couple of weeks earlier and broken a bone in his right ankle. As a result, he couldn't perform his normal work as an iron worker for the Anaconda Copper Mining Company, and not being able to climb the gallus frames he helped build was enough in itself to make him mad. I watched as he limped along the left field line toward third base. He stopped and turned toward the dugout and then turned and looked across the infield. He stared through the snowflakes for a few seconds, and then I watched him stride across the diamond. He wasn't smiling when he reached the top step of the first base dugout.

"What in the hell are you doing here?" he asked, glaring at me as he held his hands on his hips.

"I don't know," I answered, looking up at him from my seat on the wood bench.

"You don't know? What do you mean you don't know? If you don't know what you're doing here, why are you here?" he continued, still standing in the same position.

"I don't know," I answered again.

"Do you know that half the city of Butte is out looking for you?" he asked.

"No," I answered.

"Well. Do you know where you are supposed to be?"

"Yes."

"Where?"

"Home."

"Why aren't you home then?"

"I don't know."

"Aren't you cold," he asked, stepping into the dugout out of the snow.

"Not really. I was watching the snow and didn't notice the cold."

"How long have you been here?"

"Since after lunch sometime."

"How did you get here?"

"When I got back to school after lunch, I didn't have my reading book I had this morning when I left home. I told Miss Healy that I must have lost it in the park on the way to school this morning, and she said that I should go look for it and that I should come right back, even if I couldn't find it."

"Did you look for it?"

"Yes."

"Did you find it?"

"No."

"Then why didn't you go back to school as you were told?"

"I don't know. I wanted to go back to school because I told Miss Healy I would, but I didn't. I walked around the fence instead and walked through the left field gate."

"You know you're supposed to obey Miss Healy because she's the teacher, don't you?"

"Yes, I know. But I didn't want to disobey her. I didn't do it on purpose."

"Did somebody force you to walk into the ballpark and sit in the dugout?" Uncle Tim asked, sitting down on the wood bench and leaning over at the waist, placing his hands on his thighs.

"No," I answered, backing away from him a little.

"Don't back away from me when I'm talking to you. Sit up and look me in the eye."

I tried to look him in the eye, but I couldn't. I was too afraid, I guess, and mostly I just looked out the front of the dugout across the field as Uncle Tim continued to question me.

"Have you been sitting here all the time?" he asked.

"I ran around the bases lots of time, but then it started to snow. Then I came into the dugout and sat down."

"Why didn't you go home?"

"I don't know."

"Miss Healy finally called your mother to ask where you were. She thought you could be home looking for your book or that maybe you couldn't find it and decided to go home."

"I like Miss Healy. She's nice, and she always has paste on her fingernails."

"If she's so nice, why didn't you obey her? If you had obeyed her, I wouldn't have had to traipse around in the snow half scared to death that something had happened to you. Didn't you think we'd worry about you when you didn't come home when you were supposed to?"

"I didn't know about the time. I didn't think it was so late."

"It'll be getting dark soon."

"I know that now, but I didn't think of it until you came. I'm sorry. I don't know why I came to Clark Park."

"You have to be obedient. You have to do what your teachers and your mother say. Do you understand?" Uncle Tim asked, staring at me.

"Yes," I answered, trying to look him in the eye.

"You're lucky we found you. I looked all over before I thought of looking in Clark Park. I didn't think you could get in. I thought all the gates were locked this time of year. Baseball is over, and it hasn't been cold enough to ice skate until now," he said, looking out into the deepening snow that by now had completely blanketed the infield and outfield.

"The left field gate never is locked. It's always open."

"I'll know that next time," he said, standing up from the bench. "Come on, we'd better get home before your mother has a fit," he added as he picked me up by the arm and guided me toward the dugout steps. "I'm not through with you yet," he said as he followed me up the steps and out onto the snow covered infield dirt.

IV

❀

*I*t was the longest and most silent two block journey from Clark Park to my house on Aberdeen Street I had taken, have taken, or ever will take. I walked out of that ballpark many times with my sister, my mother, and my dad—and sometimes with my grandparents and even once with Joe Mandic—always carrying his black, steel-spiked shoes and baseball glove. And I walked out of it many times alone, or with my friends, from 1951 until May of 1957 when it burned down in a blaze that lit up the entire Flat, the section of Butte that fills the valley floor south of The Hill. I stood near the left field fence, just to the left of the gate, and watched the grandstand burn like a box of matches. I've never seen anything like it, but I guess wood ballparks can burn.

The ballpark burned down just like my dad died. I wish my dad were still alive, and I wish Clark Park still stood like the gallus frames as a monument to eternity. But life isn't that way. It's brutal, come to think of it, but, still, it doesn't seem to be anything we can't handle. It's been almost 12 years since my dad died and almost five years since Clark Park burned down, and my mother and sister and I haven't just lived in despair ever since those deaths. We haven't cried every day and every night. I don't remember crying at my dad's funeral, but I remember crying after the fact when I began to understand death's finality when you lowered the coffin into the ground and left the cemetery.

But I do remember choking back tears at the sight of the Clark Park grandstand burning to the ground. I was 13 then, and I knew more about the finality of death. I knew in my heart that the days of

Clark Park were gone forever. I knew the ballpark never would be rebuilt. Still, a lot of sound and fury surrounded the lives of Clark Park and my dad, and they can't just signify nothing. That sound and fury wasn't meaningless. Maybe my dad and Clark Park died, but I haven't yet. There must be something about both those lives that I can discover while I live. I'm not embarrassed to say I loved my dad and I loved Clark Park. I can't think of any other word to accurately describe my feelings.

Brother Kelley says you have to have courage. He must mean you have to have courage to love because what you love has to die, and the resulting pain hurts. If he's referring to that kind of courage, I feel better because I'm afraid of heights, and I can do without elevators. The gallus frames are tall, and the cages that raise and lower the men in the mine shafts are small and the shafts are deep. If having the courage to love in the face of death helps turn a boy into a man, then I think I'm on my way, and I feel better. I even loved Uncle Tim, even though I knew the path we were walking together, the path I had walked so many times before, was—this time—a path of punishment. I had no black, steel spiked baseball shoes to carry as Uncle Tim and I made our way toward the open gate in left field, leaving behind only footsteps in the fresh snow that now obscured the dirt playing field that extended to the gray barrier enclosing the ballpark.

Uncle Tim never said a word to me all the way from the dugout to my house. Sometimes, when South Side lost, my dad didn't talk, either. I knew when they won because he always smiled and laughed on the walk home and we delighted in listening to the soft sounds of the sprinklers throwing their water on the green lawns of Aberdeen Street. But when they lost, my dad was silent, and the swishing sound of the same sprinklers throwing the same water on the same green lawns of the same street was too loud. Usually, a walk through the first significant snowfall of a Montana winter is quiet and refreshing. You don't pick up the sounds of sprinklers throwing water anywhere. You only hear the occasional scrape of a snow shovel contacting the concrete and the continuous crunching of the snow compacting under the weight of your feet. You have to welcome the snow that closes out the green grass season just as you have to welcome the ice that closes out the baseball season. If you don't welcome the snow and ice, you can't celebrate the thaw that ushers in each new season of green grass and baseball.

But the walk Uncle Tim and I took in the first significant snowfall of the winter of 1950 wasn't usual and refreshing. It was just quiet. I heard the snow crunching under my feet and under Uncle Tim's walking cast, but I wasn't used to the sounds of labored breathing that accompanied the footsteps in the snow. Uncle Tim didn't enjoy the walk anymore than I did. It was the last thing he envisioned himself doing with me. But he never was one to take the performance of duty lightly, and in this instance duty clearly called him to administer the punishment for my act of disobedience. As I walked, I prepared myself for what I was going to have to endure, and I thought Uncle Tim was preparing himself for the punishment he was going to have to administer when we finally reached the narrow sidewalk that led to my white, three room, frame house sitting at the back of the two-lot lawn that stretched out toward the snow covered, asphalt street. Standing at the top of my sidewalk, too narrow to accommodate the both of us walking side by side, Uncle Tim finally broke the silence.

"You go first," he said, hesitating and motioning me to lead the way.

"Okay," I said, looking up at all six feet of him, standing there amidst the snowflakes without a trace of a smile crossing his face. I felt as though I was leading the way to my own execution as I stepped onto the narrow sidewalk that led to the white house resting comfortably at the back of the snow covered lawn with the white steam from the chimney rising to meet the wet snowflakes falling from the twilight sky. I've walked this path many times in my dad's black, steel-spiked baseball shoes that I liked to wear over my own rubber-soled shoes. I always liked to listen to the steel spikes clatter on the hard concrete. But this time I only heard the familiar sound of crunching snow and the unfamiliar sound of heavy breathing as Uncle Tim dragged his cast behind me and struggled the last 80 feet on the way to my house—and to my execution.

We reached the front porch, and I could see my mother and my Auntie Loo, Uncle Tim's wife and my mother's sister who is the second youngest in a family of eight children. Her real name is Lucille, but everybody calls her Loo, and to my sister and me she is never anything but Auntie Loo. In fact, she never will be anything else, no matter how old we are and how old she is. As I stood on the porch, she and my mother looked warm and comfortable in the well-lit living room, and for a moment I forgot that both of them probably were worried as well as angry, especially my mother. She was a person of admirable energy, and I'd almost rather have Uncle Tim angry with me. But I was in big trouble now that I had both of them to contend with. I was about to open the porch door and walk inside when Uncle Tim spoke to me again after he had caught his breath.

"You wait for me in there," he said, pointing in the direction of the dark garage, sitting at the end of the gravel drive-way to the right of the house.

"Isn't it locked?" I asked hopefully.

"No," he answered. "I opened it earlier today before I left to go searching for you. You go in there and wait for me. I have to go in the house and talk to your mother and aunt for a minute. Do what you're told this time. Go into the garage and don't leave. Now get in there," he added finally, throwing his right arm in that direction.

Obediently, I took my hand off the porch doorknob and walked down the short sidewalk toward the door on the side of the garage as Uncle Tim watched at the porch door before he opened it and disappeared inside, leaving me outside with my thoughts and standing at the threshold of the cold and dark garage. I opened the door and stepped inside into the darkness to accept my punishment like a man.

V

❀

Once I stepped inside the garage my imagination got the best of me, and I thought of the conversation my mother, Auntie Loo and Uncle Tim had to be having in the house. I didn't see my sister, Judy, when I stood at the front porch. Wherever she was, she must have found herself in a little trouble for not taking better care of me. But a ten-year-old girl only can take on so much responsibility. In the long run she had nothing to do with me playing hooky. Miss Healy didn't send her along with me when I left school to look for my book. Besides, with my dad's death she had lost some of her childhood and already had assumed responsibility she could have avoided, at ten, under normal circumstances. Still, I must have seen her as sharing in my trouble because I didn't include her in the imagined conversation that was going through my mind.

"What are we going to do?" my mother asked.

Uncle Tim just stood there with his hands on his hips trying to think of what his father would have done, or did do, in similar situations. He was only 26 himself and didn't have any children of his own. I had provided him with his first experience with being an authority, and he was aware of the responsibility that accompanied the role—just as he was aware of the responsibility that accompanied his role as a ironworker on The Hill. But on the job he wasn't in charge. On The Hill he had to be obedient. If he weren't, he'd lose his job. But he was the authority with regard to me, and he had to think of how the authority of his childhood taught him to listen to, respect and obey his elders. As he thought, he remembered his father's belt, and that's what I expected as I waited in the dark garage.

"Maybe we ought to go easy on him," Auntie Loo said. "Maybe he went to Clark Park looking for his dad. Maybe he's trying to figure everything out. I don't know, but I'm not so sure you have to resort to the belt under the circumstances."

"My dad used the belt when I disobeyed," Uncle Tim said, "and I never disobeyed again. I think that's what Dan needs now. He has to learn his lesson," he added, unbuckling his belt buckle. "And it's my job to teach him," he continued, drawing the belt through the loops of his Levis.

"But this is different," Auntie Loo offered in my defense. "I don't think he meant any disrespect, even if he did disobey. Besides, we all know how much Pete and Clark Park meant to him. Maybe he's been punished enough. Think of what must be going through his mind as he waits out there in the dark garage."

"I've been thinking about that, Loo," my mother said. "But I have to raise Dan to be a man. I know life is brutal, but I wish Pete hadn't died. I don't want to pamper Dan or spoil him, and I don't want him to feel sorry for himself. I have to decide on the punishment. But then maybe you're right, Loo. Maybe he's been punished enough without Tim having to take any action."

"Snuffy told me to take care of his kids before he died," Uncle Tim said. "I have to teach Dan to obey just as he would."

"But would Pete use his belt?" Auntie Loo asked.

"Only if he thought he absolutely had to," my mother answered.

"I don't hate my dad for using his belt," Uncle Tim said. "If it worked for me, it'll work for Dan," he added, rolling his belt into his right hand. "I think he has to learn."

"But with the belt?" Auntie Loo questioned once again.

"I'm hesitant," my mother answered, "but go ahead, Tim. Do what you think you have to do. Just don't overdo it."

"I won't. He'll take it like a man," he said as he walked toward the front door, grasping his belt with his right hand.

I stood in the dark garage and waited and imagined until I heard real voices outside the door. Then I waited and listened. I recognized Uncle Tim's voice first and then that belonging to Dave Hennesey, my next door neighbor.

Dave's wife, Marlene, died a couple of years after my dad, and I can still see him leaving his house, wearing his dark blue suit, on the day of her funeral. His head hung down as he walked out the front door, and when I spoke to him as he walked down the steps of the stoop in front of the house, he looked up so that I could notice his red eyes. I've always respected Dave, although no one's ever expected me to refer to him as Mr. Hennesey, and he's always taken a special interest in Judy and me. At one time I even hoped he and my mother would get married. But sometimes it's better not to see too much of people who affect you the way Dave did me. I'm not sure he could have lived up to the image I created of him.

He must have known I'd been missing all afternoon, and he must have seen Uncle Tim and me walk down the sidewalk leading to my house. As I said, Dave always took a special interest in Judy and me, and he must have been curious to see what kind of punishment Uncle Tim had planned for my act of disobedience. As my next door neighbor, Dave knew he wasn't the male authority in my life. But I'm sure he had my best interests in mind when he walked out his back door to meet Uncle Tim who walked out our front porch door, gripping his belt now tightly wrapped up in his right hand.

"What are you going to do, Tim?" Dave asked.

"I'm not sure it's any of your business," Uncle Tim answered.

"Maybe you're right. But I don't want you to hurt him."

"What do you think I am?" Uncle Tim asked angrily. "Some kind of monster? I'm not going to hurt him, but maybe he has to learn to obey. And maybe this belt can help him learn that lesson. And maybe you'd better step back into your house and stay out of this. What do you think?"

"Take it easy. I know it's none of my business, and I didn't come out here to choose you."

"You better not because it wouldn't be the smartest thing you've ever done in your life."

"Listen, I'm not here to fight you or anyone else," Dave said, raising his voice a little. "I'm just interested. You can do whatever you think you have to do, and there's nothing I can, or should, do about it. I just don't want to see Dan hurt, that's all. If he has to learn his lesson, that's fine. But maybe he already has. I think you ought to consider that before you use your belt."

"No one wants to see Dan hurt," Uncle Tim said, more calmly now. "That's why we already decided not to resort to the belt. Miss

Healy probably shouldn't have sent him to look for his book in the first place. Anyway, when he didn't find it, he went to Clark Park instead of going back to school. After traipsing all over The Flat, I finally found him sitting in the first base dugout like he was waiting for his dad to come trotting in from second base. I was wet and cold and mad and there he was, just sitting there as if it weren't snowing or anything. What do you do in such a situation?"

"I don't know. What did you do?"

"I stood on the top step of the dugout and stared at him. And then I asked him what the hell he was doing sitting in the dugout in the snow."

"What did he say?"

"He said he didn't know. And he probably didn't. He's only six years old. I'm 26, and I'm not sure why he was there, either."

"I know what you mean," Dave said. "It can't be easy to lose your dad when you're only five."

"You're right. My dad's still alive. I wonder how I would have reacted if he had died when I was Dan's age. I remember bringing him his bucket of beer as soon as I spotted him walking home from the mine. It was the highlight of my life."

"I used to watch Dan walk down the sidewalk toward Clark Park, carrying Snuffy's baseball glove and his spikes. No doubt about it. That had to be the highlight of his life."

"I'm sure you're right. I couldn't get over seeing him sitting in that dugout, and I didn't notice the snow and cold all the way home. I just kept thinking that I was going to have to punish him. I know I scared him to death because I didn't say a word. He probably was thinking about my belt all the time," Uncle Tim said, laughing now. "But this isn't simple. He did disobey, but then he didn't, when you stop to think about it. He didn't exactly disobey some boss on The Hill to prove how tough he is. You've seen those guys. Dan wants to do the right thing. If I did punish him with my belt, I think he'd accept it."

"Well, are you? I see you have it wrapped up in your right hand."

"I have to admit I was. It was the first thought that came to me when I saw him sitting in the dugout. But I was still wet and cold. I would have wanted to hit anyone then, and I don't think I saw Dan at first. Instead, I saw someone who had made me get out in the snow with this goddamn cast and look for him when he should have been home. But when I saw Dan, I began to think. And walking home I thought some more. And by the time we made it to the house, I decided the belt wasn't the way to go, although I don't think Dan realized it then. And I'm sure he doesn't now."

"What are you going to do?" Dave asked.

"I'm only going to scare him a little. I'm going to walk into the garage carrying my belt, but I'm not going to use it. I couldn't use it, but it won't hurt to scare him a little. I think he'll get the point."

"I'm sure he will, if he hasn't wet his pants already, standing in that dark garage waiting for you."

"You're probably right," Uncle Tim said with a laugh. "I'd better get in there and get it over with before he wets them too much and before you and I catch pneumonia."

"Yes, it is snowing. I'd better get back in the house. I just wanted to see what was going on. I didn't mean to interfere."

"That's okay," Uncle Tim said. "I just have one question."

"What's that?"

"What would you have done if I'd said I was going to use this belt?" Uncle Tim asked, holding up his right hand.

"I don't know. I may have played the fool and tried to stop you."

"I think I would have been a fool to decide to use it. I'm glad neither one of us had to act foolish. See you on The Hill, Dave."

"Right, Tim," Dave replied, his voice growing more faint as he walked toward his house. "Stay out of the snow with that cast."

"I will if I can keep kids in school where they belong," Uncle Tim said, his voice growing stronger as he walked toward the dark garage.

I don't know what I would have done if I hadn't overheard most of the conversation between Uncle Tim and Dave. Maybe I didn't overhear all of it, but the conservation's not a lie, even if I made up some of it. I know Uncle Tim and Dave Hennesey, and I'm sure they'd say those things. Uncle Tim's a fighter and Dave isn't, but Uncle Tim's much more tender-hearted than he likes to let on. And Dave would fight if he had to. One of these days I'll have to ask Uncle Tim just exactly what he and Dave said to each other that night. I know he won't lie to me, but I also know he won't tell me the exact truth. He likes to make up things, just as Chaucer and Shakespeare did. And none of them are trying to lie.

I didn't try to lie, either, when I told you about my imagined conversation while I waited in the garage. But my 17-year-old imagination was doing most of the talking. When I was six, I only knew I was going to be punished with my uncle's belt because such punishment typically followed an act of disobedience. And I had disobeyed. But I'm 17 now, and I can see it wasn't quite so simple for my mother or Auntie Loo and Uncle Tim. I'm beginning to realize that assuming the role of authority isn't easy. I know it wasn't easy for Uncle Tim. I'd heard my share of stories about fathers and belts by the time I was six, and they had succeeded in scaring me into obedience under normal circumstances. My dad was dead, but I knew Uncle Tim wouldn't hesitate to use the belt as he thought a father should.

But these circumstances weren't normal. The more I think about it, the more I realize that my love for my dad had to be awfully strong because I knew I was being disobedient. I knew I was going to be punished. I knew what the punishment was going to be, and I knew who would administer it. I knew all that, and still I walked into Clark Park and took my seat in the first base dugout.

VI

I may have heard Uncle Tim say he wasn't going to use his belt, but nonetheless he still cut an imposing figure as he stood in the shadowy garage doorway, grasping the belt in his right hand. If I hadn't heard his conversation with Dave, I don't know what I would have done at the sight of him standing there. I almost match his six foot height now, but then I was only six and he was as tall as he is today. He doesn't look as big to me these days because I can stand and look him directly in the eye, although he keeps reminding me that I'm not man enough to fill his shoes yet. He says he has to keep me humble, but he doesn't have to worry about that. Sometimes I think I'll never be man enough to fill his shoes. But I want to try.

I still admire Uncle Tim, and I'm not six years old anymore. I'm 17 and beginning to learn how I can be an Uncle Tim without having to climb gallus frames and fight. If I have to climb gallus frames and fight to make it, I might be a lost cause. I don't like heights, and I prefer not to fight unless I absolutely have to. I'll defend my honor when it's necessary, but so far it hasn't been challenged as much as Uncle Tim's has, I guess. Maybe times are changing or maybe I'm just growing up, but fighting doesn't hold the attraction it once did. It doesn't seem as heroic. Uncle Tim was, and is, a real man. But I don't think it was then, or is now, just because he could, and can, fight.

Still, when you're six years old and small and disobedient, a six foot figure, grasping a belt in his right hand and standing in a shadowy doorway framed against a background of early evening snowflakes, can be awfully scary. When Uncle Tim dragged his cast across that threshold, I know I would have fainted if hadn't overheard his conversation with Dave. To this day I've never seen a more intimidating and frightening figure than that which Uncle Tim presented, framed by the light of the first snowfall of the winter and the darkness of the garage. I saw something to fear and nothing to love. I wouldn't want to offend anyone who looked as mean as the figure standing in that doorway.

Luckily, the figure framed by the whiteness of the snow and the darkness of the garage wasn't real. That was merely a figure. Uncle Tim was a man. He was real. So I didn't faint when the man dragged his cast across the threshold. I felt relieved because I knew he was real. And I knew, thanks to overhearing his conversation with my next door neighbor, that he was more to be loved than feared, even if he was brandishing a belt in his right hand as he approached me.

I acted afraid because I didn't want him to know that I'd heard his conversation with Dave, and I didn't want him to get the idea that I wasn't aware of the seriousness of my offense against Miss Healy and my mother. It's not easy to act afraid when you know you have nothing to be afraid of. When Uncle Tim sent me to the garage, I was petrified, but now that the threat of the belt had vanished, the fear had disappeared as well. But I still had to act afraid. If I didn't, Uncle Tim would have thought I was arrogant, and he hated arrogance. If he thought I was acting arrogant as he walked toward me in the garage, he would have used the belt. So I had to act afraid. As Uncle Tim moved toward me, brandishing his belt, I backed up against the wall of the garage without saying a word and covered my rear end with my hands.

"Do you think you've learned your lesson?" Uncle Tim asked as he continued to walk toward me, now grasping the belt in both hands.

He was putting on a pretty good act himself because he couldn't appear to be too soft and feel sorry for me just because my dad had died. His death didn't provide me with any real excuse to disobey, although any disobedience was understandable, considering the circumstances. But I was too young to pick up the idea that it was okay to disobey authority anytime it was convenient. Uncle Tim was acting, but I didn't dare laugh—no matter how humorous he appeared as he stood in front of me, snapping his leather belt by alternately loosening it and then pulling it together with both hands.

"Did you hear what I said?" he asked, moving closer to me and still snapping his belt.

"Yes," I answered weakly, looking up at him and still covering my rear end with both hands.

"Well, are you going to disobey your teacher or your mother again?"

"No," I answered sheepishly, still looking up at him and at the belt he held in his hands.

"Are you sure?" he asked, standing over me now.

"Yes," I answered, still covering up with my hands.

"Do I have to use this belt just to make sure?" he asked, now showing me the belt.

"No," I answered, leaning against the wall.

"Okay," Uncle Tim said, slipping the end of his belt through the loops in his Levis. "But you listen to me."

"Okay," I said, dropping my hands to my sides.

"You have to obey your mother and your teachers. You know that, don't you?"

"Yes."

"Do you really know why you disobeyed?"

"Not really. I didn't mean to."

"I know you didn't, Dan," he said, kneeling down in front of me on his left knee. And as long as you mean that, you shouldn't have to be punished with the belt. Do you understand?"

"I think so."

"If you wanted to disobey, you should be punished with the belt because then you would have been disrespectful. It's wrong for boys and girls to act that way towards their parents, teachers and other adults. If I thought you were being disrespectful in that manner, I would have to show you how not to display that behavior. And maybe the belt would help you learn. Do you understand?"

"Yes, I think so," I answered, looking him in the eye.

"I believe you, Dan. I don't think you wanted to disobey. Maybe you had to go to Clark Park. Just don't use the ballpark as an excuse to skip school. Do you understand that?"

"Yes," I answered with admiration rather than with fear.

"You have to grow up, and part of the process involves understanding that your dad is gone. But if you love him, you don't have to let him die. Do you see?"

"Yes," I said, still looking him in the eye as he knelt on his left knee in front of me.

"Okay," he said, smiling and slapping me on the rear end with his right hand. "Your mother hasn't seen you in a while. She's in the house with your aunt. You'd better get in there and show both of them that you're all right," he added, giving me a little push toward the garage door.

I walked toward the shadowy doorway and stopped just on the edge of the garage's darkness to look back at Uncle Tim, still kneeling on his left knee where he had left me.

"Go ahead," he said. "Get into the house before I take you over my knee."

I smiled, stepped out of the garage into the snow, and tried my best to walk in Uncle Tim's adult footprints as I made my way to the front porch door.

VII

George Lewis is as about as opposite from Uncle Tim as you can get. He doesn't climb gallus frames and he doesn't fight. His nose is prominent because his head is small and balding, not because it's broken and scarred like Uncle Tim's. He has no specific ethnic identity to be proud of, and even Uncle Tim's own receding hairline seems appropriate and comfortable with his Irish heritage. I've never laughed at Uncle Tim's baldness, but I did the first time I saw George take off his hat that night he came to our house to take my mother out, almost two years after my dad's death and my own first grade act of disobedience.

I was used to my dad and Uncle Tim. I was used to bus drivers, baseball players, iron workers and fighters. I was used to real men. And now here in my house I saw a man wearing loose brown slacks and a top coat, that hid his round shoulders, and a gray, felt hat, that hid the bald head I was about to discover and that completed a figure of a man more comical than imposing. That figure, standing in the shadowy doorway of a dark garage brandishing a belt in his right hand, wouldn't have inspired fear in anyone. And on the strength of its first impression, it wouldn't have inspired anyone to walk in its footsteps, either.

But George is the type of man who grows on you if you give him a chance. Neither Judy nor I was looking for a father, I don't think. I already had chosen Uncle Tim, although I'm beginning to understand that in some way my dad still was very much alive. It's hard to let go of something or someone you really love, which explains what I was doing that day sitting in the dugout at Clark Park. I wasn't willing to let my dad die that easily. Maybe that's what Brother Kelley has in mind when he talks about the power of the hero. Death can't destroy the devotion a hero inspires. In fact, it seems that death actually can strengthen it.

I know my dad's dead, but my devotion to him isn't—almost like his death gave me something to live for. Maybe that helps explain why Macbeth's words about life being meaningless affected me so much. They seemed to oppose what my experience was telling me. But Macbeth was eloquent and passionate, and you have to listen to eloquence and passion. It may be expressing the truth. Still, neither Judy nor I needed a hero when George came into our lives, but we must have known that our mother needed, and deserved, something. I suppose that explains our curiosity when she first told us she was going on a date. I'll say this for her—she told us she was going out. She didn't ask us if it was okay. But she did explain to us one night after dinner, about a week before George came to the house.

"Before we do the dishes," she began as we were finishing our hamburger patties and mashed potatoes and gravy she had fixed after work, "I have something very important to tell you, and I want both of you to listen carefully."

Judy and I finished our last bites of mashed potatoes and looked at each other, wondering what our mother had to tell us. She'd never sounded quite so serious before, and neither one of us, I don't think, anticipated what was to follow. But we were ready to listen, just as we were told.

"Okay, Mom. We'll listen" Judy said, putting down her fork.

"We'll listen, Mom," I contributed, following Judy's example.

"Both of you know that no one ever will take your dad's place," she said. "Judy, you know that, don't you?"

"Yes, I know," Judy answered.

"And you, Danny?"

"Yes, I know," I answered emphatically.

"But it is possible for a woman to love another man after her husband dies," my mother continued. "You don't ever forget your husband, but life has to go on. And it's not wrong to love someone else the same way you loved your husband. Your dad is dead and he's gone, but I learned a lot about love in the 13 years we were married.

I know what love is, and it wouldn't be wrong to find that same love with someone else. It would be wrong to say you've found it when you know you really hadn't. Do you understand?"

"I think so," Judy answered.

"And what about you, Danny?"

"I think so. Do you love someone else already?"

"No, not yet," my mother answered with a laugh. "But I hardly would call two years already. Do you think we should call two years already?"

"No, I guess not," I answered. "It just doesn't seem that long."

"I think two years is a pretty long time. I'm 12, and you're only seven," Judy offered in support of our mother.

"I know. But I'll be eight this summer."

"Let's not argue about time," my mother broke in. "The older you get, the more aware of it you'll become. I'll be 38 in November, you know."

For the first time I remember being aware of my mother's age. Before, I never thought of her or my dad in those terms. I was only seven, going on eight, and my mother was almost 38. If she was 38, I thought, then my grandmother must really be old because her face revealed many more wrinkles than did my mother's. I think I've been impressed with age ever since then. When I was eight, 38 seemed old and 68 seemed ancient. Now that I'm almost 18, 38 doesn't seem quite so old anymore, even if 68 still does. It's interesting, as well as impressive, to live a long time. If you live 68 years, for example, you have to accumulate a wealth of experience. Uncle Tim's almost 38 now, and he still seems pretty young. But he can tell some great stories. They're true in some way, but at the same time I can tell they aren't. He makes up much of what he says, but Brother Kelley says that something made up doesn't necessarily have to be false.

For example, I have to make up some of the conversation between my mother, Judy and me. But that doesn't mean I'm lying. I just can't remember the conversation exactly as it happened. But my mother knew about love. She wasn't afraid to love my dad. And now that he'd died, she was telling us she wasn't afraid to love again. She was a courageous woman, and she'd never entered a mine shaft or climbed a gallus frame. She wasn't afraid, which explains why Judy and I listened to her. We listened and knew that she'd never settle for anything less than what she had experienced with my dad. Even if she were to marry again, Judy and I knew that the man she married would love us just as our dad did. Thus we felt secure as my mother continued.

"But I'm still young enough to experience love again," she said. "I may be 38, but that's not quite as old as either of you might think. When you're my age, I guarantee you'll understand. Do you see what I mean?"

"Yes," Judy answered confidently.

"And, Danny, how about you?"

"I think so," I answered.

"Sometimes life can get lonely after you've been used to being married for 13 years."

"Do you want to get married again, Mom?" Judy asked as I sat up straight.

"It's not that I want to so much. It's just that I would if I ever loved someone as I loved your dad."

"Do you still love Dad?" I asked.

"I'll always love your dad. Don't ever forget that. But I could love another man at the same time because love is bigger than any one person. In other words, your dad isn't the only man I could love. Do you understand?"

"I think so," I answered.

"I think so, too," Judy said. "But why are you telling us all this. Are you going to marry someone?"

"Hardly," my mother answered, laughing. "I have to fall in love first. I thought you were listening."

"I was, but I just got mixed up there for a minute," Judy said.

"That's okay. I'm not going to marry anyone just yet, but I am going to go out with someone."

"When?" I asked abruptly. "Does he play baseball? Does he work on the gallus frames?"

"Next Friday night," my mother said in answer to my first question. "And no, he doesn't play baseball, and he doesn't work on the gallus frames."

I sat back in my chair as my mother continued to answer questions, and Judy continued to listen attentively. I wasn't too sure this person, who was going to go out with my mother, was much of a man. He didn't meet my standards, but Judy was older and still interested.

"I really don't know much about him," my mother went on, "other than his name is George Lewis and he's a machinist."

"What kind of a name is Lewis?" I asked. "And what's a machinist? Does he build big machines?"

"What difference does it make?" Judy asked, looking at me. "You should just be glad Mom has a chance to go out."

"I am glad, but I'm curious. I've never heard the name Lewis before, and I don't know what a machinist is. I know Kristich is a Croatian name, and I know Shannon is an Irish name. But I don't know what kind of a name Lewis is. And I've never seen a machinist. So there."

"Well, good for you," Judy said.

"Stop it, both of you," my mother interrupted angrily. "It probably doesn't, and shouldn't, matter as Judy says, but it doesn't hurt to ask, either, as long as you really want to know. You have to remember that not everyone is a Kristich or a Shannon, and not everyone can play baseball and climb gallus frames. Do you both understand?"

"I think so," Judy and I answered together as I sat up in my chair again.

"In that case, I can tell you more about him. I haven't met him yet."

"You mean you haven't seen him yet?" I asked in disbelief.

"It's called a blind date, stupid," Judy said, looking straight at me.

"I'm not stupid. Besides, you don't know everything."

"I know more than you do. I'll be in the eighth grade next year and you'll only be in the third. When I go to high school, you'll still be in grade school."

"So? I'll be in high school some day."

"By that time I'll be in college," Judy replied with a smirk.

"All right, that's enough," my mother said. "If I knew it was going to be so much trouble, I wouldn't have told you about George Lewis. You'll both grow up soon enough. Let it happen naturally. Don't try to force it. Trying to make it happen, or thinking it's already happened before the fact, is almost as bad as trying to prevent it from happening. But for now, Judy's right. My coming date is a blind date, Danny, because you don't know and in some, if not most, cases have never seen the person you're going out with."

"Why do you want to go on a blind date?" I asked. "Why don't you go out with someone you've already seen?"

"Some men I know have asked me, but they're all friends of your dad. I don't feel right going out with them. I think I'd rather go out with someone who didn't know your dad. I don't want anyone feeling sorry for me, and I don't want anyone taking me out because I'm Snuffy Kristich's widow. Your dad was awfully well-known in Butte, and many men would like to be seen with his widow. They might not really care about me. I want someone who wants to go out with me. Do you understand?"

"Yes," Judy answered immediately.

"I think so," I answered a little doubtfully.

"Plus," my mother went on, "going on a blind date can be adventurous, just as going out with your dad always was. But I'm honestly interested in George Lewis. I think I remember him from my younger days when I still lived in East Butte. I think he lived on the West Side, and I'm sure he used to come to some of our dances in East Butte and McQueen."

VIII

*B*utte was, and still is, a city of neighborhoods and boundaries that you crossed, and cross, with caution. But I think the circumstances were different during the era my mother had in mind. I don't think people crossed the neighborhood boundaries as easily as they do now. Everyone was loyal to their neighborhood, and they didn't exactly trust outsiders. Uncle Tim enjoys telling stories about those days. He's from the North Side and Centerville, more than half way up The Hill in the heart of the mining operations, and you still can identify his neighborhood by the Mountain Con gallus frame. The Mountain Con, short for Mountain Consolidated, is the deepest mine in town, and both it and its gallus frame belong to Centerville. When you grow up playing in the shadow of that gallus frame and on the rocks of the mine's slag heaps, you develop a fierce loyalty to it. You may live in Butte, but you love Centerville.

As a result, you can have a tendency to hate the other neighborhoods, like East Butte and McQueen or Meaderville located on the East Side of The Hill close to the foothills of the Continental Divide. Those Butte neighborhoods had the Leonard Mine, but its shaft wasn't as deep as the Mountain Con's and its gallus frame, sitting at the bottom edge of the east side of The Hill, wasn't easily visible from all over town. When Uncle Tim spoke of monuments to eternity, he had the Mountain Con gallus frame in mind. If he didn't build it personally, he grew up in its shadow. And it stood tall and straight and proud, straddling the mile-deep shaft—the deepest shaft on The Hill.

But at least East Butte, McQueen and Meaderville had its mine and gallus frame like Centerville, Corktown, and Dublin Gulch—situated on the lower slope of The Hill just south of Centerville—identified by the Kelley Mine and its accompanying gallus frame. Uncle Tim did, in fact, work on the Kelley gallus frame, and to listen to him tell it, he drove in every rivet all by himself—making it the only gallus frame in the world that one man built with his bare hands. I never tire of listening to Uncle Tim tell stories about Butte. In fact, sometimes I think Butte is one, big story and that its people are natural storytellers, even if they don't realize it. There must be something to those gallus frames, mines and slag heaps. The people who have embraced them never run out of stories.

Brother Kelley grew up in Centerville and knows Uncle Tim. I'm not sure if Uncle Tim knows Brother Kelley in return, but I've told him some of my uncle's stories to find out whether or not they're true. He never commits himself one way or the other, but he always smiles when I tell him one of Uncle Tim's stories. Like Shakespeare and Chaucer, Brother Kelley understands things. He understands Butte, for example. Like him, I believe it's 'The Richest Hill on Earth,' and, like him, I want to understand why. I want to understand the magic.

In the old days, if you grew up next to a slag heap and under the shadow of a gallus frame, you were convinced that any existing magic didn't extend beyond the boundaries of your neighborhood. It stopped where Centerville or East Butte or McQueen or Meaderville or Corktown or Dublin Gulch or Fintown ended, and you crossed those boundaries at your own risk. If you did cross them, you did so with humility. Uncle Tim spent his youth either defending his neighborhood or crossing somewhat arrogantly into others, and he has the nose to prove it. When he talks about fighting, you listen because you easily can recognize his expertise. I like to listen to his stories about those days. The people he refers to are alive. They love something and they hate something, and they aren't afraid to defend what they love.

It must be important to love and to hate. The people from the gallus frames and slag heaps sometimes hated each other, but if they shared the same love and hate, at least they were together. They lived in their own ethnic neighborhoods—mainly either Irish, English,

Finn, Italian, Serbian or Croatian—and near their own mines, but they had something in common. None of them held any special love for those who lived on Butte's West Side or on its South Side, comfortably removed from the gallus frames and slag heaps. They associated such citizens with arrogance as they moved away from the gallus frames into the Victorian homes of the West Side and onto the green-grassed lawns of the South Side that extended further south toward the country club. I live on the South Side, on The Flat, and I enjoy my green grass. But I can't help being impressed by the gallus frames and have no desire to escape their embrace.

Butte still has its neighborhoods and it's still a city of sound and fury, but it's changing. The city I live in today isn't like the Butte Uncle Tim describes in his stories. Some of the prominent places are gone now, and I haven't had a fight since I was six years old, when Uncle Tim sent me back outside to fight Jerry Stanich who had chased me all the way from school to Uncle Tim's house. He told me not to be afraid and that he didn't care if I lost. But I had to fight. I did and received a black eye for my trouble. But so did Jerry. I was as proud of that black eye as Uncle Tim is of his nose, but it didn't last much longer than a few days and I have little desire to get another one. I suppose I will if I have to, but I'm not so sure Uncle Tim is trying to encourage it with his stories.

I don't think he understands what he's trying to communicate, but I bet Brother Kelley does. He believes in stories, and I think he understands what the story is saying even if the storyteller doesn't. So, I'll have to ask him someday. I'll ask him if he thinks Uncle Tim fought out of love and duty because if he did, then his stories—and Butte's story—are love stories. Macbeth slit his enemy "from the nave to the chaps," but he was a Scot who lived up to his duty and fought out of love for his country and his king. Maybe that's why I feel sorry for him. If you have to fight and if you fight for duty and love, at least the sound and fury will signify something. It's too bad Macbeth didn't grow up in Centerville under the shadow of the Mountain Con gallus frame. Maybe it would have made a difference.

But Butte's different. The neighborhoods are changing, and the city is pushing further out to the south past the country club where the gallus frames are hard to distinguish. At least I can still see them clearly from Clark Park whenever I want to. I know I'm going to leave

Butte when I go to college this fall, but I've already promised myself that I'll never forget the gallus frames, even if they're out of my sight. I could never look Uncle Tim in the eye if I ever forgot them.

The Butte my mother and Uncle Tim liked to refer to sounded like a divided city. But the neighborhood boundaries could be crossed, as long as you crossed them quietly. Those boundaries, although not as recognizable, still are intact, and from Uncle Tim's stories I've learned to cross them quietly and not loudly as if I deserve instant acceptance. People loyal to a neighborhood like Centerville deserve as much from someone raised in the green-grass comfort of The Flat. You can grow up with green grass or with slag heaps and learn to love something bigger. You can learn to love Butte. If you live on The Flat or the West Side and want to remain in sight of the gallus frames, you're welcome in the neighborhoods that depend on them for their existence. The gallus frames united Butte and still do because they're monuments to eternity. They're made of iron and, unlike the wood structure of Clark Park, can't burn down.

I've heard hundreds of stories about fights in Butte's neighborhood bars because the bar must have been the field of honor for men like Uncle Tim. But I've never heard stories about fights in Clark Park, unless someone was referring to a prize fight of some kind. Everyone came to Clark Park. It didn't belong to any neighborhood like The Goodwill belonged to Centerville or like the Club 156 belonged to East Butte or like the Yellowstone or the Helsinki belonged to Fintown. The neighborhoods needed their bars, and the people felt proud to identify with them, but Clark Park belonged to Butte. And the people from the neighborhoods were as proud of their ballpark as they were of their bars.

Clark Park was Butte's ballpark and not McQueen's or the North Side's or the South Side's or the Silver Bow Parks. It didn't belong to the Miners' Union either, but they, along with the neighborhood athletic clubs, fielded teams in the Butte Copper League. There were no boundaries in Clark Park, only turnstiles and gates through which passed the people of Butte to celebrate the magic of baseball. I lived well within sight of that ballpark and I could hear all its sounds. It's gone now, but I've promised myself I'll never lose sight of it and I'll never stop hearing its sounds. I just wish it would have been made of iron. It may be rusty by now, but it still would be standing. Still, maybe I'm better off with it gone. I don't think I could stand to see it sitting empty and rusty and silent.

Meaderville, lying at the bottom of the eastern slope of The Hill, belonged, and belongs, to Butte as well—although it was, and is, an Italian neighborhood. But it belonged to Butte, and still does, because of its supper clubs. The restaurants, like the bars, belong to the neighborhoods. But the supper clubs in Meaderville—featuring steaks and fried chicken accompanied by generous portions of spaghetti and ravioli—like the ballpark on The Flat, belong to Butte. I've never heard stories of any brawls at Clark Park, and I've never heard about any in Meaderville's nationally famous Rocky Mountain Cafe, either. You go to celebrate and you don't have to worry about defending anything or challenging anyone. You forget your neighborhood identity and there's nothing left to fight for—or maybe there's something bigger to defend that isn't threatened. I don't understand all the details yet, but I think there's something about the supper club and the ballpark that's bigger than any neighborhood. I get the same feeling whenever I visit the Columbia Gardens.

The Gardens belongs to Butte, too, even though it's maintained by the Anaconda Company. I have no great love for the Company, but it does operate the Gardens. Once again, I don't know all the details, but I've been told that it's part of the agreement the Company made with W. A. Clark, the acclaimed copper baron and politician from Butte's early days at the end of the 19th century and the beginning of the 20th, when it bought all of his mining holdings and took control of The Hill and the city. I can feel sad sometimes when I think of Butte being so dependent on the Company, and the popular story claims that Anaconda burned down Clark Park. I wouldn't be surprised, but the ballpark was made entirely of wood and such a structure can burn down. Besides, Butte likes to blame the Company, or give it credit, for anything that happens.

When Uncle Tim tells stories, he doesn't seem to blame anyone for anything. But when people talk about the Company, they always either blame it or praise it. In some way the Company did build Butte, but in another way it had nothing to do with it. I think Brother Kelley would say that individuals built Butte with their courage. But then he doesn't see the Anaconda Company as Butte. Instead, he sees courage defining it. If you ask me, I don't think the Company cares one way or another. They just want to make money, and they'll maintain the Columbia Gardens as long as Butte makes money for them. I hope it always makes that money because Opening Day at the Gardens is every bit as inspirational as Opening Day at Clark Park used to be.

The Columbia Gardens belongs to Butte—and no one ever should call it an amusement park in the presence of any loyal Butte citizen, regardless of any neighborhood identity. Uncle Tim says you have to fight when your honor is challenged, and if an outsider wants to scare up a fight in Butte, he only has to insult the Columbia Gardens—purposefully—by calling it an amusement park. Such a park is a place for cheap thrills. The Columbia Gardens is a place of magic to be treated with the reverence commanded by any Roman Catholic Church, complete with its stained glass windows, altar tabernacle, crucifix, votive candles, statues, incense burner, stations of the cross, and spires reaching toward the sky—as if to touch Heaven.

I said earlier that I liked majesty. I like the majesty of the supper clubs. I liked the majesty of Clark Park, and I like the majesty of baseball. I like the majesty of religion, and I like the majesty of the Columbia Gardens. I'd never think of an amusement park in conjunction with majesty. Anyone who sees the Columbia Gardens as an amusement park never would understand baseball or religion and never would understand Shakespeare or Chaucer. No one can tell me that Shakespeare and Chaucer didn't like majesty. If they didn't, they never could have written 'Macbeth' or 'The Canterbury Tales.'

It's interesting that the majesty of the Columbia Gardens equals that of the Catholic Church. The Gardens, then, has to be nature's church because I feel equally inspired by the majesty of the Immaculate Conception Church or St. Pat's or St. Joe's or Sacred Heart or St. John's or St. Ann's or Holy Savior or St. Mary's or St. Lawrence. Come to think of it, I felt the same inspiration in Clark Park. And I know I'd feel it in Yankee Stadium as well. Macbeth never must have seen a Catholic Church. How could anyone see such a structure without being inspired? In the same vein, it's too bad Macbeth never had the chance to see Clark Park or the Columbia Gardens.

W. A. Clark might have exploited the mineral wealth of the Butte Hill and the men who mined it, but he gave us the Columbia Gardens and I don't care why he did it. Anyone who gives a city something like the Gardens deserves to have its ballpark named after him, regardless of his motives. Other cities may have their amusement parks, but taking a picnic to Butte's "Garden Spot of the Rockies" certainly was more adventurous than taking one to an amusement park—or even simply to the Columbia Gardens. No matter how many times you visit the Gardens, it's always like going for the first time. It was, and is, amongst the truest of adventures.

I'm sure you can find more lavish floral displays and I'm sure you can find greener grass somewhere in the country or the world, but I don't think you'll find a floral display or green grass anywhere more inspiring than what you'll find at the Gardens. And I think I know why. First of all, the flowers die every fall, and you can pick them on the last day of the Gardens' season. Picking those flowers reminds me of welcoming the ice at Clark Park. You have to welcome the ice and you have to pick the flowers. That's the way life is supposed to be. As I said before, I don't think baseball would be the same if you didn't welcome the ice, and I don't think the Gardens would be the same if you didn't pick the flowers. Maybe it sounds sad, but you have to do it. Besides, life is more adventurous because the ice has to melt and the flowers have to come back. Clark Park burned down, but the ice still melts, and the pansies always bloom again at the Gardens. It's interesting. People like to go to the Gardens when the flowers begin to bloom and the grass begins to turn green. I think Chaucer would understand the Columbia Gardens. Maybe Butte is a medieval town after all.

It certainly is a mining town. And as a mining camp that has lasted well into the 20th century, it's more than earned its designation as the Mining City. By its very nature mining is not what anyone would call clean, and a city completely dominated by that industry can't help but reflect its presence. Because of the mines and their slag heaps—and because of the houses clustered around them, seemingly without any sense of order—no one ever would accuse Butte of being beautiful. Brother Kelley refers to it as "the ugliest city in the continental United States," and he has to be right. I've been to Seattle and San Francisco and never would refer to either city as being ugly.

But without this ugliness, I don't think the Columbia Gardens would be so beautiful. Bright red, white, purple and violet floral displays are pretty and the ordered flower beds certainly decorate the green, manicured, gently flowing lawns. But without the ugliness of the black or dull orange or murky yellow of the slag heaps and without the wood frame houses clustered around the gallus frames, the Columbia Gardens would be just another attractive amusement park—and not 'The Garden Spot of the Rockies.' I think you have to live with the ugliness to see the beauty, and as long as Butte has the Gardens, I wouldn't do anything to alter the Mining City's appearance.

When my mother talked about dances in Butte, she usually referred to those held at the Gardens in the imposing dance pavilion that's still visible from almost any point in the city. You can't miss its bright white siding and red, tile roof. The pavilion is huge and rows of Chinese lanterns, hanging from the ceiling, light up the inside with the soft glow of candle light. And if you can't fall in love at the Columbia Gardens under those conditions, there's no hope for you. I've never seen anything like it. We don't have many dances at the Gardens anymore because music is changing. When the rock n' roller Gene Vincent came to town a few years ago, for example, he didn't perform at the Gardens. It didn't see appropriate.

But we still hold our proms there because we have to hire dance bands. I have to admit that I'd rather dance to Elvis Presley and Buddy Holly, but I'll endure a dance band just to experience the Gardens. The big bands my mother talks about always played at the pavilion, and from listening to her stories, I can tell that going to those dances had to be the highlight of her life. I'm glad I've had the chance to enjoy the same experience because it helps me understand my mother, even if she is 47 years old. I hope she always can dance at the Columbia Gardens. And I hoped George Lewis could dance like she always said my dad could.

Unlike the neighborhood dance halls, such as the Winter Garden Uptown and the Boobnega in East Butte, the Gardens' pavilion belonged to no section of the city. Instead, it belonged to Butte, and someone from the West Side found himself more welcome at the Gardens than he did at the Boobnega. East Butte, with its black, Pittsmount slag heap and Leonard gallus frame, didn't trust the West Siders with their green grass and Victorian houses. And furthermore, East Butte boys were especially protective of East Butte girls.

The same somewhat holds true today when we go to CYO dances. I live in St Ann's parish on The Flat, and I walk softly when I go to a dance at the Immaculate Conception or St. Mary's on The Hill because neither represents my territory. But I feel different at a mixer at Central after a football or basketball game or at a dance at the Finlen Hotel or the Masonic Ballroom or even at the Miners' Union Youth Center. None of those dance halls resemble the Columbia Gardens Pavilion, but you don't have to be quite as careful, with neighborhood and parish boundaries not being so evident. I understand my mother now when she talks about dances she attended when she was my age and older, but I didn't understand quite as well when I still was in the second grade. But I did understand fighting, and I wanted to know where she thought she'd seen George Lewis before.

IX

❁

"**D**o you remember George Lewis from the Boobnega or from the Columbia Gardens?" I asked, scooting up to the edge of my chair.

"Why don't you just let Mom talk?" Judy asked, sneering at me. "Stop interrupting her."

"I'm not interrupting her, and I am letting her talk. I just want to know, that's all. I don't know everything like you do."

"If the two of you would quit snapping at each other and listen, you might learn something," my mother said impatiently. "I'll tell your brother when he's out of line, Judy. That's not your job, even if you are almost in the eighth grade. Just be Dan's sister. You don't have to try to be his mother, although I appreciate your concern."

"See, she told you."

"That's enough out of you," my mother said, looking me directly in the eye. "I don't know where you'd be without Judy. So don't be so smart. Do you understand?"

"Yes," I answered as Judy smiled.

"Now maybe I can answer Danny's question," my mother said, relaxing once again. "I attended a lot of dances at the Boobnega and the Columbia Gardens, and it's hard to remember sometimes. East Butte boys didn't like the boys from other neighborhoods coming to their dances. As an East Butte boy, your dad belonged in that category, and I didn't like him at first. I thought he was just a little too cocky. Sometimes an East Butte girl could be attracted to a West Side boy and didn't want the protection of any East Butte boy. In those circumstances their loyalty bordered on the obnoxious. I never experienced a dull moment in those days, but you had to be careful if you were a West Side boy coming to an East Butte dance."

"Was a dance at the Gardens different?" Judy asked.

"Yes. The Gardens didn't belong to East Butte as did the Boobnega. Everyone went to the Gardens. I think we went to the Boobnega because we liked to be defended by the East Butte boys, even if they were cocky and obnoxious. But we went to the Gardens to fall in love. Nothing surpassed dancing at the pavilion. I didn't find your dad quite as cocky at the Gardens, and I'll never forget dancing with him. He was a good dancer. But I don't remember George Lewis from the Gardens. So I must remember him from the Boobnega."

"Did he fight?" I asked with great interest.

"No, I don't think so. Remembering fights at the Boobnega is the same as remembering dances at the Gardens. If he fought, I'd remember. But his name sounds familiar, if not special. He probably was one of the West Siders the East Butte boys chased away from the Boobnega."

"And he didn't even fight?" I asked again.

"One of these days, Danny, you'll learn that sometimes those who fight can be greater cowards than those who don't. Your dad didn't fight, and just because George Lewis didn't fight at the Boobnega doesn't mean that I shouldn't go out with him. If I don't like him, I won't go out with him again."

"If he lived on the West Side, he must have been rich," Judy said.

"Not everyone from the West Side is rich," my mother said. "Some people live more on the fringes. They might hope to be rich someday, but they aren't always rich at the time. I have a hunch George Lewis fits that description. If he were rich, I don't think he'd be taking me out."

"Why not?" I asked.

"Because he probably wouldn't even know me."

"But Dad was famous," I said. "Everyone knows you."

"Maybe everyone who follows baseball does. But not everyone follows baseball."

"Does George Lewis?" Judy asked.

"I don't know. But I'm sure I don't remember him from Clark Park."

"Do rich people go to Clark Park?" I asked.

"Not all of them. Some of them think they have better things to do."

"Do people who want to be rich go to Clark Park?" Judy asked.

"Not always. Sometimes they're too busy trying to get rich."

"Would you like to get rich, Mom?" I asked.

"I wouldn't mind it. We could have a larger house, for example. Wouldn't you like to live on the West Side?"

"No," I answered emphatically. "It's too far from Clark Park. I'd rather live here and go to Clark Park than be rich. Would we have to stop going to Clark Park if we were rich?"

"No," my mother answered. "We could be rich and still go."

"I just want to go to Clark Park," I said. "I hope George Lewis isn't rich, and doesn't want to get rich. And I hope he follows baseball."

"Well, we'll find out next Friday. In the meantime, you two better get the dishes done while I run the carpet sweeper over the living room rug," my mother concluded, getting up from the table.

"Okay," Judy said. "Come on, Dan. I'll wash and you dry. And be careful. Don't drop any dishes."

"I'm coming, and I won't drop any. And stop being so bossy," I said as I got up from the kitchen table to help her clear off the dinner dishes. "If getting rich makes you stop going to Clark Park, I never want to get rich. Nothing is that important," I muttered to myself as I carried my plate and glass the few steps to the kitchen sink.

For the next week Judy and I lived in anticipation of next Friday when George Lewis would come to take our mother out. And I know she lived in the same anticipation because she didn't seem as tired after a day at the county courthouse where she had worked for about a year now. She stayed home for a time after my dad died, but then she found a job, half days, at the courthouse working in the Clerk and Recorder's office. I think we needed the money, but I also think my mother had to get away from the house. Three people living in a three room house can get pretty close, especially for the adult who has to put up with two children. Now that she was working full time, Judy and I had a lot of time to spend alone in the house, and we made the most of it. I don't remember ever feeling abandoned just because my mother wasn't home when I came home from school. She was doing what she had to do for us, and Judy and I came to look forward to having the house to ourselves. In fact, sometimes we even resented my mother being there. Then we had to treat the house as a house—and not as a bowling alley or as a bar complete with shuffleboard.

When you welcomed the ice at Clark Park, you had to move indoors, to the bowling alley, for example. And if we were lucky, sometimes we were allowed to accompany our uncles to the neighborhood bars where we became acquainted with shuffleboard. When my mother wasn't home, Judy and I easily could transform our kitchen into a bowling alley or into a bar with our dining table serving as a shuffleboard and cans of potted meat serving as the pucks. As long as we were bowling with our miniature pins set in the far corner of the kitchen next to the porch door and with our smooth, round, steel marble serving as our bowling ball or as long as we were playing shuffleboard on the kitchen table with our potted meat cans, we enjoyed the time we had alone. Believe it or not, a bowling match or a shuffleboard game played in that kitchen always proved to be adventurous. Even when Judy reached high school and when I was older myself, we still would get out the pins and potted meat cans every now and then. Isn't it strange how a kitchen bowling match or shuffleboard game can take on such importance?

I don't think I understand why Macbeth had to be king, although I can see where he deserved to be someday. I'll have to ask Brother Kelley if he doesn't happen to explain my problem in class. He says we have to listen to the experience we have accumulated in the "ugliest city in the continental United States." When I listen as he says, I get the impression that kings are the most unhappy. I've always missed my dad, and I probably always will. But I've never been as unhappy as Macbeth. But then I've never had to live on the West Side, and I've never wanted to leave Clark Park or our three room house. I've always been content to stay put.

X

❁

"Do you think we'll like George Lewis?" I asked Judy one day when we were picking up the bowling pins and putting away the potted meat cans before my mother came home from work.

"I don't know," she answered. "We just have to wait and see."

"He sounds so different from Dad or from Uncle Tim. I can't picture him going out with Mom."

"You've never met him."

"I know, but I can picture him. I just can't picture him going out with Mom. Can you?"

"You just don't know much about dating," Judy answered. "When you get older, you'll understand more. I can picture him, and I can picture Mom going out with him. But I can't wait to see what he looks like. I hope he's handsome."

"I think you have a different picture in your mind than I have in mine because you're a girl. I can't picture Mom with the George Lewis I have in my mind."

"Maybe so," Judy said. "But I can picture the two of them together. I think Mom will have fun. She hasn't been out in a long time."

"I know. But he doesn't sound like her type."

"Maybe we'd better let Mom decide that. Besides, haven't you noticed? She hasn't raised her voice to us this week."

"You're right," I said. "And she doesn't seem to notice if the house is a little messy. She hasn't redusted the end tables, and she hasn't run the carpet sweeper over the living room rug after you've vacuumed it. She still can raise her voice though."

"I wouldn't know how to act if she didn't," Judy said with a laugh.

Now that I look back and remember, my mother had a lot to be angry about. First of all, she was angry with my dad for deserting her and leaving her with two kids to raise. I know she felt that way because I heard her tell Auntie Loo. During the course of the same conversation I also heard her say that she was mad at the Church's God. She didn't understand why that God would take my dad when He left countless men who couldn't measure up to him. Auntie Loo always told her that my dad was better of in Heaven with God and that he was needed more up there than he was down here and that God had called him home.

Auntie Loo's explanation might have made sense to me, but it only made my mother more angry most of the time. That's the very God she was mad at, she would say. Couldn't that God see how much Pete was needed down here? They always went to church and they never went to show off, like some of the hypocrites who sat in the front pew. Why didn't that God take those hypocrites first? she would ask, sometimes in desperation. And Auntie Loo always would say that God knows best. I think she meant well, but sometimes she only succeeded in making my mother more angry. And she could direct that anger toward Judy and me—sometimes accompanied by language I've only heard in a dugout.

Auntie Loo's explanation sounded good and made sense until you stopped to think about it. I didn't think about it too much when I was young because I just took it for granted that she, as an adult, knew what she was talking about. Besides, according to the catechism, God always did know best, and you were supposed to obey God. If you didn't, you were in big trouble. Look what happened to Adam and Eve when they disobeyed God. We're still paying for that act of disobedience.

But now that I think about it, that standard explanation, authorized and supported by the church pulpit, doesn't seem fair. I didn't eat the apple, and if I'd have been in that Garden, I wouldn't have eaten it. So why should I have to be punished for something I didn't do? But wait a minute. I disobeyed Miss Healy when I was in the first grade, but that didn't make me bad or evil. I respected Miss Healy and wanted to obey her. I wasn't trying to defy her authority. Instead, I was obeying another authority which then created the appearance of disobedience.

But I really wasn't disobedient. On the contrary, I was obedient when you stop to think about it. Uncle Tim, Auntie Loo and my mother couldn't be mad at me for what I did. And you know what? I can't be mad at Adam and Eve for what they did, either. Look what happened when they ate the apple. Think how happy we'd be if they had obeyed God. But then maybe I would have eaten the apple as well. After all, I did disobey Miss Healy. When you think about so-called established truths, they don't always make sense. And now we're exploring space where Heaven and God are supposed to be. What if the story of Adam and Eve is made up?

Brother Kelley says that something made up isn't necessarily false. But does that mean the God in the story of Adam and Eve isn't real, that He's simply made up? Is He the God who lives in Heaven and who created everything down here? Brother Kelley's certainly right about one thing. When you think, sometimes automatically accepted answers don't make sense. In that case what do you do? Do you give up or do you look for sensible answers? I think the hero Brother Kelley talks about chooses the second path. I don't think the hero is afraid. But, still, I don't know. It's scary, and life appears to be easier when you don't think. But Brother Kelley says if you don't think, you can't be a man. So, I guess you have to think and find answers that make sense. Maybe Adam and Eve—especially Eve—weren't afraid. Maybe they were heroes. It's something to think about.

I think Judy and I must have realized my mother needed an outlet for her anger, and Judy and I happened to be available. If the answers the Church provided to her questions could have been more satisfying to her, I think Judy and I would have been spared some anxious moments. My mother could be gentle, as you imagine all mothers to be, but when she was angry, she was a match for any father—as you imagine all fathers to be.

But I'm thankful she didn't pretend. When she was angry and bitter, she let us know. She didn't try to deceive us. Now that I think about it, I don't see how she could help but be bitter, considering the circumstances. How could you possibly love a God who took away your earthly husband because He felt he was more needed with Him? My mother couldn't accept such an explanation that depicted God as being cruel and selfish. Does this God enjoy seeing His children suffer? If He does, I'm not so sure I trust Him. But I think my mother thought she had suffered enough. No wonder she welcomed the anticipated arrival of George Lewis more with a smile than with a frown. Her enthusiasm only made Judy and me more curious. Our mother never was a weepy woman, and when she stopped raising her voice, you knew something big was in the wind.

"I think she'll always be Mom," I said, responding to Judy's laugh. "I don't want her any other way, but it is nice to see her smile a little more often."

"That's because she has something to look forward to again. I'm excited for her."

"So am I. But I still want to see George Lewis. I don't know anyone who doesn't go to Clark Park."

"I don't either. But maybe a person doesn't have to go to Clark Park."

"How could someone not want to go?" I asked. "And I can't picture Mom going out with anyone who doesn't want to. I can't picture her with anyone who'd rather be rich instead. Did Dad want to be rich?"

"I don't think so," Judy answered. "I think he just wanted to play baseball. That's why we live here. He wanted to stay close to Clark Park."

"Do you think Mom wants to leave Clark Park? Do you think she wants to be rich?"

"I don't know. But I think it's hard for her to remember Clark Park all the time, and I think it sounds good to have more money so that we could live in a bigger house."

"But this house is big enough. Don't you think?"

"I think it is," Judy answered. "But wouldn't you like to sleep in your own bedroom when you grow up? Do you always want to sleep on a hide-a-bed?"

"I've never really thought about it. I don't mind sleeping on the couch. I don't have my own room, and neither do you. But we can bowl and play shuffleboard in the kitchen because we have the entire house to ourselves."

"I know. But I think Mom worries that the house is too small. She'd like to think she could give us something more comfortable."

"Aren't you comfortable? What else do you need?"

"I'm comfortable and you're comfortable for now. But I'm not sure Mom is. She's not a kid, you know. She's an adult."

"I know. But why can't an adult be comfortable in this house?"

"Can't you see it's a little small?"

"It looks big enough to me."

"That's because you're only seven years old."

"Yes, but I'll be eight this summer."

"Mom will be 38. She can see that the house is a little small."

"I don't want to leave here just to be more comfortable. That's not a good reason to move. Do you think Mom would move just to make us more comfortable?"

"I don't think so. She knows how much this house means to us. It means a lot to her, too, but she's an adult. I think adults see things differently than we do. We're not grown up yet."

"I know, and I want to grow up right here close to Clark Park. And I don't care if I have to sleep on the couch the rest of my life. I don't want to move to some big house on the West Side. I'm from The Flat. I'm from Clark Park, and I want to stay here."

"So do I. And I think Mom understands that. She wouldn't move us just to make us more comfortable. She might be tempted, but I don't think she'd give in."

"What would make her move?"

"I think she'd move if she loved someone else like she loved Dad. Then I think she'd move, even to the West Side. But I don't think she'd move for any other reason."

"That makes me feel better. Do you think she'll love George Lewis like she loved Dad?"

"I don't know. We'll have to wait and see."

"How could she love him like she loved Dad?"

"I don't know," Judy answered again. "But we have to trust her. We have to believe in her. Still, we'd better put the kitchen back together before Mom comes home from work or even the coming of George Lewis won't help us."

"That's for sure," I said as I smiled and quickly moved to gather up the bowling pins as Judy cleared our shuffleboard of the potted meat cans.

XI

*A*s usual my mother came home to a neat and orderly house. In fact, I don't think you could find a cleaner house in all of Butte. Sometimes the waxed kitchen floor resembles a skating rink, and my best friend, Dave Jacobsen—Jake to those of us who know him—always makes it a point to step cautiously onto the rug that sits just inside the door. He lives in Floral Park, further south on The Flat near the country club, and my other best friend, Paul Brennan, lives on the Upper West Side near the base of Big Butte, our volcanic mountain cone that rises above The Hill and marks its western boundary. I have by far the smallest house, but we still manage to gather here. At times I know my mother wishes we would gather elsewhere, but, still, she'll miss us when we leave for college in the fall. But she wasn't thinking of anyone going to college in the spring of 1952, and neither was I.

Judy and I straightened up the house, and both of us were thinking primarily about George Lewis, as was my mother. Judy was right. We had to trust her. She needed a life separate from the house and us, and maybe George Lewis could provide it. She certainly deserved such a life, and if ever a mother had earned the love and trust of her children, our mother had. I still trust her, and I always will—even after I leave home.

I think Brother Kelley would like my mother, and it's too bad Macbeth didn't marry someone more like her. If he had, I'm not so sure he would have killed his king, Duncan. He would have been tempted because Duncan wasn't a great king in the first place, and

Macbeth undoubtedly would have been greater. He just needed someone who matched his nobility to help him decide, and if he would have married someone more like my mother, he would have decided differently. She would have loved him more than she loved being queen. I'm sure of that fact because ten years after George Lewis came to our house for the first time, we still live here—two blocks east of where Clark Park used to stand. If we would have moved just because my mother had to feel like a queen, I think I'd feel as despairing as Macbeth. And she had to be tempted more than once because as things turned out, all of us found it hard not to love George Lewis—even if he didn't play baseball and couldn't fight.

I counted the days until his arrival, and the more I think about it, the more I realize that as long as you have something worthy of wonder, time doesn't pose much of a problem. But time can be a burden otherwise. Macbeth would have been better off wondering about being king than actually obtaining the throne. Once he made it, he no longer saw anything worthy of his capacity for wonder and cracked up. Whatever the reasons, I remember time flying by during the adventurous week when the three of us, collectively, wondered about the coming of George Lewis. And all the wonder centered on a man who couldn't even boast of a fine Irish or Croatian name like Shannon or Kristich.

The Friday of his coming arrived before we knew it, and I had a hard time keeping my mind on school. Ever since I disobeyed Miss Healy in the first grade, I hadn't been in any trouble, even though I never was teacher's pet and never liked anyone who tried to be. Uncle Tim probably would have liked me to be more of a fighter, even if he never would have tolerated me being a bully. But ever since the black eye incident when he made me defend myself against Jerry Stanich, I haven't been very eager to fight. I've always been quiet, and more than one teacher has thought me to be shy and withdrawn. But I'm just curious, and I listen. And on this Friday ten years ago, my curiosity had reached its peak. When the bell rang ending the week, I didn't waste any time and hurried over to Judy's room faster than usual. I wanted to get home as quickly as possible, even though I knew my mother still wouldn't be home from work and George Lewis wouldn't arrive for several more hours.

"Come on," I said to Judy as she walked out of her seventh grade classroom on the second floor of Emerson Public School. "Let's get going. I want to get home."

"What's the hurry?" she asked. "George won't be there until later on tonight anyway."

"I know. But I still want to get home. Besides, it's Friday. Why would anyone want to stick around school? Come on. Let's go."

"Okay. But I'd like to get my coat first, if you don't mind."

This was one of those times when Judy liked to act more grown up than she really was. She was almost in the eighth grade now and couldn't allow herself to be excited about the coming of someone with an ordinary name like George Lewis, although I knew her excitement equaled my own. Why do we consider it more grown up to act calm and controlled? I'm almost 18 and I'm not ashamed to admit that I still get excited about baseball and the World Series—just as I did before I was even ten years old. I'm no longer a little boy, but I know I'd probably panic if I ever had the chance to meet Mickey Mantle face to face. He's not some casual acquaintance. He's the center fielder for the New York Yankees.

I've outgrown, and want to outgrow, many things, but if you have to stop wondering about life to grow up, then I'm not so sure I want to. Without having something worthy of wonder, growing up can't be an adventure. Life's full of wonder for a child, and I don't know why you can't be a man and still wonder. Brother Kelley still does, and if he isn't a man, no one is. I have no desire to stop wondering. It seems to me that if you stop, you can't grow up.

"Aren't you excited?" I asked her as we walked toward the stairway.

"I suppose so. But I'm not going to let everyone know it. Just take it easy and walk down the stairs. Don't fall down them."

"Don't worry. I'll make it down the stairs. Aren't you excited to see what he looks like. Don't you wonder about that?"

"Yes, I wonder about it," Judy answered as we neared the bottom of the stairs. "But I'm not about to jump out of my shoes as you are. Remember, I'm almost in the eighth grade now, and I have to act my age."

"Does that mean you can't have any more fun?" I asked as we reached the bottom of the stairway and stopped for a second.

"No, stupid. It doesn't mean you have to stop having fun. It just means that you have to act more sophisticated, that's all."

"What does sophisticated mean?" I asked, looking her directly in the eye. She was awfully small for a sophisticated 12-year-old.

"It means you can't act so silly."

"But I'm not acting silly. I don't like people who act silly. Uncle Tim doesn't act silly. Is he sophisticated?"

"He's a man. Men are supposed to drink and fight. It's okay for them. But I'm a girl, and girls have to be sophisticated."

"But what's sophisticated?" I asked again. "What does it mean?"

"It means grown up."

"What does grown up mean?"

"It means the exact opposite of you," she answered.

"Are you grown up?"

"I'm more grown up than you are."

"Was Dad grown up? Was he sophisticated?"

"Of course. He was a man."

"That makes me feel better," I said.

"Why?" Judy asked, walking toward the school's front doors.

"Because if Dad was grown up and sophisticated, then I want to be grown up and sophisticated. He loved baseball. Remember Mom telling him that he looked like a little boy when he was dressed in his uniform?"

"I remember," Judy answered.

"Remember her saying that the knickers hid his bowlegs?"

"I remember that, too."

"You know what?" I asked.

"What?"

"I just thought of something."

"What?" Judy asked, stopping in front of the solid oak door.

"That day Mom teased Dad about his uniform turned out to be the last day he ever wore it," I answered. "He never played another game after South Side beat Silver Bow Parks 4-3 to win the Copper League pennant. But, remember, he pinch hit to drive in the winning run."

"That's right. He drove in Kenny Sykes. I'll never forget that."

"Because you were in love with Kenny Sykes."

"So what if I was?" Judy asked as the blood reached her cheeks. "He was handsome. And besides, he signed a contract to play for the Yankees. I'll never forget Kenny Sykes."

"Know what else I think?"

"What?"

"I think Dad was sophisticated because he loved baseball. And I want to love baseball so I can be sophisticated, too. Maybe Uncle Tim is sophisticated because he fights when he has to."

"I think he fights sometimes when he doesn't have to," Judy said, resting her hand on the iron door handle.

"Maybe. But he doesn't run away. Don't you think that has to have something to do with being sophisticated?"

"It probably does. Do you have any more questions?" she asked impatiently. "I thought you wanted to hurry home."

"I do. But I have just one more question."

"What's that?

"Well, two more questions," I said. "Do you think Mom is sophisticated? And don't you think Dad would expect us to wonder if George Lewis is, too?"

"You ask so many questions. Do you ask this many in school?"

"Not really. But I like to think. Anyway, it's your fault. I just wanted to go home. You brought up sophisticated. I just want to know what it means. But you haven't answered my question."

"Sophisticated is something that grown ups are," Judy said. "It's something we have to become, and I think it means more than acting grown up. I think you have to be grown up. You can't just act like it."

"Like you act?" I interrupted, smiling at her.

"Yes, like I act," she answered, returning my smile.

"Do you think we'll ever be sophisticated?"

"I hope so. I know Mom is, and I know Dad would expect us to wonder if George Lewis is sophisticated," she answered, pushing open the heavy oak door.

"That's what I thought," I said as Judy and I walked through the doorway, across the threshold, down the cool, shaded school steps and into the warmth of the spring sunshine.

XII

*W*e welcomed the ice in winter, but having tired of it by now, we welcomed the spring warmth. I liked ice where it belonged, and on a perfect winter day in Butte, with the crisp snow crunching under your feet and the spiked icicles hanging from the eaves of houses where soft, white smoke from the chimneys floated peacefully upward to meet the clear blue sky, you can wish the ice never would go away. But not all winter days are perfect. And on those that aren't, when the sky darkens and the wind howls, blowing the snow into drifts stacked along the hedges and the sides of houses and no clothing can protect you from the penetrating cold, you long for the warmth of spring when you no longer need so much protection from nature that can be both benevolent and brutal with its warmth and its ice. But I've never seen the ice last forever. I like the balance of nature, and I like the rhythm the changing of the seasons creates.

Macbeth, on the other hand, wanted all spring. He wanted all benevolence. He didn't want any of the brutality and destroyed the natural balance of things. Maybe when we try to alter that balance, we make life signify nothing. Maybe you have to love life just the way it is, just the way it's naturally supposed to be. Maybe Macbeth's choice led him to speak about the nothingness of life. Maybe that's what religion teachers mean when they say we have a free will. Maybe Macbeth's choice made his life meaningless, but that doesn't mean that life itself, as we experience it in nature, is meaningless. I'm beginning to think that Macbeth was right with regard to his own life but that he was mistaken with regard to life in general.

If life is meaningless, then why was I so excited on that Friday in 1952 just because the sun was shining and the water from melting ice was running down the streets and boys were playing marbles and chasing girls with the hopes of catching them and stealing a kiss and as I was hurrying home to wait the arrival of George Lewis? I'm glad Brother Kelley makes us think because when you think, you can understand. And the more you understand, the more inspired you are. I would have been inspired on this day simply because of the onset of the spring thaw. The anticipated coming of George Lewis only added to the already natural inspiration.

I could tell Judy was inspired, too, because she took off her coat to experience the spring warmth. And if she weren't almost in the eighth grade, she would have welcomed the right boy's chase. I used to like to chase Sandra Potter on days like this, and sometimes I even managed to steal a kiss, which tells me that I got an early start with girls and the adventure of love. But I only joined in the chase in the spring and summer and on perfect winter days at the skating rink at Clark Park. And I can't help thinking that the adventure lay in the pursuit.

I guess the same is still true because I pursued Julie Shaw for most of these last two years of high school. Everyone thought I was crazy, and maybe I was because I wasn't the only guy involved in the pursuit. But Julie's the most beautiful girl I've ever seen, and taking her home from a dance just once made the effort worthwhile. I may never have the chance again, but I'll never forget the chase and I'll never forget the purple bow she wore in her black hair. Maybe that bow's a monument to eternity like the gallus frames and Uncle Tim's nose. Do you think it's sophisticated to keep a purple bow a girl once wore in her hair?

If it's sophisticated to welcome the arrival of spring's promise, Judy and I had to be as sophisticated as anyone could get as we walked home. She had taken her coat off, and, forgetting the fact that she was almost in the eighth grade, she'd skip along the sidewalk. And if the right boy was chasing her, she'd allow herself to be caught. Kenny Sykes was the stuff of her dreams when he played for South Side in the Copper League before he signed with the Yankees. I shouldn't have been so bold, but I sneaked her diary one day and read it. I thought my life was over when she found out. She had great plans for herself and Kenny. At least I discovered why she wanted to go to Clark Park as badly as I did. Someone she loved was there.

Judy and I had to walk through Clark Park on our way to Aberdeen Street, and I could see the grass struggling to turn green as the ground thawed under the warmth of the welcomed spring sunshine. The snow had almost completely melted from the park's lawn, and I could see the baseball diamond for the first time since the ice arrived in late fall. No grass was left around the home plate area, and puddles of water sat in the worn areas of first, second, and third base. The field still was unplayable, but at least you could see it and anticipate. We both stopped to observe the ballpark that occupied the opposite, or northeast, end of the park at the intersection of Texas Avenue and Wall Street—the widest street anywhere in the world, I thought—and adjacent to the Naval Reserve Center that stretched one block westward to Florence Avenue. We stared at the imposing, wood grandstand that hid the houses sitting behind it on Wall Street and dwarfed the gallus frames, still visible, like black dots, on The Hill further north.

We stood in awe and wonder because that's how you stand in the presence of something as sacred as the Blessed Sacrament, housed in its altar tabernacle, and something as sacred as your dad's grave, sunk into Holy Cross cemetery's hallowed ground. And that's how you stand when you look at the Mountain Con gallus frame, sitting across the street from Uncle Tim's house in Centerville, and that's how you stand at the Garden Spot of the Rockies, hugging the foothills of the East Ridge. I know Brother Kelley would understand what I mean because that's how I stand in his presence. Judy and I wondered how we would stand in George Lewis' presence as we walked across Texas Avenue, away from Clark Park, and stepped onto Aberdeen Street.

We walked up Aberdeen, dodging the water puddles sitting in dips in the sunken sidewalks. The winter ice wasn't kind to concrete, and over the years the sidewalks would crack and sag, collecting the water from the melting snow. The ice wasn't kind to asphalt either, and Aberdeen Street, with its generous collection of potholes, resembled most of the streets on The Flat. If you live in Butte, you can complain about the potholes, but if you don't live in the Mining City, you have to be careful. If you complain, you have to smile because if you claim superiority because you live in a city that boasts smooth, black-topped streets, you insult Butte's honor. I notice the potholes more now than I did ten years ago, and sometimes I find it hard to understand why road crews can't be more conscientious. Maybe they expect the Anaconda Company to take charge. I don't know, but I don't like to hear any outsider, who doesn't understand Butte, snicker at what I've earned the right to criticize. I still don't like to fight, but those disrespectful, critical outsiders can make me consider coming out of retirement.

I think understanding should precede criticism. I don't like people who just like to criticize. Chaucer, Shakespeare and Brother Kelley are different because they've taken the time to understand. When you take that time, you become more tolerant and more humble, which explains why I respect Brother Kelley. He's the most tolerant teacher I've ever had, and he teaches all students. But you can tell he doesn't like those who aren't willing to take the time to understand. He says he can't tolerate arrogance because it destroys harmony. He doesn't destroy anything, and he's the most humble man I know. When he explains the humility of the hero, I wonder if he knows he's describing himself. I know that it's easier to believe in the hero when your teacher is a concrete expression of that idea. As I said before, Brother Kelley lives what he teaches. No wonder Shakespeare and Chaucer come alive in his classroom.

Of course, I wasn't thinking of Brother Kelley as I walked up Aberdeen Street in the spring sunshine ten years ago. I didn't know he existed then, and at that time he was teaching in some other Irish Christian Brothers school, probably in Chicago or New York. I wonder what he was like in those days. I can't stop thinking about him because I've never had a teacher express what he does. And unlike other Brothers he never has to threaten us or physically intimidate us to get us to listen. He makes you respect learning because he obviously respects it himself. I'm afraid of some of the other Brothers, but I'm not afraid of Brother Kelley. Fear does command obedience, but not forever. Outside of class, when we're no longer afraid, none of us respect the Brothers who rely on fear.

Brother Kelley says that individuals like Chaucer and Shakespeare write out of love. I think he must teach out of love as well, and I think Judy and I must have walked up Aberdeen Street ten years ago under that same motivation. I remember walking that final block and looking at the black-topped and potholed street in front of our house and realizing that with the melting of the ice, I could put away my sled and ice skates and bring out my dad's baseball shoes. I didn't have my own pair of steel-spiked baseball shoes then, but I had my dad's to wear over my regular, rubber-soled shoes. Now that the spring sunshine was melting the winter ice, I could transform our lawn into a baseball diamond once again. And I could listen to the steel spikes clattering against the concrete as I walked down the narrow sidewalk that split the base path between first and second base as it led to our front porch door.

The diamond wasn't playable yet, however, because the spring thaw had left a lake that stretched all the way from our driveway to Dave Hennesey's house next door. And the lake had to reach six inches deep close to the front of the house where the sidewalk sunk lower than the lawn. The coming of spring has its drawbacks, and when you live in a house sitting at the back of two lots, the water from the melting snow doesn't always flow toward the street and down the gutters as it's supposed to. Judy and I had to walk through the soggy grass and around the lake to get to the porch and dry land. My field wouldn't be playable for a few weeks yet, but it was close. The sun would dry it out, the grass would green up and the cheers would return to the ballpark. But for now I only could see the water collecting on the gravel pathway separating the house from the garage.

"Ha-ha," Judy laughed. "You have to bail water until Mom comes home from work."

"I don't know why you shouldn't do it," I said. "You're older than I am."

"I know. But you're a boy and boys are supposed to bail water. So there. You better do your job."

"I will," I said, wiping my feet on the front porch rug. "Why do we have a garage anyway? We don't even have a car. Who needs a stupid garage? Besides, the water wouldn't flood the basement."

"Maybe not, but if I were you, I wouldn't take the chance. You know what Mom would do if she came home and saw the water. She just might throw you in," Judy added, laughing.

"You'd like to see that, wouldn't you?" I asked, finding the key that always hung between the storm door and the house door. "You'd probably let me drown."

"It would be one way to get rid of a brother."

"Then you'd really be happy. But if you got rid of me, you wouldn't have anyone to bowl with, or to play shuffleboard with. Then what would you do?"

"I don't know. I guess I can't live without you after all. But the thought was interesting for a minute. Are you going to open the door or just stand there and stare at the water? It won't go away by itself, you know."

"I know," I said, opening the door and stepping into the house. "I wouldn't mind if I just had to bail it once. But after I get rid of the water, the pool fills up again. Where does all the water come from?"

"From the snow, dummy," Judy answered as she stepped onto the kitchen rug sitting in front of the threshold. "Stay on top of the rug until your feet are dry. I don't want to leave any footprints on the linoleum. I don't feel like scrubbing the floor if I don't have to."

"You better make sure the end tables are dusted and the living room is clean," I said, resisting the temptation to step onto the kitchen floor. "Mom will want the house especially clean tonight. See, you can't just sit around doing nothing," I added, checking to see if I could safely step onto the linoleum.

"I know. But the house should look nice tonight. I don't mind dusting and cleaning if I have a purpose and if I actually can see dust and dirt. Otherwise it can drive me crazy. At least you usually can see a reason for bailing the water."

"Maybe so, but that doesn't make it any fun. I'd rather bowl or play shuffleboard until Mom comes home."

"I would, too. But we'd better get started. Besides, we can bowl or play shuffleboard tonight after Mom and George Lewis leave."

"That's right," I said, realizing that Judy and I would be home alone at night for the first time. But I couldn't get used to George's name. It didn't seem to fit with Anne Kristich from East Butte and Clark Park. "I'll get my boots," I said, walking toward the closet attached to the back of my mother's bedroom to the right of the kitchen.

"I'll get started with the dusting," Judy said. "And I'll even vacuum the living room rug."

"Okay," I added, spotting my rubber boots at the back of the closet and sitting right next to my dad's white and red-trimmed South Side baseball uniform.

The uniform always lay in the same place, and I walked into that closet many times just to look at it. I wanted to wear that uniform someday and display the South Side emblem on the left side of my jersey. My dad always wore his uniform with the same pride that Brother Kelley displays in wearing his black, ankle length cassock that distinguishes the Irish Christian Brother. I know he lives up to the responsibility that accompanies the cassock, and I know my dad did the same with his baseball uniform. I can't expect less of myself when the time comes, but I think responsibility was simpler ten years ago. I only had to put on my boots and bail water that day, which was easy compared to what I face now. But Brother Kelley says the courage you admire in others is an expression of the courage you have yourself. You just have to live what you see and admire. I must be awfully courageous because I can see a lot of courage.

But the Church says I'm a sinner. That's interesting because when I look at Butte, I don't see sin. I see courage instead. I see courage in the gallus frames, in Clark Park and in the Columbia Gardens. And if I look closely enough, I even can see it in the story of Adam and Eve. Maybe it took courage to eat the apple. It would have been easier to remain in the Garden, but they ate the apple. Maybe my mother is like Eve. It would have been easier for her never to want to love again. Then she'd never have to face the pain she experienced as a result of having loved my dad. But she wanted to love again. She wasn't afraid. Maybe not wanting to love again would have been a sin, just as choosing to stay in the Garden would have been a sin for Adam and Eve.

Maybe it's a sin not to live the courage we can see in heroes, in individual human beings. I'd like to avoid that sin because I don't want to be as miserable as Macbeth had to be. I wonder if the Church can be wrong. How can an institution with all that majesty be wrong? But then Christ is courage. It would have been easier for him to go along with the Pharisees, but he had courage. He didn't back down from a fight when honor was at stake. Like Adam and Eve—especially Eve—he wasn't afraid. And I don't see sin when I look at the crucifix. I've broken church rules. But I don't hate God or Christ or the Church when I do. Sometimes I think you have to break the rules just to be normal.

Maybe the Mass is more important than the rules. I know it's more inspiring, and I like its majesty. But I still try to keep the

Church's rules. They tell us to be obedient, but the Mass celebrates Christ's disobedience. I wonder what obedience and disobedience really mean?

See what I mean? Nothing was so complicated ten years ago when I sat on the bench next to my mother's bed and buckled my boots. Then I only had to decide whether or not to bail out the water. That was an easy decision to make compared to what we're faced with now. It's going to take a lot of thinking, but I'm not seven years old anymore, either. I wanted to be obedient when I was seven, which explains why I buckled up my boots. And I want to be obedient now. But what does obedience really mean? The answer doesn't seem so simple anymore.

Maybe that means I'm growing up. Life was simpler in 1952 than it is in 1962. And you can't go back ten years because that would stop progress. But you can journey back there in your own mind and explore the past. You can remember and try to understand. I've come across lots of sound and fury, and I still have ten years to go. So far I can't say life signifies nothing as Macbeth concluded. But if I don't get back to 1952 now, I'll never make it through the next ten years. Butte makes me think, and I have a hard time stopping once I get going on an idea. The spring sunshine doesn't take care of the winter ice all by itself, whether the year is 1952 or 1962, and I've bailed a lot of water the past ten years. But this will be my last spring because I'll be leaving for college in the fall. Then I'll probably miss bailing out the water and come home on spring vacation just to keep in practice.

With my boots buckled I walked into the kitchen to get the garage door key from the candy dish that always sat on top of the refrigerator resting against the east wall of the kitchen to the left of the doorway leading to my mother's bedroom. Judy already was busy dusting the living room when I stood on one of the kitchen chairs and reached up to find the key. I found it without any trouble, stepped off the chair and slid it across the kitchen back to its place at the head of the table that doubled as our shuffleboard. I opened the cupboard doors underneath the kitchen sink, grabbed the bailing pan, and walked across the kitchen and out the door. Once I found the bucket, waiting for me and sitting in the outside corner where the porch met the kitchen, I was fully equipped to battle the spring runoff.

As usual, what began as a battle, quickly became no contest. On an especially warm spring day the winter snow runoff proved to be too much, and as soon as I'd fill the bucket with the bailing pan, the puddle would return. At least Judy could vacuum the rug without having the dirt flow into it as fast as her machine could suck it out. After a while I stopped trying to battle the water because, no matter how much I tried, I proved to be no match for the sun's power. I just bailed and tried to enjoy the welcomed spring warmth. I've never believed flooding to be the danger my mother fears, but I bail the water anyway. The sounds of the spring runoff remain the same, and I still can hear the dripping and cracking as the spring sun loosens winter's grip on the icicled eaves. But I didn't forget about George Lewis as I bailed the water out of the pool, tossed it down the alley behind the house and listened to the quiet, satisfying sounds of the always promised spring thaw.

XIII

"**A**ren't you finished yet?" Judy yelled from the house. "It's almost five o'clock. Mom will be home soon."

"This should be my last bucket full," I answered. "It's cooling off now, and the water isn't running as fast anymore. The snow melted fast, though. We'll be able to play baseball again pretty soon. I can't wait."

"Right now you'd better come in and get cleaned up for dinner. I don't know what time George Lewis is coming, but we have to eat dinner first. And Mom will be in a hurry."

"She's always in a hurry," I said, stepping onto the sidewalk carrying the bucket and my bailing pail.

"Don't be so smart," Judy scolded.

"I'm not trying to be smart. I'm just telling the truth. Watch how fast she moves. She can get things done faster than anyone I know."

"Maybe so. But she'll be in more of a hurry tonight. So come on."

"Is the house clean?

"As clean as I can get it."

"Do you think it'll be clean enough?" I asked, reaching the front door.

"I don't think she'll notice tonight," Judy answered as I walked into the kitchen. "She'll be too interested in other things."

"I'm glad she'll have other things to think about," I said as I sat down at the kitchen table and took of my rubber boots.

"You could have taken those off outside, you know," Judy remarked, standing in front of me, hands on hips, as though she were my mother.

"I know, but they're dry. See, I didn't even get the floor wet," I said, pointing to the dry linoleum.

"Well, put the boots away before Mom gets home. I want everything to be just right when she gets here."

"I thought you weren't excited," I said, picking up my boots.

"I am excited. I'm just not acting silly like you are."

"Are you acting sophisticated?"

"I don't know. Just go put your boots away like you're supposed to. Here comes Mom," she said, looking out the porch windows.

I heard the front door open as I set my boots on the closet floor next to my dad's baseball uniform and walked back into the kitchen.

"Did you bail out the water between the house and the garage, Danny?" my mother asked, taking off her own rubber boots that protected her high heels.

"Yes," I answered, "but I could hardly keep up with it. Whenever I thought I was done, the pool would fill up again."

"Well, thanks for your help. I'm glad spring has arrived. I'm getting tired of wearing these boots. Did you get the living room clean, Judy?" she asked, walking into her bedroom to put her boots away and to take her coat off.

"Yes. I dusted and even vacuumed the rug."

"You're a big help, too," my mother said from her bedroom. "It's nice to have the house clean. Did you two come home from school right away?" she asked as she walked back into the kitchen wearing bedroom slippers in place of her high heels.

"Judy wouldn't leave school right away, but once I talked her into it, we came right home. We were both pretty excited, even though she wouldn't admit it."

"If you're excited, Judy, you should admit it. I'll admit that I'm excited tonight. I hope I don't ruin your dinner," she said as she reached for the spaghetti and the can of Chef Boyardee mushroom sauce.

I knew my mother was excited because usually she didn't start dinner so quickly. Instead, she'd get the carpet sweeper and pick up the residue left by the vacuum cleaner Judy had used. But tonight was different. I think she was enjoying the chase, even at 38. I remember smiling as I watched her fix our dinner. She always cooked fast, and she seemed to get water to boil faster than anyone else in existence. In no time at all she had the spaghetti on the table and had mine cut up and ready to eat.

"What time are you going out?" Judy asked as she and I sat down at opposite sides of the table, on either side of my mother's vacant spot at its head.

"George is coming at six-thirty. So I don't have too much time."

"Are you and George going alone?" I asked. I thought it strange to be calling a man by his first name, but I felt as though I knew him after all the anticipation. "Is it okay to call him George or should I call him Mr. Lewis?"

"You don't have to call him anything for now. I may never go out with him again. But I guess we can call him George. I don't think he'd mind. And no, we're not going out alone. We're going with the Olsens."

"Aren't they the people from the South Side Athletic Club?" Judy asked. "Didn't they know Dad?"

"They're the ones, and they did know your dad," my mother answered from her bedroom.

"Then why didn't George know Dad?" I asked.

"Because he's been living in Alaska for several years," my mother answered.

"I thought he lived on the West Side," Judy said.

"He did, but he's run a grocery store in Alaska the last few years."

"I don't want to move to Alaska," I said.

"We're not moving to Alaska," my mother said, laughing.

"Was George married?" Judy asked.

"Yes, but his wife died about a year ago."

"Does he have any kids?" I asked.

"Yes. He has a boy and a girl. I think the boy is a couple of years older than you and the girl's about the same age as Judy."

"I don't want a brother and a sister," I said. "Why can't you go out with someone who doesn't have kids?"

"Don't jump to conclusions. I haven't gone out with him yet, and I don't know what's going to happen. We'll have to wait and see."

"Where are you going?" Judy asked.

"We're going out to eat, and then we're going to the Elks Club."

"Are you going to dance?" I asked.

"I hope so."

"I hope he's a good dancer," I said.

"So do I. But you two better finish your spaghetti now before it gets cold. I have to get ready," my mother added as I heard the bathroom door close.

After all the anticipation it seemed as though we had nothing left to say. So Judy and I just ate and waited. Spaghetti with Chef Boyardee mushroom sauce was, and is, one of our Friday night staples—along with Kraft macaroni and cheese. I don't remember ever complaining about not being able to eat meat on Friday, although I'm not sure I understand why we commit a mortal sin if we do. I can understand not breaking a rule the Church has established, but I have a hard time imagining God sentencing someone to Hell simply for eating meat on Friday. I can recognize the idea of sacrifice involved, I suppose, and it seems to me that if someone dies for you, skipping meat once a week is the least you can do. But that's not much of a sacrifice. It's too easy. Still, with that rule in place you can measure the passing of the weeks. And besides, avoiding meat on Friday makes it taste all the better when you break the fast.

Butte is a city of food, and nothing beats a pork chop sandwich from Pork Chop John's following a Friday night dance at Central or somewhere else. Sometimes, after midnight, the line can stretch a block long Uptown on Mercury Street, and you can smell the pork chops from a greater distance. I've never seen a brawl at Pork Chop John's because you don't have to live in Centerville or East Butte or on the West Side or The Flat to enjoy a pork chop sandwich. Pork Chop John's belongs to Butte and not to any specific, boundaried neighborhood. If you're not from Butte, you probably haven't heard of such a sandwich, and if you've never received Holy Communion in a Catholic Church, you may not understand its power. But waiting in line after midnight on a Saturday morning to eat a sandwich built around a breaded pork loin, covered with mustard and onions and pickles, has the same inspirational affect on me as does waiting in line at Mass to receive the Blessed Sacrament. I hope I don't sound sacrilegious, but it's the truth. It works like magic. I just can't explain it yet.

But I want to understand the magic of the gallus frames and pork chop sandwiches. In know they're objects as sacred as the Blessed Sacrament. I've broken my share of church rules, but I've never eaten meat on Friday, although I've had many chances. I'm either afraid of going to Hell or I don't want to destroy the magic of the pork chop sandwich. I suppose it's probably a little of both, but it's too bad that Macbeth never had the chance to stand in line at Pork Chop John's on Mercury Street and savor the magic smell of the pork chop simmering in the deep fat fryer. If he could have experienced that glorious smell and if he could have tasted the pork chop, he would have realized that he didn't have to be king. And if ascending to the throne meant he would have to give up pork chop sandwiches, Duncan would have enjoyed a long reign.

It was after six o'clock when Judy and I finished our spaghetti and began to clean up our dishes. We still hadn't said anything to each other, but both of us had managed to keep an eye on the clock. George Lewis was supposed to come at six-thirty, and the time was getting close. We were picking up the dishes and putting them on the counter next to the sink when my mother walked out into the kitchen, ready for her date.

"Boy, you really look nice!" I exclaimed as I turned around and caught sight of her.

"Wow," Judy said. "You look like you should be going to a dance at the Columbia Gardens."

I never saw my mother as being attractive or unattractive. She was my mother and thus always looked the same. But on that night ten years ago I realized, for the first time, that she was attractive. And I was proud of her. She never wears loud clothes that don't flatter her, even if they might be in style. I think she dresses with what Brother Kelley would call dignity, and I think Chaucer, who seemed to pay close attention to the clothes people wore in his time, would approve. I remember that I did when I turned around and saw her that night. Maybe I never really saw her before, but she made me feel proud to be a Kristich—just as proud as my dad ever did.

She isn't exceptionally tall at five three, but she's never looked small or frail. Even at 47 she doesn't look old because her blue eyes remain alert and alive. She's a woman of strength, and she looks it in the way she proudly holds herself. I've never seen her stand with drooping shoulders, for example, even if she's spent the entire day walking the concrete floors at the courthouse. If you look hard enough and if you're honestly interested, you can see courage. Beauty's nothing to be proud of, but courage is a different story. I can see her beauty, but her courage really inspires me. I think Brother Kelley's right. Butte is rich in courage, even if it isn't rich in beauty. If you have courage and beauty, too, that's fine, but if you have to choose, I think only a fool would choose beauty. Otherwise, life would signify nothing no matter how attractive the sound and fury.

You can't live as a monument to eternity if you're proud of beauty. The gallus frames aren't beautiful, and Butte itself isn't beautiful—unless you're looking for courage. If we have to be reminded of that virtue, then the gallus frames and Butte are monuments to eternity. To be sophisticated maybe you have to be more interested in courage than in beauty. And you have to be grown up to be more interested in courage. Growing up must not be easy because while Macbeth had the courage to slit his enemy "from the nave to the chaps," he couldn't find the courage to grow up. I don't think people of adult age are automatically grown up. But if you truly love Butte, you have to want to grow up. You owe it to the city and to the men and women who built it and died in it, just as Brother Kelley says.

My mother looked sophisticated to me, standing in the kitchen dressed for her date. I remember her short-sleeved, navy blue dress just as if it were yesterday. She had the bow tied neatly in the back, and she wore a pair of black high heels to go with it. I'd never really noticed my mother's clothes before, but I knew she owned many pairs of shoes because I noticed them whenever I walked into the closet to examine my dad's baseball uniform. She always afforded herself the luxury of owning shoes. She's always complained about her hair, although beyond knowing that my hair matched hers in fine texture, I never paid much attention to it. I just listened to her complain about it before we walked the three quarters of a mile to St Ann's every Sunday morning. But she must have been satisfied with her hair that Friday night ten years ago because she made no fuss over it. She puts it up with bobby pins every night, and on the night of her date with George Lewis every curl knew its place, and her feathered bangs wouldn't dare extend beyond the middle of her forehead.

She's Croatian, of course, or Bohunk in the vernacular peculiar to Butte natives, and you can read her heritage in her nose. As I told you, Butte is a city of noses, with the straight and noble Bohunk nose being one of the most prominent. My mother likes to wear silver jewelry, and on that night she wore small, round clip-on earrings that complemented her navy blue dress. I don't know too much about make-up and the tools women use, but I do know my mother used some kind of pencil to touch up her light-brown, plucked eyebrows. And I don't know what she'd do without her compact. She had to be wearing rouge that night. She takes her compact everywhere, and she never would have left it home when she was going out on a date—with George Lewis or anyone else.

She had to be wearing lipstick as well, but similar to her taste in rouge, it couldn't have been anything too noticeable. But most distinctly I remember her blue eyes, that never need any kind of make-up, as being especially lively that night. No wonder I felt proud to be a Kristich. Because I wanted to look like my dad, I always checked in the mirror to see if I bore any resemblance to his pictures. When I look in the mirror today and smile, I can recognize the creases in his face that extend from the corners of his nose to the corners of his mouth. But even without smiling I can recognize my mother's nose.

"Do you think I look good enough?" she asked, standing in the kitchen as if she didn't hear any reaction from Judy and me.

"Look good enough?" Judy asked. "I think you look elegant."

"I do, too," I said. "I hope George Lewis looks elegant, too."

"Men don't look elegant, stupid," Judy said. "Women look elegant. Men look handsome," she added with a twinkle in her eye.

"That's enough," my mother said. "Glamour and looks aren't everything, you know. Do you think your dad was handsome like a movie star?"

"I don't know," I answered. "But if he was going out with you tonight, he would be. I wish you were going out with him tonight instead of with George Lewis," I added with a quiver in my voice.

"I guess I do, too, Danny. But I can't. Do you understand?"

"I think so. I'm trying to anyway."

"I am, too. And if we want to and if we try hard enough, I think we will. But I'm going out with George Lewis tonight. That doesn't mean I'll ever forget your dad. Okay?"

"Okay," I said.

"We just want you to have a good time tonight," Judy said. "But I still hope George Lewis is handsome like a prince or something," she added with a smile.

"We'll have to wait and see, Judy," my mother said just as we all heard a knock on the front door. "I guess we won't have to wait any longer. I think he's here. Are you ready?" she asked nervously as she walked toward the front door.

"I think so," Judy and I answered simultaneously as we stood side by side in front of the kitchen sink and watched our mother open the door to welcome George Lewis.

XIV

❀

$\mathcal{I}$ can look back on that night now and laugh, and the more I think about it, the more I realize that no one could have lived up to the images Judy and I had created when George stepped across the threshold and into the kitchen. Judy expected a handsome prince, and on first glance, George Lewis—wearing a gray, felt hat and brown slacks, almost completely hidden by his light gray topcoat that protected him from the spring chill and hid his sloping, round shoulders—hardly resembled a prince. As a seven-year-old boy who knew nothing about the machinist trade, I was expecting to see a man who appeared capable of building large machines, and George didn't appear to have that capability. Still, both Judy and I stood in the kitchen, with eyes as big as targets, waiting for our mother to introduce us to George Lewis who finally had arrived.

"Hi, you must be George," she said nervously as he stood just inside the front door.

"That's right," he replied, stepping across the threshold and wiping his feet on the kitchen rug that welcomed him.

"Won't you step further into the kitchen?" my mother asked, motioning him to move away from the door. "I'd like you to meet my children."

"Thank you," he answered, moving toward the center of the kitchen. "I would like to meet them."

"This is my son, Dan," my mother said, pointing to me.

"Hi," I said, nodding my head in George's direction.

"Hello, Dan," he said, extending his right hand.

I responded by shaking his hand the way Uncle Tim tried to teach me. He told me never to offer what he called a dead fish. He said a man's handshake should be firm, and I tried to follow his instructions, even though I couldn't get a solid grip on George's hand that was rough, but not callused, while his handshake was firm, but gentle.

"It's nice to meet you," he said as we shook hands.

"It's nice to meet you, too," I said as he released my hand.

"And this is my daughter, Judy," my mother said, motioning to my sister standing next to me on my left.

"Hello, Judy," he said as he removed his hat and offered her his hand as well. "I'm pleased to meet you," he added, taking and holding Judy's hand without shaking it. "How old are you?" he asked.

"I'm pleased to meet you, too, and I'm 12," Judy answered, looking up at him.

"You're getting to be a real young lady," he said.

"I hope so," Judy replied. "I'll be in the eighth grade next year, and I'll be 13 in January," she added, smiling as she continued to look up at him.

"And how old are you, Dan?" he asked, holding his felt hat at his side with his right hand.

I didn't know what to expect from a man named Lewis because I couldn't recognize his name. I could recognize Irish names, or Harp names as Uncle Tim jokingly says, or Bohunk names as Butte says—sometimes not so jokingly. And I could recognize Italian, Serbian, and Scandinavian names. Such names meant something to me because they reflected a specific identity I could picture in my mind. But Lewis didn't mean anything to me, and George's appearance didn't inspire awe. He didn't present an immediate expression of imposing masculinity that I associated with Uncle Tim and my dad.

I had nothing but a neutral reaction to George, until he took off his hat. Then I noticed his now prominent nose, neither broken and scarred nor straight and noble, and bald head that appeared to be disproportionately small in relationship to the wide-shouldered topcoat he was wearing. When George removed his hat, I started to laugh inside, and no one would have noticed if he didn't ask me my age.

"Seven," I answered, trying my best to suppress my laughter. But I must not have been very successful because my mother blushed through her rouge and quickly told George that I would be eight this coming July. He smiled and calmly placed his hat back on his head and helped my mother with her coat that she had placed on the foot of her bed just inside the archway to the right of the kitchen door. George said he enjoyed meeting us once again and tipped his hat in our direction as he walked out the door. He smiled as my mother kissed us goodbye, still with a slight blush visible through her rouge. They walked out the door together, and I don't think that any one of us suspected that they'd still be walking out that same door ten years later, still dating but never marrying.

"He's bald!" I exclaimed as the kitchen door closed behind them. "Did you see that?"

"How could I miss it?" Judy answered, laughing. "It seemed funny because I didn't expect it. He was nice but not as handsome as I had him pictured. Then I saw your reaction when he took off his hat. Why did you have to laugh?"

"I couldn't help myself. I didn't mean to be impolite, but he just looked funny. He wasn't what I expected him to be, either. But then I'm not exactly sure what I expected. Did you feel his hand when he took yours?"

"Yes," Judy answered.

"What did you think?" I asked.

"I thought his hand was rough. And the fingernails looked a little dirty. What did you think?"

"He shook my hand."

"That's because you're a boy."

"I know. But Uncle Tim told me that sometimes you can tell a lot about a man by the way he shake hands. He told me never to offer someone a dead fish."

"What's a dead fish?"

"A hand that feels limp. I don't remember shaking hands before tonight, but George's hand didn't feel like I think a dead fish would feel. He squeezed my hand, and I tried to squeeze his. I couldn't get a solid grip on it because it was so much bigger than mine. But I didn't want to give him a dead fish."

"Do you think Uncle Tim would like him?"

"I don't know. He doesn't look like Uncle Tim, even though both of them are bald. But I never laugh at Uncle Tim. George is different."

"No one looks like Uncle Tim."

"If George looked like him, I wouldn't have laughed when he took off his hat. I probably would have been afraid."

"Are you afraid of Uncle Tim?" Judy asked.

"I was when I saw him hobbling toward the dugout the day I played hooky from school," I answered. "And I was afraid walking home from Clark Park when I thought he was going to punish me with his belt. And I was afraid when he sent me into the garage to wait for him when he went into the house to talk to Mom and Auntie Loo. If I hadn't have heard him tell Dave he wasn't going to use his belt, I think I would have fainted from fright. Even after I knew I wasn't in danger, watching him step into the dark garage—holding his rolled up belt in his right hand—scared me to death."

"Are you still afraid of him?"

"I think I would be if he would have used his belt that day. I think I'd be petrified, to tell you the truth. He could scare anyone who didn't know him."

"Do you think you'd be afraid of George?"

"No. He's not the scaring type. Do you think he is?" I asked.

"No. I don't think he's scary at all."

"Do you think he's handsome?"

"Not like Uncle Tim is."

"Do you think he's handsome like Dad was?"

"I don't know. I never laughed at Dad like that. But I suppose George is kind of handsome. Do you agree?"

"I don't notice if men are handsome. I just know he didn't give me a dead fish to shake. Do you think he's sophisticated?"

"I don't know," Judy answered. "But I hope he is. I think I'll have to get to know him a little better before I can decide on something so important."

"Did you like him?"

'Yes, I think so. He was nice. Did you like him?"

"Yes. I think he's funny. And he didn't get mad when I started to laugh. Would you like to get to know him better?"

"I think so. Would you?"

"Yes," I answered. "I think he'll make us laugh."

"Well, maybe we'll get the chance," Judy said, turning to the dishes stacked up on the kitchen counter. "I'll wash and you dry. And don't drop anything."

"Maybe we will," I said. "And don't worry. I won't drop anything. Do you want to play shuffleboard or do you want to bowl after we're done?"

"Let's get the dishes done first before I decide," Judy answered, turning her attention to the soap suds that now filled the dish pan.

"Okay," I said, reaching for the dish towel hanging on the rack on the opposite wall to the left of the stove. "I wonder if George bowls or plays shuffleboard." I asked as I grabbed the dish towel and stepped to Judy's left to wait for her to place the clean dishes in the drying rack.

XV

❀

The presence of George Lewis has been nothing like his coming, but the more I saw of him, the more I came to develop a genuine affection for him. For the past ten years he's been as much of a male presence as a man could be without being a father. I'm proud to be associated with him, and I've never hesitated to have him know any of my friends. I know he loves my mother, and I have no doubt that she loves him, which has to make it hard for her because she has to think of getting married. Life would seem easier then. On several occasions both Judy and I have told my mother that she should marry George, but she must know something neither one of us does. She told us that she'd never marry again unless she found the same love she experienced with my dad. I've seen her with George, and I've been with the two of them. I know they feel a genuine attraction for each other, and when they're alone, I know they both need—and enjoy—each other's company. Without loving the individual, I don't think you could go out with someone for ten years.

I know I can't go out with a girl for long if I don't care about her. It's not honest. I admit that I've taken girls out just to have a date, but I didn't want to take Julie Shaw home from a dance just because I wanted to take someone home. I wanted to take her home. Do you see the difference? If you take a girl home from a dance because you have to take someone home, the sound and fury signifies nothing. But if you take a girl home from a dance because you want to be with that particular girl, the sound and fury signifies everything. I know because I've experienced both situations.

So, the love my mother shared with my dad must have been special. It must have been similar to what I felt for Julie Shaw. I'll never forget that. I still have her purple bow, and I'll always keep it. But the love my mother and George felt for each other must have been missing something. I trust my mother, and I know she isn't afraid. I know she has courage. She isn't like Lady Macbeth. She doesn't have to be queen, but I know George would like to be rich. And I know he doesn't follow baseball. My mother doesn't expect him to follow baseball, but I don't think she'd marry simply to get rich. I think George, unlike my mother, has something to prove. He's tired of living on the fringes of the West Side, and he always thinks of some plan that will put him in the midst of that neighborhood. Or he always thinks of some scheme that will allow him to escape, once and for all, the city he calls "Hungry Hill."

George and I are very different in that regard. I think Butte is "The Richest Hill on Earth," and he thinks it's "Hungry Hill" or "Hell's Kitchen." He's not like Uncle Tim or my dad or Brother Kelley. Uncle Tim sees courage in Butte and wants to be a part of it. Brother Kelley sees courage as well, if maybe in a different way, and he wants us to see it so that we'll have the courage to face the life that Macbeth found meaningless. But I don't think George sees courage in Butte. I think he sees a city that's done him wrong in some way, and he wants to prove to the Mining City that George Lewis can be somebody worthy of living on the West Side. He's like Macbeth, only he's comical. If Brother Kelley knew George, I think he'd see comedy, rather than tragedy, in him. I feel sorry for Macbeth, but for some reason I don't feel the same way about George. I'm not sure why, but I think George wants to be rich because he thinks an individual has to be rich to be somebody. He wants to be somebody more than he wants to be rich.

Maybe Macbeth is tragic because he couldn't find the courage to accept, and affirm, life that isn't all riches. But I don't think George is entirely without courage. He's lived in Butte for a long time, and no matter where he goes, he always ends up back here. I wish he could have experienced Brother Kelley because if you listen to him, and if you listen to Butte and the gallus frames, you can see that no one has to be rich to be somebody.

If you were my mother, you couldn't help loving George, but she's truly sophisticated because she doesn't have to be rich to be somebody. If George were as sophisticated, he and my mother would have been married years ago. My mother and my dad must have experienced that kind of sophisticated love, and she must have been referring to it when she told Judy and me that she'd never marry again unless she found the love she had with my dad. I suppose this love has a name, but she doesn't know it and neither do I. Brother Kelley probably knows, but he'd say you don't have to know its name to recognize it. He'd say that wanting to recognize that sophisticated love is more important than learning its identifying name.

I think my mother is courageous and wise. She must know what people have in mind when they speak of true love. I don't think everyone truly loves because if they did, they'd be happier. But I'll have to be careful. I don't want to pursue, or marry, someone who isn't interested in this true love. No matter what we call it, I know it's real because my mother and my dad had to have experienced it. I think my mother has to love George, but she'll never marry him unless he becomes the man she sees he could be. I don't feel sorry for her because she can stand on her own. But I guess I feel sorry for George because I think he'd trade my mother for the chance to get rich and be somebody. I wish he'd listen to the gallus frames at least. He doesn't have to follow baseball. The West Side may be a long way from Clark Park, but it's awfully close to the gallus frames. You just have to listen.

I wish I could tell George about Brother Kelley and what he teaches, but it's not my place. George is the adult, not me. Although he doesn't occupy a classroom, he does try to teach me all the time. He tells me about "Hungry Hill," and I always listen because he's interesting and even entertaining. He's comical, and I think he'll die in the shadow of that same Hill because he belongs here. He's as much a part of Butte as is my dad and my mother and Uncle Tim and Brother Kelley and myself. If Butte is one big story, then George's chapter is as important as anyone else's. Maybe that's why I listen to him—just as I listen to my mother, Uncle Tim, and Brother Kelley, and just as I continue to listen to my dad.

I listen to George, but I don't believe him, which explains his frustration with me. He wants me to believe him because he thinks he's right, which further explains why he's taken me to Seattle and San Francisco and why he takes me to Spokane all the time. He wants me to see how those cities are better than Butte because they're far removed from "Hungry Hill." I like visiting them, but I'm more fascinated by San Francisco than I am by either Seattle or Spokane. With its steep hills, Victorian houses, and unique charm and personality, San Francisco reminds me of Butte. I could live there and feel at home. Also, I think I might be able to live on Queen Anne Hill in Seattle, but I never could live anywhere in Spokane.

Whenever we travel with George, I can't wait to get back to Butte. When he catches sight of the gallus frames and proclaims: "There it is, 'Hungry Hill,'" I always silently say to myself: "There it is, 'The Richest Hill on Earth.'" So George and I make a great pair. He teaches and I listen. He wants me to believe him because he's convinced that he's right. I listen out of respect and recognition of his noble intentions, but I don't have to believe him, nor do I have to believe Brother Kelley or Uncle Tim, or my mother and dad for that matter. But they make more sense, and, as Brother Kelley says, my accumulated experience in the "ugliest city in the continental United States" supports them. And you have to believe that which makes sense. In this case, then, I have to be loyal to Brother Kelley, Uncle Tim, my mother, my dad, the gallus frames and baseball.

George doesn't particularly enjoy baseball. Unlike my dad's friend, Joe Mandic, who, I remember, liked to associate baseball with religion, he finds it dull and boring. He's not alone in that regard, but it's comical, and never offensive, with him. It's even more comical when I remember that George—and not Uncle Tim or Joe Mandic—took me to my first big league baseball game at Candlestick Park that night in the summer of 1960. Now that I think about it, I can't help laughing. If I was colder than I ever have been in my life, just think how cold George must have been.

XVI

George Lewis may have taken me to my first big league baseball game in Candlestick Park in the summer of 1960, but Uncle Tim took me to the Butte-Central football game at Naranche Stadium in the early fall of 1953. Butte High and Butte Central have been playing football since the 1920s, but I didn't become aware of the cross-town rivalry until the 1950s. Baseball still is, and always will be, my first love, which explains why I refer to it as The One True Sport. I know Butte is The Richest Hill on Earth as well, but I don't completely understand baseball and Butte just yet. I'm just beginning to understand Butte's riches, and you can't think about too many things at the same time. But I know baseball and Butte are equivalent, and I'll always be loyal to both of them—no matter the consequences.

Butte and baseball are worthy of love, as are my mom and dad. I think you love your mom and dad automatically at first, and as you grow up, you discover whether or not they've proven themselves worthy of that love. I know my mother has proven herself and I know my dad has, too, because if he hasn't, my mom would have married George Lewis by now. But loving a city like Butte and a game like baseball doesn't come automatically. You're exposed to either. Then something grabs you, and you decide to love. That's it. You decide to love Butte and baseball. You don't decide to love your mom and dad until they've proven worthy. Once they prove themselves, you decide to love them just as you decide to love Butte and baseball.

Deciding to love must have some connection with Brother Kelley's comments about free will. No accident determines your decision to love or not to love. And nothing accidental surrounded that September night in 1953. With that exposure to Central, supported by the majesty of football, I discovered something worthy of love and decided to embrace it. I'll never forget that night, and ever since I've loved the maroon and white and hated the purple and white. When you decide to love Central, you also decide to hate Butte High. I don't remember a dull September in Butte since 1953, even though baseball always left Clark Park after Labor Day and even though the ballpark burned to the ground in May of 1957.

I think my interest in the Butte-Central rivalry had something to do with Judy entering Central that same fall. As far as I know, she went to Central because we were Catholic and Catholics went to Catholic schools. Neither of us attended a Catholic grade school, however, although we did go to catechism class every Monday across The Flat at St Ann's. Our principal, Miss Sullivan dismissed us early from Emerson so we could make it to St Ann's on time. But I don't know if Judy chose to go to Central. She may have gone simply because she didn't go to a Catholic grade school.

I may have been destined to walk that pre-ordained path as well, but when my grade school years ended in 1958, after one year at the new junior high, it didn't make any difference. I was going to Central, and I didn't care if every one of my friends was going to Butte High. That's what can happen when you sit in Naranche Stadium in September of 1953 and watch your sister's school, Butte Central, or just Central, beat Butte Public, or just Butte High, 6-0 for the first time in 28 years. From that day forward I wanted to wear, and be loyal to, the maroon and white. And from that day forward I cringed at the sight of purple and white.

The 1953 Butte-Central game is the first football game I remember watching. I knew about Notre Dame because I was a Catholic and because Uncle Tim was a Notre Dame fan. And I remember listening to Notre Dame games on the radio before 1953. In fact, Saturdays in the fall meant listening to Notre Dame football games just as summer days meant listening to baseball's Mutual Game of the Day. I remember listening to the Lone Ranger and other radio programs, but I've come to associate radio with rock n' roll. When rock n' roll was born, we had Randy 'The Racer' Riddle at KOPR and 'Bouncing Billy' Venture at KXLF to listen to. I never trusted 'The

Racer,' who since has left Butte, and I don't trust 'Bouncing Billy,' who's still around. Their nicknames are too contrived. They aren't earned Butte names like Snuffy and Spud. They're just names they've chosen for themselves because disc jockeys have to have names to promote and sell records. But if I don't trust them, I do trust the songs they play. Besides, neither 'The Racer' nor 'Bouncing Billy' ran for the touchdown that sank the Butte High Bulldogs in 1953. Central's Bobby 'Scooter' Johnson ran 60 yards to pay dirt to live up to the nickname he previously had earned.

I knew about 'Scooter' Johnson before the game, but I certainly didn't see him in the same light as I saw my sister—that of a high school student. He was a football player. I must have read about him in the newspaper in the days leading up to the game because I can remember knowing him and Central's quarterback, Tom Welch. Now that I attend classes, and even run around with, high school football players, I can see—and smile at—the difference between them and the players the sportswriters describe. Their accounts read like stories associated with the likes of Shakespeare and Chaucer. My dad must have enjoyed reading about Snuffy Kristich because he collected the newspaper clippings of his games in the Copper League. I've read those clippings countless times, and now I realize I could be reading them in Brother Kelley's English class. No wonder I've entertained thoughts about becoming a baseball writer.

The anticipation that accompanied the 1953 renewal of the Butte-Central football rivalry more than compared to that which accompanied the coming of George Lewis in the spring of 1952. I was loyal to Emerson, my public grade school, but I was a Catholic, which might have accounted for my feelings of loyalty to Central. But then not all my Catholic friends, who went to Emerson or some other public school, felt the same way. In fact, most of them felt loyalty to Butte High. I think I must have been affected by the catechism that taught me to see the Catholic Church as The One True Church.

When you're young that teaching can make sense because narrow boundaries define your world. I believed the Catholic Church to be The One True Church just as I believe Butte to be The Richest Hill on Earth and baseball to be The One True Sport. At 17 I still believe, even more strongly, what I first believed about Butte and baseball. But I'm not so sure about the Church, now that the boundaries of my world have expanded. I can understand that it's the first and oldest church of our civilization, and I even can understand how it could be The One True Church for us. But what about the world beyond our Christian boundaries? Does that world need our church? I don't know, but any church must be okay if its majesty can awaken someone's curiosity and sense of wonder. I don't know if the Catholic Church is The One True Church, but I do know that I like its majesty.

I like the majesty of sport, too. Once you're struck by it, you take the majesty with you, and every baseball game becomes a World Series game and every vacant lot becomes Yankee Stadium or Clark Park. You don't have to sit in Yankee Stadium with 60,000 fans to make baseball signify something. Butte's baseball fans didn't need Yankee Stadium as long as they brought he proper love to Clark Park. And that love created the magic.

I'll stick to that conclusion until my dying day because the Copper League players weren't even professional. And now that I'm older and able to understand baseball in more depth, I can tell from the box scores, preserved in my dad's clippings, that, with few exceptions—such as he and Kenny Sykes—most of the players hardly were exceptional. They certainly weren't in the same class as the Dodgers and the Giants I saw at Candlestick Park. But the simple fact is that I had no love for Drysdale and Snider, Mays and McCovey. But in the days of Clark Park I loved Babe Krilich and Pete Petrowski and the others who played for the South Side Athletic Club in the Copper League. But the majesty of the ballpark whetted the appetite and put me in touch with something worthy of love.

Naranche Stadium's majesty almost matched that of the grandstand at Clark Park. Named after Eso Naranche, a Butte High football legend killed in action in World War II, Naranche Stadium—unlike Clark Park—had lights. But the artificial light didn't matter. Unlike baseball, football isn't a game of the sun in the first place. Besides, the arc lights surrounding Naranche Stadium illuminate the white chalk lines of the gridiron and actually contribute to the majesty, if they don't create it. The magic still lives in that stadium, even though we haven't defeated Butte High during my four years at Central. But I don't think winning the game made the evening in September of 1953 so special. Win or lose, I think I still would have decided to love Central. Beating Butte High for the first time in 28 years only helped.

Being in high school meant that Judy had to take the bus home from Uptown because Girls' Central is half way up The Hill on West Park Street, next to the Fox Theater and just west of the Knights of Columbus sitting on the corner of West Park and Idaho Street. Boys' Central is just one block south, at the corner of Idaho and Mercury Street, if you measure from the rear entrance to Girls Central on Galena Street and almost two blocks in the same direction if you measure from its main entrance that looks eastward, toward Idaho Street, from its U-shaped courtyard. After school Judy had to walk east on West Park, for four or five blocks, until she reached Burr's department store, at the corner of Park and Dakota, or the Rialto Theater, at the central Park and Main intersection, to catch either the Race Track or Englewood bus to The Flat.

If she caught the Englewood, she would get off at the corner of Florence Avenue and George Street where she'd then walk through Clark Park to get home. If she caught the Race Track, she would get off at the corner of Wall Street and Monroe, just about two and one-half blocks north of our house. After school taking either bus didn't make much difference, but at night catching the bus provided a challenge. If she got off the Race Track at the corner of Wall and Monroe, she had to walk past Crazy Molly's house adjacent to the bus stop. And if she made it past Crazy Molly's, she had to contend with the dark alley that served as a short cut from Monroe to our house, resting at the back of its two lots on Aberdeen Street. By the time I made it to high school in 1958, the bus routes and the bus stops hadn't changed.

I don't mind taking the bus home from school, if I don't walk or hitch-hike, but I still don't like taking it home at night. I remember jumping off the bus and running all the way home after it stopped opposite Crazy Molly's. I felt greatly relieved to walk into the house and turn on the lights, knowing that I was safe again. Maybe Crazy Molly was harmless, but she was eccentric enough, with her front yard dance routines, to scare us. She's gone now, but I still don't waste any time getting off the Race Track bus. If I get stuck taking the bus home from Uptown after a dance, I run all the way from the bus stop to our front door. I don't have to sprint very much anymore, now that

I'm a senior, but I was a match for any Olympic champion during my freshman and sophomore years when no one could drive.

Judy took the bus home more often than I did because we didn't have a car, and none of her friends drove cars, even if their families owned them. If a boy didn't take her home from a dance, she had to catch the late bus in front of Burr's or the Rialto and bravely get off in front of Crazy Molly's. But almost ten years ago I was waiting for her to come home from Girls'Central Uptown on the day of the Butte-Central football game. I was still in grade school at Emerson on The Flat, and I made it home before she did.

XVII

I was sitting at the table when she opened the kitchen door and walked into the room. She wiped her feet on the rug just inside the front door, took off her coat, dropped it on the bed to her right, and just inside the archway that separated the kitchen from the bedroom, and walked toward the kitchen table. Sisters are like mothers in that you never notice whether or not they're attractive. But now that Judy had begun her freshman year in high school, she looked more grown up. She used to be a neighborhood tomboy who could play baseball as well, or even better, than any of her male competitors, having learned the finer points of the game from my dad and then having learned even more after she discovered Kenny Sykes in the Copper League. She always chose to be Kenny whenever we played baseball, and whenever she and I happened to be on the same team, we always adopted the South Side Athletic Club. But she was in high school now, and her tomboy days lay behind her, even though she still could have played baseball with the best of them—in spite of her developing sophistication.

She didn't wear make-up to school because I don't think the Sisters of Charity allowed it, and they still don't, as far as I know. The girls do wear lipstick and rouge at dances, but I don't know what they wear to school because I never get the chance to see them. I don't particularly like make-up anyway, but I have to admit that I have a weakness for perfume. Julie Shaw wore perfume that drove me crazy whenever I danced with her. Maybe girls, especially Julie, shouldn't wear perfume. Sometimes, it almost proves to be too much to handle.

I never looked at Judy in the manner I looked at Julie, but I do know that she wore the same uniform that Julie and the girls wear today at Girls' Central. Even though the Brothers don't allow us to wear any kind of blue jeans to school, we don't have to wear uniforms. Still, I like to see the girls in their uniforms, and I remember being impressed when I first saw Judy wearing hers. She naturally looked more grown up dressed in her white, short-sleeved blouse that she wore under her dark blue jumper with GHS stitched in red near the left shoulder strap. I think uniforms, in their majesty, help distinguish the individual, and in this regard Judy was no exception.

I don't think she wore nylons in 1953. Instead, she wore the same ankle length socks that girls at Girls' Central still wear today, even though I'm sure they wear nylons most of the time. Otherwise, their legs wouldn't look so tan during the winter months. With or without nylons, the girls wore their uniforms longer then than they do now. I know Judy's uniform jumper hung down below her knees almost halfway to her ankles. But today when the girls kneel down in church before school begins in the morning, you can see that their uniform jumpers hang straight. When they stand up during, or after, Mass, the jumpers very seldom reach below their knees. The Sisters at Girls' Central probably wouldn't agree, but I like today's uniform length. In fact, one of the Sisters always reminds Julie that she's wearing her uniform too short, but I've never mentioned it. And I've never said that she shouldn't wear perfume, either.

Judy didn't wear her hair much differently than girls do now, although she never wore it in the pony tail style that can be popular today. When she was in grade school, my mother would pin up her hair in curls every night before she went to bed. But she looked more grown up now without those long curls and with her shorter bangs resting comfortably on her forehead. Instead of reaching down to the small of her back, as it did during her grade school days, her hair was cut closer to her neck, giving it a more mature, fuller look. Judy's grade school hair style didn't fit with her Girls' Central High School uniform.

She doesn't sport the prominent and proud Bohunk nose that identifies my mother and me. Instead, she has my dad's wider and flatter variety of the same that's more compatible with the high cheekbones she also inherited from him. Her eyes reflect a darker blue than mine do, and her hair is both thicker and a darker brown. If my mother had Judy's hair, I'm convinced Sunday mornings, before walking to church, would have been far less traumatic for her.

Judy always was small but never frail, which explains why she could play baseball with the neighborhood boys. My dad stood five eight while my mother stands five three at the most, and I know Judy isn't as tall as she is. I just reached five ten, and I look like a giant compared to Judy. If she wasn't fully grown by the time she reached high school, she was awfully close to it. We had our battles every now and then, but I always respected her and still do. I made it home before she did when she went to high school, but sometimes I wished the situation were reversed.

"Which bus did you take home?" I asked as she sat down at the kitchen table.

"The Race Track," she answered, making herself comfortable in her chair.

"Did you see Crazy Molly?"

"No, not today. But I do someday. Sometimes she's dancing in her front yard, and sometimes she's just standing there."

"What do you do when you see her?"

"I really don't know what to do. I don't want to run because I don't want to embarrass her, and I don't want her to see that I'm scared. At night I just run as fast as I can all the way home. But during the day I just try to act as calm as I can. It's not always easy."

"Do you really think she's crazy?"

"I don't know. I don't know what crazy is, I guess, but she does act different that anyone else I've ever seen. I don't know too many people who stand in front of their porch in the middle of the day and dance. But I don't think you guys should tease her. She'll get back at you someday."

"I don't tease her all the time."

"Maybe not all the time. But who throws dead frogs in her yard and then cherry bombs when the Fourth of July comes around?"

"I'm not the only one. Besides, I haven't done that very often."

"Well," Judy said, "you'd better not do it at all anymore because she might decide to retaliate."

"She wouldn't hurt me. I've talked to her, and I've even been inside her fence. One day she showed me her garage that was stacked to the ceiling with newspapers. I wonder what they were for."

"I don't know. But you'd better be careful."

I should have heeded Judy's words, but I didn't. That following summer, as I was standing at the corner of our alley—two blocks south of Crazy Molly's—watching my next door neighbor ride my bike in front of her house as he was teasing her, she shot my bike chain in half with her pellet gun and then shot me in the side. I thought I was dead and hit the ground with all the style of John Wayne. Judy burst into the biggest tears I've ever seen away from the movie screen when she saw me rolling in the dust. Luckily for me, Crazy Molly didn't fire a real gun with real bullets, but she wasn't so lucky. My mother called the police. They came to get me, and then they picked up Crazy Molly. They took me to the hospital and her to jail in the same police car. I became a neighborhood celebrity because I'd been shot, and no one ever saw Crazy Molly again. That summer I learned what it was like to be a hero, but I don't think Brother Kelley has that kind of hero in mind. I didn't do anything but get shot. At least Bobby 'Scooter' Johnson ran 60 yards for a touchdown.

"I'll be careful," I said in response to Judy's warning. "Don't worry."

"I'm not going to worry tonight. I have other things on my mind. Don't tell me you've forgotten about the football game."

"Are you kidding? I thought maybe you had. I thought maybe you were too grown up to be excited."

"Just because you're grown up doesn't mean you can't get excited. I think I'm more excited now that Central is my school, even though my friends from Emerson went to Butte High. Sometimes I wish I went there, too."

"But then you couldn't wear that uniform. They don't wear uniforms at Butte High."

"I know. It's different. But we held a pep rally today, and I felt a part of Central for the first time. You'll see when you get to high school. I can't wait to get to the game now. I wish Mom would hurry and get home so we could eat and get going."

"Who are you going with?" I asked.

"Ellen McGivern's dad is going to pick me up and take us to the game."

"Who's Ellen McGivern?"

"She's a friend I've made at school."

"Do you know Tom Welch and Scooter Johnson?" I asked with wide open eyes.

"Everyone knows them," Judy answered. "Tom Welch is our quarterback and Scooter Johnson is our star halfback. I don't know them, but I know who they are. I've seen them Uptown after school, and I saw them today at Boys' Central at the pep rally."

"You saw them?" I asked in disbelief.

"Sure. They're seniors. I saw them at the pep rally when the coach introduced the team. They were standing at the front of the study hall wearing their letterman's jackets."

"Really? What do you do at a pep rally?"

"There's a skit that has something to do with the game," Judy answered. "The cheerleaders lead cheers, and the coach gives an inspirational talk to all of us about the importance of school spirit and loyalty to the maroon and white. Then the band plays the school song, and we all stand up and sing. If I were a boy, I couldn't wait to wear our colors and play against the purple and white of Butte High."

I listened to everything Judy said as she described the pep rally, and ever since that day I wanted to attend one to see if she was telling the truth. I've since discovered she was. Nothing surpasses Girls' and Boys' Central coming together at a pep rally before the Butte-Central game. The school song works like magic, making all of us realize that Central belongs to Butte and not to any neighborhood. Usually, only the girls cheer, but Central's version of the Notre Dame Fight Song is too much to resist. And when we get to the part where her loyal sons are marching to victory, we sing as loud as we can—and not just to make noise. The fight song helps us to be true to our school, and Central is worthy of our loyalty, as far as I can see. And I'm sure their version of the Wisconsin Fight Song works the same magic for the Butte High students, contributing to the fierce rivalry.

"The pep rally sounds exciting," I said, responding to Judy's description. "I'm going to the game with Uncle Tim, and we're going to meet some of his friends there. I like to be with him when he's with his friends."

"You won't always go to the game with Uncle Tim. Someday you'll have your own friends as I do, and you'll want to go with them."

"Maybe so, but I'll always remember going with Uncle Tim. I like to listen to him and his friends talk. They talk like men, and I get to listen. Sometimes they even swear, even though Uncle Tim never swears when he's just with me. I'd like to be an uncle someday. Then I could take my nephews and nieces to baseball and football games. I could even take them to a bar where they could play the pinball machines while my friends and I drink a beer and a shot of whiskey. I wonder what whiskey tastes like. Uncle Tim lets me taste beer, but he says I have to get a little older before he'll let me taste the whiskey. I know he's funny when he drinks it."

"Yes, but he fights sometimes, too," Judy said. "Remember the time when he was supposed to get us some ice cream when he and Auntie Loo were baby-sitting us?"

"That's the night he came back with blood all over his jacket," I answered.

"That's right. And the ice cream had melted."

"I remember. I was sitting on the stoop in front of Dave's house when Uncle Tim came walking up the sidewalk. I still can see the blood on his jacket."

"What did he say when he saw you?"

"He said he licked the both of them. He must be tough. I hope I can be as tough as he is someday."

"I hope so, too. But if you have to get that bloody, you're wife will mad at you just as Auntie Loo was mad at Uncle Tim that night. I remember that."

"Why was she mad?" I asked.

"Because got into a fight and didn't bring the ice cream home in time and because he had blood all over his jacket. Auntie Loo asked him if he had to fight, and he said he did because two men chose him. She said that maybe he shouldn't have stopped to have a drink on the way to get the ice cream. But he said he just stopped in Boogs' to have one drink before he came home."

"Then what did Auntie Loo say?"

"She just said 'men!' and turned and tried to save some of the ice cream as Uncle Tim tried to apologize. He kept telling her that he did lick the both of them. I don't know if Auntie Loo knew whether to laugh or cry. But she finally laughed a little and dished up the ice cream that wasn't completely melted."

"But Uncle Tim's funny," I said.

"I know he is," Judy replied, laughing. "What time is he picking you up?"

"I think he's coming a little after seven," I answered, looking up at the kitchen clock that hung on the wall above the ringer washer that sat against the south wall of the kitchen next to the front door. "What are you going to do after the game?"

"I'm going to the dance at Boys' Central."

"Are you going to dance with Tom Welch or Scooter Johnson?" I asked, sitting on the edge of my chair.

"I don't think so. They're seniors and I'm just a freshman. Seniors don't dance with freshmen. But I'll see them there."

"What do you do at a dance?"

"I really don't know. This is my first one."

"Are you nervous?"

"A little."

"Do you think anyone will ask you to dance?"

"I don't know. But I hope so."

"Do you know how to dance?"

"Of course. I learned when I was in the eighth grade, and I danced with Uncle Tim at my graduation."

"Don't get mad. I was just asking. How are you going to get home?"

"I don't know. Mom says I can come home with a boy if someone asks me, as long as I come straight home and if I call her to let her know. But if no one asks me home, I'll take the bus."

"The Race Track?"

"Yes. It stops closer to the house."

"That means you'll have to get off by Crazy Molly's."

"I know."

"Does that scare you?"

"A little."

"Why don't you just come home after the game?"

"Because I want to go to the dance. I'm not that scared."

"I bet you run all the way home from the bus stop if no one takes you home."

"I don't think anyone will take me home because no one knows me that well yet. Besides, I wouldn't come home with just anyone.

Anyway," Judy said, looking at the clock, "it's almost five o'clock and Mom will be home soon. If we don't get the house picked up before she gets here, neither one of us will be going anywhere. She and George are going out tonight, too."

"Where are they going?"

"I don't know. You'll have to ask Mom. But for now, you shake out the kitchen rugs and sweep the floor and straighten up the table. I'll run the carpet sweeper over the living room rug and dust the tables. We'd better get started."

"I guess you're right," I said, getting up from the kitchen table. "We have to have the cleanest house in all of Butte," I added, picking up the rug in front of the kitchen door and reaching for the doorknob.

"I'm sure we do," Judy said, walking through the kitchen toward the bedroom to get the carpet sweeper. "Shake the rugs," she hollered from the closet.

"Okay," I said, opening the front door to the Friday night, autumn chill. I could feel football in the air as I shook the dirt free from the rug that always lay just inside the kitchen door.

XVIII

❀

*M*y mother had been going out with George for more than a year and a half, and I could tell she was happier. Still, some things never change, and she couldn't tolerate coming home to a messy house. So Judy and I took great pains to clean up whatever mess we made before she came home from work. Even if we hadn't made a mess, we cleaned as if we had. My mother could see dirt where none existed. Superman, with his x-ray vision, had nothing over her. No one had been in the house all day, but if I didn't sweep the kitchen floor and shake out the rugs and if Judy didn't run the carpet sweeper over the living room rug and dust the tables, she would have known. We tried to fake it before but without success. Neither one of us was willing to take the chance tonight so Judy worked in the living room and I worked in the kitchen cleaning a house that no ordinary woman ever would have thought needed it.

"Are you almost done?" I asked as I swept dirt, more imagined than real, into the kitchen dust pan.

"Yes," Judy answered. "I just have one corner left to go over and then I'll be finished. I don't know of any other carpet where the dirt gets caught before it has any chance of settling in," she continued with a laugh.

"Was Dad the same as Mom? I can't remember."

"He was more like us, if that's what you mean. He made sure the house was neat and clean. He knew he'd be in trouble if he didn't."

"You're lucky. You remember more than I do. I don't remember any of those details."

"I was older than you when he died. So I remember more about him."

"Did he ever get mad at Mom?"

"Not really that I remember. He usually could make her laugh about herself and the house. But she could get mad at him. I especially remember one time when he came home drunk."

"Did Dad come home drunk like Uncle Tim?"

"Not very often, but I know he did at least one time. He came home drunk without his money, and Mom threw his wallet at him."

"Really? Did she hit him? What did he do?"

"She didn't hit him with it. And he had no choice but to apologize."

"Did it work?"

"Not right away. But eventually it did."

"How did he lose his money?"

"He lost it gambling Uptown at the Board of Trade on East Park Street. Men used to cash their checks there, and Dad lost his playing cards or dice, I guess. I don't think he ever did it again, though. One time was enough."

"I wish I could remember all you can."

"You remember enough."

"But I wish I remembered more. Sometimes I feel like he never died. I feel like he's still here."

"Maybe it does seem that way, but I wish he were here. I like George, but he's not Dad. Sometimes I really miss him, like when I graduated from the eighth grade."

"But Uncle Tim was there for you."

"I know, but every other girl had the chance to dance with their dad. I think a father is different for a girl. We both miss Dad, but you have Uncle Tim. I do, too, but it's not the same. I wish I had Dad now. I don't think it's fair," Judy said as tears welled up in her eyes.

"I'm sorry. I didn't mean to make you cry. We'll make it okay."

"I know we will. I just feel sad sometimes. That's all. He'd be so excited for the game tonight and for me going to my first high school dance and all that. And he could take you to the game. I just miss him now, I guess."

"I do, too, but Uncle Tim says that Dad told him to take care of us. I figure that's sort of like Dad still being alive through Uncle

Tim. Dancing with him, then, is like Dancing with Dad, and going to game with Uncle Tim is like going with Dad. I know Uncle Tim cares, and that makes it special."

"You're right," Judy said, smiling and wiping her eyes. "Besides, Dad wouldn't want me to feel sorry for myself and not enjoy the game and the dance. Maybe Central will win this year. They haven't won since 1925. That's 28 years. I know we would have won if we could have played immediately after the pep rally today. Wait until you get to high school. Then you can see for yourself."

"I can't wait, but you'll be in college by the time I get that far. That seems like forever. I hope high school's the same when I get there. I hope they still have pep rallies and dances."

"They will, and you'll be a big hit. Maybe you'll be a football star."

"Like Tom Welch and Scooter Johnson?"

"Maybe. But if that doesn't turn out, you always can sweep the locker room floor. You'll have had enough practice by then."

"Real funny," I said, swinging the broom in her direction, but not wanting to hit her.

"Be careful. You'll break something, and then we'll be in big trouble," she said, laughing. "Put the broom away. It's almost time for Mom to come home," she continued as she walked through the kitchen on her way to the bedroom closet. "I can't get the living room any cleaner. This carpet sweeper probably makes it dirtier," she concluded as she put the carpet sweeper in the closet, leaning it against the east wall where it belonged.

"I hope it's clean enough," I said, looking out the kitchen door window, "because here comes Mom and George now driving into the driveway."

Now that my mother was going out with George, she didn't have to take the bus home from work because he always was waiting for her at the courthouse. Even though she liked being picked up from work, I think she would have been happier if she had made the decision. She's an independent woman, although some people attribute her behavior to "Bohunk stubbornness." But I think she just likes to be free and doesn't like to have any man tell her what to do. If George would have let her choose to be picked up, I think he'd be better off, as would we all. But the days were growing shorter now, and you could feel the autumn chill in the air. Having George waiting outside the courthouse on such nights was better than having to walk to Burrs to catch the Race Track or Englewood bus. I didn't think she'd be angry when she walked into the kitchen.

"How was work today?" I asked as she walked in and wiped her feet on the rug in front of the door.

"It was fine," she answered, taking off her coat. "We really weren't very busy today. It's nice to have some quiet days. I get tired of walking on those cement floors in these high heels. It's always a relief to get home and take them off," she added, walking into the bedroom. "Did everything go okay at school today?" she asked from inside the closet.

"Yes," I answered. "The day went fast because it's Friday and because Uncle Tim's taking me to the Butte-Central game tonight. Time can go pretty slow sometimes, when I don't have anything to look forward to."

"That's why it's nice to look forward to coming home," my mother said, smiling. "Especially when your children have cleaned the house," she added, looking around the kitchen. "It looks clean in here. Did you shake out the rugs and sweep the floor?"

"Yes."

"Good for you. Where's Judy?"

"I don't know. She just put the carpet sweeper away before you came home. She must be in the bathroom," I said just as I heard that door open.

"Hi," my mother said as Judy walked into the kitchen.

"Hi, Mom. How did work go today?"

"Fine. I was telling Dan how we didn't have too much work today and how it's nice to have some days when the office isn't too busy. Are you excited about the game tonight, too?"

"Yes," Judy answered enthusiastically. "We had a pep rally at Boys' Central this afternoon, and that helped. Plus I'm excited to go to the dance after the game. I've never been to a high school dance."

"It's a big night for you. I hope Central wins the game and I hope the dance is fun."

"Did you go to the Butte-Central game when you were in high school, Mom?" I asked.

"Well, I didn't go to high school, Danny."

"I thought everyone went to high school," I said. "I thought everyone had to."

"Maybe that's the case now. But it was different in my day. I couldn't go to high school because I had to go to work."

"Didn't that make you mad?" Judy asked.

"No, not really. I wasn't alone. Life was different in those days. We didn't have much money and everyone had to help out. So, a lot of us didn't go to high school."

"Do you wish we still lived in those days?"

"No, Danny. You have to live now. I don't want to forget those days, and I suppose there are times when I wish I could go back. But we can't go back and that's that. But I want to remember the past, and you should be open to revisiting it. You should listen when people talk about those days. You, too, Judy."

"Uncle Tim tells stories about those days all the time, and I always listen," I said.

"So do I," Judy added.

"Are Uncle Tim's stories true, Mom?" I asked

"Knowing Uncle Tim, I wouldn't be surprised if he stretched the truth just a little bit. He has quite an imagination, you know."

"I know," Judy said. "That's why I enjoy his stories so much. He sure likes to tell them."

"Uncle Tim will tell stories for as long as people will listen," my mother said.

"I'll always listen to him. Even when I grow up."

"I hope you will, Danny," my mother said. "But when you grow up, you'll have your own stories to tell. You'll be able to tell about the football game tonight and about playing hooky and sitting in the Clark Park dugout."

"That's right," I said as my eyes lit up. "When Judy has kids, I can tell them stories just as Uncle Tim tells me stories. That way they can revisit the past, too. I hope they'll like to listen."

"They will. I'll make sure of that. You just make sure you tell the truth."

"I'll tell the truth. But is it okay if I use my imagination like Uncle Tim does?"

"You have to use your imagination," Judy answered, "to make the truth a story."

"Neither of you will have a chance to tell anyone anything if I don't get dinner started," my mother said. "Judy, you can make the salad while I get the spaghetti started. Okay?"

"Okay, Mom," Judy answered, opening the refrigerator door and reaching into the crisper to get the lettuce, tomatoes, radishes, and green onions.

XIX

I left my mother and Judy in the kitchen and walked into the living room to wait for dinner. As always, I encountered a room that was clean, orderly and warm. In the summer the sunlight shines through the porch windows, allowing us to open the porch door and feel the sun's warmth. In the late fall, and in the winter with the arrival of the ice, we have to close the porch door to keep out the cold and turn the heating over to the gas furnace in the basement. The heat registers are built on either side of the wall that separates the kitchen from the living room, and each register juts out just enough to make it possible to sit on the ledge and feel the warmth rising from the basement furnace. I still like to sit on the living room ledge during the fall and winter to feel the warmth. Besides, I've always found it a good place to think while I wait for dinner.

I'm attached to our living room, even if it isn't the roomiest in Butte and even if it does double as my bedroom with the hide-a-bed sitting against the north wall that meets the alley at the back of the house. We didn't have a TV set yet in the fall of 1953, but we did have a Philco console radio that sat against the west wall across from the heat register and underneath the mirror that reflected the chimney depression that extended from the wall just above the register. My dad's cushioned rocking chair still filled the corner to the left of the radio, and a shiny, black, fold-top desk—the size of a small piano and trimmed in gold artistry—sat almost in the opposite corner just to the right of one of the end tables that framed the hide-a-bed.

Judy always did her homework on that desk. She'd fold the top and pull out the desk to give herself more room to work, and the dark green, felt cover helped cushion the black, wood bench. Ornately carved legs supported the desk and its bench, and the heels of Judy's shoes had left the wood bar connecting the bench legs scuffed and scarred. The brass lamp sitting on the adjacent end table gave off enough light, and at night—with the light burning and Judy working—that desk never looked so smooth and shiny.

No matter how often Judy used it, I never saw a finger print or a dust particle mar the appearance of our black desk. My mother put it down the basement when Judy went to college, which means that I have to do my homework sitting at the kitchen table. She says the light's better in the kitchen, but I'll take the black desk any day. Someday I'll put that desk in the living room of my own house. I can't picture my house without it nor can I picture it without a hassock, just like the one that sat in the corner across the room from my dad's rocking chair.

The living room carpet didn't quite cover the hardwood floor, and my mother and I still have to turn it periodically to make sure it wears evenly. Every Saturday she waxes the exposed floor with Johnson's paste wax. I've never seen that hardwood when it didn't shine just as I never saw the black desk when it wasn't completely free of dust and fingerprints. The carpet's mixed, floral design of soft greens, violet, and pink colors blends in with the light green, tweed material that covers the hide-a-bed and with our new blonde, straight-angled coffee table and matching end tables. But in 1953 I saw the dark, ornately carved cherry wood tables my mother and dad bought after they were married. I liked those tables better than I like their blonde counterparts, but the new tables match the blonde, combination TV and stereo and complement the soft pink color of the walls and ceiling. Now that I think about it, I liked the dark wood better. It seemed warmer, but I suppose it's out of date now. However, I'm glad the gas furnace isn't out of date because I still can sit on the register's ledge and think—just as I could in 1953. Some things don't change, I guess.

I've always liked to think. When I played Little League baseball, I used to think about my dad and Lefty Reardon all the time. Lefty, my dad's best friend, died of a heart attack at the Anselmo mine in February of 1950, just a few months before my dad died. Lefty was only 37 when he died which made him the same age as Uncle Tim who's 20 years older than I am. Like 41, 37 seems awfully young to die. It doesn't seem fair, but, still, it happens all the time. I've always wondered about death and how untimely it can be, and I remember asking Brother Williams, my religion teacher during my sophomore year at Central, if my dad would have died if Adam and Eve hadn't eaten the apple in the Garden of Eden. I was trying to figure out death and why my dad died and, I suppose, why Lefty Reardon died because he taught me how to pitch. Brother Williams said that my dad wouldn't have died if Adam and Eve hadn't eaten the apple. I wanted to believe him because he was a teacher, because he was a Brother, because he spoke for the Church and because I didn't think he was trying to lie to me. But no matter how hard I tried, and believe me I tried, I couldn't bring myself to blame Adam and Eve for my dad's death. I can't blame them and I can't hold them accountable. But nonetheless, according to Brother Williams and the Church, they are responsible for his death.

If he and the Church are wrong, however, then all that follows from their fundamental conclusion is wrong as well. If that's the case, you really have to think about life being "a tale told by an idiot full of sound and fury signifying nothing." As long as you can believe the Church and Brother Williams, you're safe. But if you can't, I can see how you're in for trouble. What if we don't have, and can't find, any evidence to support their basic premise? What do you do then? Do you decide that life's "a tale told by an idiot full of sound and fury signifying nothing?" I'm not convinced because on the chance that the space explorers won't find any evidence to support the Church and Brother Williams, I think my journey has produced something.

I can understand how Macbeth's life could have been meaningless, but I can't see how life in general can be meaningless simply because individuals die—sometimes untimely. Maybe death is natural, and in the face of it maybe we're supposed to live more for love than to get rich and to live on the West Side. Maybe my mother's like Eve and maybe Eve's heroic and maybe people just die. I don't mean any disrespect for Brother Williams and the Church, but when I think about it, their basic conclusion doesn't make sense. Do people die just because someone ate an apple off a tree? I don't see how Eve can be evil because eating the apple doesn't strike me as being an evil thing to do. Maybe Brother

Williams never has thought about it, but Brother Kelley has. If he hasn't, he wouldn't teach the way he does. I think he admires Eve, and I don't think he blames her for anything, even though he hasn't explicitly said so yet. I think he'd get in trouble if he did. But that's why he tells us we should want to be heroes. That's what he means by wanting to know, love and serve God.

Somehow Butte must be knowing, loving and serving God because the city looks happy to me and people die here all the time. Maybe Butte knows, loves and serves God without realizing it. I've never thought about that, but I think Brother Kelley has. And he wants us to think just in case John Glenn and the other explorers don't discover any next world. Maybe that's what monument to eternity means. Neither the gallus frames nor the crucifix can talk, but if anything's a monument to eternity, it has to be the crucifix. If I think and look carefully, I can see courage and love in both the gallus frames and the crucifix. But I wasn't thinking about gallus frames and crucifixes in 1953. I was only nine years old, and no one had heard of Alan Shepard and John Glenn. Still, I was thinking. I liked to sit on the heat register ledge and think, and I used to lie in bed and think. You have quite a bit to think about when you kiss your 41-year-old father goodbye in his coffin and when you realize that the man who taught you how to pitch was even younger and died first.

I started to play Little League baseball in 1952 when I was eight years old, and I still can remember my first authentic uniform. I've never been more proud of anything, unless it's my first, and my dad's last, baseball glove. I wore that glove as the third baseman for the Front Street Bakery Yanks in my first game in the Longfellow Little League. We played Community Creamery, and I'll never forget the first ground ball ever hit to me in a baseball game played with uniforms and umpires—just like the games the Copper Leaguers played in Clark Park. I fielded the ball cleanly on the third big bounce, took a little crow hop as my dad had taught me, and looked toward first base—directly into the sun. I couldn't see the baserunner, and I couldn't see the first baseman. I couldn't even see first base. But I threw the ball anyway, and it sailed over the first baseman's head and over the fence behind the baseline. I turned my first ground ball into an error, and the runner stood on second base as a result. Uncle Tim was the coach, but he didn't reprimand me that time.

Every night before a game I used to pray to my dad and Lefty Reardon both of whom, I was sure, now lived in Heaven. On the chance that they still were stuck in Purgatory someplace, I used to pray that they'd get out in a hurry so that they could enjoy Heaven's bliss. I prayed because I believed they could hear and that they'd give me the help I was asking for, that somehow they'd help me play better. Maybe I would have played just as well without the prayers, but saying them, and directing them to my dad and Lefty, helped me play from the heart.

But now we're exploring space where Heaven is supposed to be. What if we don't find anything? Then, what happened to my dad and Lefty Reardon? It's comforting to believe in Heaven, which is why I hope we find something in space. But I'm not so sure, now that I'm 17. It's not as easy to believe as it used to be, and traditional answers don't make as much sense as they used to. But I can see that as long as we believe in Heaven, life, which includes death, can't be meaningless. But it's a different story if there's nothing to Heaven in any way. That's why I think it's scary today, but you can't stop exploring. We have to venture out into space. We can't stop just because we're afraid of what we might discover. Maybe it's more comfortable not to explore and not to think about what the explorers find or don't find, but we're not supposed to live for comfort alone. If we do, it seems to me that we'll eventually agree with Macbeth.

I wonder how Shakespeare learned so much. Brother Kelley says that Macbeth's tragedy can be anyone's tragedy. For some reason Shakespeare and Brother Kelley make a lot of sense, but I don't think Shakespeare agrees with Macbeth. I think he agrees with Brother Kelley who doesn't think life is meaningless, even though he won't explicitly say so. He wants us to find out for ourselves because if we don't, we'll never believe him or Shakespeare. So we can't be afraid. We have to explore.

Maybe Heaven isn't a place out there somewhere where my dad and Lefty Reardon still can play baseball and listen to prayers and watch me play my own baseball games. Maybe the soul the Sisters explained in catechism never has to die. Maybe our physical existence isn't everything, and maybe we should take better care of, or as much care of, the soul. If Macbeth had taken better care of the soul, I think he'd have escaped the misery of despair. Shakespeare didn't despair and neither has Brother Kelley. The soul has to be real, even if it doesn't depart for Heaven, or Hell, after death. If it isn't real, all of religion is a lie. But how could anyone conclude that religion is a lie? I'd hate to try to live without its promise. Just look at Macbeth.

I don't know whether or not my prayers worked. But if you think winning proves they did, they must have worked especially well in the first game I ever pitched. Little League games last six innings, and in this particular game Uncle Tim put me in to pitch in the second inning, after our starting pitcher proved he couldn't throw strikes. In the next five innings I struck out 15 batters. Either I prayed extra hard the night before the game or I enjoyed a great advantage because Lefty Reardon had taught me how to pitch. But I always prayed hard, and I never struck out 15 batters in five innings again, although I never lost many games, either. I prayed just as hard when I was older and playing in Babe Ruth League, but my first trip to the mound at that level resulted in me being banished to the dugout in tears after two innings. Puberty arrived late with me, and Little League strikeouts from 45 feet became Babe Ruth line drives from 60 feet six inches. The hitters were getting even with me, and neither my dad nor Lefty Reardon could do anything about it. After puberty the strikeouts began to return, but never like before. I think I struck out 15 in my first trip to the mound in Little League because Lefty Reardon had taught me how to pitch. And no one had taught the batters how to hit.

Sometimes my 17-year-old thoughts take over from my nine-year-old thoughts. When I was nine sitting on the ledge above the furnace in the living room waiting to eat my spaghetti and salad before going to the Butte-Central football game with Uncle Tim, I actually was thinking about something Judy had said before she began to make the salad. She said you have to use your imagination to make the truth a story. I wanted to tell stories as Uncle Tim did, which is why I asked if I could use my imagination. I wanted to tell the truth. But I wanted to use my imagination because I wanted to tell a story.

I don't know if Judy understood what she said, but I thought about it that night and ever since, especially since I've had Brother Kelley as a teacher. Now when I remember and think of what she said, I think of him and Shakespeare, and I think of Uncle Tim and his stories in a different way. 'Macbeth' is a product of Shakespeare's imagination just as Uncle Tim's stories about Butte and Centerville are products of his. But I think I recognize a difference. Shakespeare knew what he was doing, but I think Uncle Tim just likes to tell stories. I think Brother Kelley's more like Shakespeare in that he knows what Shakespeare was doing, and he knows what he's doing when he tells us stories in class. They're all telling the truth, only I don't think Uncle Tim is as aware. None of them lie. They tell the kinds of stories I want to tell to anyone willing to listen.

I didn't have too much time to think about imagination and truth that night because my mother and Judy didn't take too much time preparing dinner. Sometimes I think my mother is a magician when she cooks. I've heard people say that a watched pot never boils, but I think my mother skipped the boiling when she made our Friday night spaghetti—as she still does, even without Judy—with Chef Boyardee sauce. She was, and still is, a whirlwind. I'm glad Judy was the girl because I wouldn't have wanted to try to keep up with her. Sometimes I think she made water boil by the sheer force of her will. I've never seen anything like it, but no one, then or now, ever was a better cook. For some reason Chef Boyardee spaghetti sauce gives off a smell that rivals that of the Saturday morning pork chop sandwich offered at Pork Chop John's on Mercury Street. No one had to tell me to leave my spot on the ledge above the furnace to join my family in the kitchen for Friday night dinner.

XX

✿

"This sure smells good," I said, taking my place at the table to the left of my mother who always sat at its head nearest the refrigerator. "Is this vinegar and oil dressing on the salad?" I asked, reaching for my napkin.

"Of course it is," Judy answered. "We never have anything else on salad. I don't know why you even had to ask."

"I don't, either, I guess. I just thought I would. I wouldn't want to eat salad without vinegar and oil, and I wouldn't want to eat spaghetti without this salad. Friday night wouldn't be the same without either."

"We don't always eat spaghetti and salad on Friday night," my mother said.

"I know, but this is my favorite. I like the taste of the vinegar mixed with the spaghetti sauce."

"So do I," Judy said, sitting down across from me.

"Dinner's better when you like the smell and taste of food," my mother said, taking her seat at the head of the table. "Take some spaghetti, Judy, and pass it on to Dan. I'll start the salad."

"Okay," Judy replied as I watched her trap some spaghetti between her fork and the serving spoon as she transferred it to her plate. "Do you want me to serve you or can you serve yourself?" she asked after she had taken enough.

"I can serve myself. I'm almost ten years old, you know. You don't have to serve me anymore."

"Well, don't make a mess on the table," Judy said. "Serving spaghetti is pretty tricky."

"I think Dan realizes that fact, Judy," my mother said. "He's dropped it on the table often enough, just as someone else I know did on occasion. But he is almost ten and should be able to handle it," she added, smiling at the both of us.

"I can do it," I said emphatically. "Just watch." I held the serving spoon in my left hand, picked up my fork with my right hand, and dug into the spaghetti. I still can hear the squishing sound as I caught the noodles between the spoon and the fork, lifted them from the spaghetti dish, and placed them on my plate without dropping one of them on the table. "See how I did that?" I asked, proud of my accomplishment. "Just like a professional spaghetti server. Do you want me to serve you some, Mom?" I asked as I caught some more spaghetti and placed it just as securely on my plate.

"No thanks, Dan," my mother said, smiling. "I think I can handle it okay. Take some salad."

"Okay," I said, taking some from the bottom of the bowl so that I'd be sure to get some of the vinegar and oil along with the lettuce, radishes, onions and tomatoes. "Have some salad, Judy," I added, pushing the bowl in her direction.

"Thanks. Do you want me or Mom to cut your spaghetti for you?" Julie asked, smiling.

"I don't want anyone to cut it. I can roll it up on my fork without making a mess," I answered, demonstrating my technique. "See, I did it," I added, "and I kept it off my chin and my shirt."

"Just keep it up," my mother said. "And be careful. Remember, you're not an expert yet like your sister," she added, looking at Judy.

"Thanks, Mom, for recognizing talent," Judy said, smiling. "It tastes good as always. Plus I have to be careful. I don't want to stain my uniform."

"You should have changed it after school," my mother said.

"I know, but after I came home, Dan and I started to talk. I forgot all about changing until it was about time to straighten up the house."

"Well, I'll forgive you this time, I suppose. We all know how much Dan likes to talk," my mother said, looking at me as I concentrated on my spaghetti. "Isn't that right, Dan?"

"What? I must not have been listening. I'm trying to roll up this spaghetti the right way. It's hard to hang onto the fork without dropping it on my plate. I guess it takes practice."

"I just mentioned to Judy how much you like to talk. She said it was your fault that she didn't change her uniform after school. Is that right?"

"It wasn't my fault. We were just talking about the game tonight and about the dance afterwards. She likes to talk, too. But we picked up the house. We didn't want to talk that much."

"I appreciate your help. It's much more pleasant to come home to a neat and clean house," my mother said as she tasted her spaghetti and salad.

"If you didn't go to high school," Judy asked, "did you ever go to the Butte-Central game?"

"Yes. We used to go all the time."

"Who did you root for?" I asked.

"I only can remember rooting for Central. I guess that's because I was a Catholic, but I probably would have attended Butte High if I'd have gone to high school. We wouldn't have had to pay tuition there. By the way, Judy, do you like Central?"

"Honestly, I don't think I did until today. Most of my friends from Emerson went to Butte High. But after attending the pep rally, I felt glad to be at Central, and I hope we win tonight. It must be exciting to play in this game if it's this exciting just anticipating and getting ready to go watch it."

"Are you and George going to the game tonight?" I asked, carefully taking another bite of my spaghetti.

"No, I don't think so," my mother answered.

"Why not?" I asked.

"Because George doesn't especially like football, and it's hard to sit out in the cold if you don't like what you're watching. It's easier if you want to be there. Then you really don't notice the cold."

"Do you want to go?" Judy asked.

"In a way, but I certainly won't be heartbroken if I miss the game. It's not like going to watch your dad play baseball. Still, if I knew someone who was playing, I'd go for sure, regardless of the cold or anything else. I'd go to a baseball game to watch people I didn't know before I'd go to a football game under the same conditions," she added, continuing to eat her spaghetti.

"What are you going to do tonight?" I asked.

"I think George wants to go look at the new cars. He says the 1954 models have come in, and he wants to look in the showrooms. He loves Plymouths and hates Fords almost like your dad loved the Yankees and hated the Dodgers. It's funny. George's entire life seems to revolve around cars sometimes, and we've never owned one. How could I go from your dad and baseball to George and cars? It doesn't make much sense, but it's hard not to like George. He makes me laugh."

Now that I think about it, about George and cars I mean, I have to laugh, too. He knows as much about cars as I do about baseball. And I can recite the starting lineup of the 1927 Yankees without consulting any book. To George, seeing the new cars on display in their showrooms every fall represents the highlight of his life. He's convinced he has to own a car to be somebody. But if he ever made it, he'd lose his charm and no longer be George. I don't think you have to own a car to be somebody, but I do have to admit that owning one would make it easier for me in the dating world.

"He makes me laugh, too," I said, agreeing with my mother. "He really is funny. Are you going to marry him, Mom?"

"I don't know. I won't get married again unless I find the same love I had with your dad. George makes me laugh and I like to be with him, but so far it's not quite the same. It would be easy to marry George, but I'm in no hurry to marry anyone. I really have to think about it."

"We can make it if you don't get married again, Mom."

"I know we can, Judy. And knowing that keeps me strong. I told you before that I wouldn't get married unless I found the love I experienced with your dad."

"I trust you."

"Thank you, Dan. That makes me feel good. And I'll feel even better if we get the dishes done before Uncle Tim and George come and before Mr. McGivern comes to get Judy," my mother added, getting up from the table. "So finish your spaghetti and lets get to the dishes. You two dry and I'll wash."

"Okay," Judy and I replied together as we rolled up the last few strands of spaghetti and cleaned our plates.

We picked up the dishes and placed them on the counter to the right of the sink where my mother stood filling the plastic dish pale with hot water as the soap suds rose to the top. She washed dishes like she cooked, and Judy and I had to work together to keep up with her. Sometimes I had to ask her to slow down to give us a break. She'd always laugh, but she'd still wash and rinse so fast that the movement was nothing more than a blur. I still dry and my mother still washes. And I still try to keep up.

Mr. McGivern was supposed to pick up Judy around seven o'clock. We finished the dishes by six-thirty, giving her half an hour to change out of her uniform into something more suitable for watching football and dancing. My mother wasn't going out with George until after Judy and I left, and I was almost ready to go dressed as I was, wearing my brown school cords, light blue shirt, and maroon crew neck sweater. My mother told Judy to get ready as she wiped off the kitchen table, and I hung up the dish towels on the rack attached to the wall to the left of the kitchen stove and just above the cupboard where Judy and I kept our bowling pins and where I kept my dad's last, and my first, baseball glove,

"Did Dad like football?" I asked as my mother cleaned off the table and as Judy readied herself in the bathroom.

"He liked Notre Dame. He used to listen to their games every Saturday, but baseball remained his game—his religion—with bowling taking a close second. He bowled with, and against, the same men he played baseball with, and against, every spring and summer. Basically, they all just changed uniforms, and your dad liked his uniforms. From the City Lines, to baseball, to bowling—they all had to be washed and ironed regularly. I spent a lot of time taking proper care of his uniforms," she added, smiling.

"I remember watching him bowl at Harry's Alleys," I said, "just as I remember watching him play baseball. He'd always take me into the bar so that I could check to see if anyone left any money in the slot machines."

"He liked those machines," my mother said, still smiling. "In fact, he liked to gamble. He always said that gambling itself was better than winning money and that you had to enjoy the experience even if you lost. Sometimes he lost and sometimes he won."

"Judy told me about the time he lost all his money and came home drunk besides. She said you got mad at him."

"That was the only time," my mother said, laughing. "I didn't think it was funny at the time because he'd lost his entire paycheck, and we needed that money to live on. I wouldn't speak to him for a couple of days after that escapade."

"What did he do to get you to speak to him again?"

"Oh, he cleaned the house and washed the dishes to get back in my good graces. Finally, he made me laugh, and I got over the anger and the shock. Then we borrowed some money to see us through. He always could make me laugh—sometimes mostly at myself. He was a good man, Danny. Just ask Uncle Tim. No one thinks more of your dad than he does. He always looked up to him, and whenever he drank too much, your dad always was there to remind him that he was a married man now. Uncle Tim admired him. I think your dad represented everything a man should be."

"What about George?"

"He's different. He's almost there, but something's missing in George. He could be what a man should be, as your dad was, but I'm not sure he realizes that. Do you understand?"

"I'm trying to. Do you miss Dad?" I asked.

"I'll always miss him, Danny, because you always miss someone you love. That's why I'd never marry again unless I found the love I experienced with your dad. I'd be dishonest to marry without that love, and I'd cheapen the love I shared with your dad. I couldn't do that. You always have to be honest, Danny, and you always have to love. Your dad gambled and he would drink with his friends and he would enjoy life with them, but he was honest and he loved."

"I want to be just like Dad. I miss him and Judy misses him. I know because she told me so. But I always pray to him in Heaven, and it makes me feel better."

"We have to have faith, Danny. Your dad's never coming back, but somehow I know he's still alive. As long as you and I and Judy live honestly and with love, we'll never let him die."

"I'll never let him die. I promise."

"I believe you, Danny. You're only nine and already you remind me of your dad."

"Do I?" I asked as my eyes lit up.

"Yes," she answered.

"How?"

"By how you love baseball and bowling and by how you get excited about football games, like the Butte-Central game tonight, and by how you listen to George and me and Uncle Tim and by how you make me laugh and by how you try to understand. I think you're becoming a real man. Just like your sister's becoming a real woman," she added as we both turned toward the bedroom in time to see Judy, dressed for the game and the dance, walk under the archway and into the kitchen.

In place of her Girls' Central uniform she was wearing a gray, full skirt and a black, pullover sweater along with her white anklets and black and white saddle shoes. Julie Shaw might wear a similar sweater today, but she wouldn't wear a full skirt unless she was going to a costume party. It would hang too far below her knees and would hide her figure more than Julie, or I, would like to see it hidden. But most of all, I'll remember Judy's smile that lit up the kitchen.

"You look nice, Judy," my mother said." And your smile suits the occasion. I don't see how any boy could resist asking you to dance," she added as Judy blushed in response.

"I bet Tom Welch or Scooter Johnson will ask you to dance," I said confidently.

"I don't know what to expect," Judy said. "How should I act, Mom?"

"Don't act any way. Just be Judy, that's all. Don't try to make an impression on anyone. If you try to make an impression, either you won't impress anyone or you'll end up impressing someone unworthy. Be quiet and honest and see what happens. Okay?"

"I'll try," Judy answered, putting on her long, gray coat and adjusting the collar. "I think they're here. I hear a horn," she said, looking though the venetian blinds that covered the windows on the kitchen door. "Yes, that's them. I'd better go now. Have fun tonight, Mom. I'll see you when I get home. Goodbye, Dan. Have fun with Uncle Tim. Make him tell you some stories."

"Remember to come right home after the dance," my mother said. "Don't miss the late bus. It leaves Burrs at 12:20, so that gives you plenty of time. And use your good judgment. If someone asks to take you home, make sure the offer is honest, and don't try to make someone ask to take you home."

"I wouldn't do that, Mom," Judy said, opening the kitchen door. "I don't want to go home with just anyone. I'll take the bus first."

"Okay. Enjoy yourself and be careful"

"Goodbye, Judy," I said. "Maybe Tom Welch or Scooter Johnson will ask to take you home."

"No, I'm too young for either of them," she added, walking out the door. "I'll see you later tonight," she concluded, closing the kitchen door behind her.

"Do you worry about Judy going to the dance?" I asked.

"No, not really," my mother answered. "She'll be okay. She has to go sometime. Besides, Mr. McGivern may pick up the girls after the dance. But if he doesn't, she'll be all right on the bus, and I should be home by the time she gets home. What time is Uncle Tim coming to pick you up?"

"He said he'd be here about quarter after seven. We're going to meet some of his friends from work at the game," I added, looking up at the clock.

"Well, you'd better brush your teeth and get your coat. It's ten after now. Don't forget to wash your face and hands," she said as I walked into the bedroom on my way to the bathroom sitting at the back of the house parallel to the alley.

The bathroom's small, but it's big enough to hold a classic bathtub that sits on lion's claw legs and that to me, at nine, seemed as big as a swimming pool. I'm going to miss that bathtub when I leave home for school, but I have to admit that I'm looking forward to enjoying the convenience of a shower. Still, I won't forget the bathtub. The toilet's just a toilet, but it beats the outhouse at my Aunt Elizabeth's. She and my Uncle Tony live in Klein which is a coal mining town in eastern Montana, near Roundup where my grandparents settled—and where my mother was born—after arriving in this country from their native Croatia, and their house didn't have running water. I used to like to visit them in the summer because I could pump water and use the outhouse and take a bath in a big tub in the kitchen as my aunt poured hot water over me. I enjoyed the experience, but two weeks proved to be enough. I always welcomed getting back to Butte to our flush toilet and hot water. The sink in the bathroom was, and is, awfully small in contrast to the accommodating size of the bathtub. Still, it was big enough for brushing teeth—and I'm finally discovering that it's big enough for shaving as well.

We have no heat in the bathroom, which means the hot water from the tub or sink steams up the window and the narrow medicine cabinet mirror above the sink, making it next to impossible for me to see my face to shave. I wouldn't know how to wash my face or shave without wiping the steam off the medicine cabinet mirror. I don't understand why Macbeth's castle wasn't good enough. The houses on Butte's West Side come equipped with heat in the bathroom, and that's fine. But I don't want to leave here just to have bathroom heat. I don't think life's any different on the West Side, even if the houses have heat in the bathrooms.

I turned on the hot water and watched the steam rise from the sink and fog up the medicine cabinet mirror as I looked out the adjacent window at the darkening night. The street lights glowed, but, with the sun still lingering in the west, they hadn't taken complete effect yet. I had been to Naranche Stadium before, and as I washed my hands and face, I could picture the white, gridiron lines freshly chalked on the dirt and sawdust playing surface. And I could picture the crowd filing in under the illuminating glare of the lights attached to the posts that surrounded the football field. In my mind Naranche Stadium presented a magical setting, and I knew I wouldn't be disappointed as I felt the hot water splash on my face. I dried off with one of the hand towels that hung on the rack just above the bathtub and to the right of the sink and then, once again, wiped the steam off the medicine cabinet mirror. I took my comb from my shirt pocket, ran it through my hair to straighten my left side part, and pronounced myself ready to go. I heard the kitchen door open as I opened the bathroom door and walked through the bedroom toward the closet to get my coat.

"Hi, Tim," I heard my mother say as I found my coat. "Are you ready for the game?"

"I think so," I heard Uncle Tin answer. "Are you going to get George to go?"

"No, not this time," my mother answered. "He isn't much of a football fan."

"If he doesn't like baseball or football, what does he like?" Uncle Tim asked. "Does he like to bowl?"

"Yes, he does. But he doesn't bowl in a league right now."

"He certainly is different than Snuffy," I heard Uncle Tim say.

"He's not as different as you might think," my mother said. "I enjoy his company, and he's a good dancer."

"As long as you enjoy him, that's what counts, I guess," Uncle Tim said. "But you're going to miss a good game. This could be Central's year."

"You say that every year, Tim," my mother said, laughing

"I know, but this is different. Central has Tom Welch and Scooter Johnson. I think Butte High's in trouble. Besides, Central's due—after 28 years."

"But I thought you went to Butte High."

"I did, but I always wanted to go to Central. It's too bad I'm too old now," he laughed. "Don't you think I'd look impressive dressed in maroon and white?"

"No doubt about it," my mother answered as I walked into the kitchen.

"Here's one guy I know who would look good dressed in Central's colors. Right, Dan?" Uncle Tim asked, looking down at me standing to his right near the kitchen door.

"I hope so," I answered, looking up at him. He didn't look as fearsome as he did three years earlier as he stood in the garage doorway brandishing his belt, even though I knew he wasn't going to use it. I didn't feel any fear nine years ago as I looked up at him standing there wearing his red and black, plaid jacket and his brimmed, tan felt hat that covered his bald head. His red nose testified to the chill in the air, and the shadow of his black beard appeared barely visible on his clean shaven face. No matter how old I am, Uncle Tim still looks imposing. He's only six feet tall, but he looked at least seven feet to me then and he still can, although I almost can look him directly in the eye. His nose must give him his stature. It has to be a monument to eternity—just like the gallus frames he built all by himself.

"Are you ready to go, Dan?" he asked.

"Yes," I answered. "I'm ready."

"Well, we'd better get going so we can find a good place to park. When should I bring him home, Anne?" Uncle Tim asked, moving toward the kitchen door.

"Judy's going to the dance after the game. So she won't be home. I'd appreciate it if you could take him to your house after the game for a little while. George and I won't be out too late tonight. I'll make sure I'm home by 11 o'clock."

"Why doesn't he just stay with us tonight? Wouldn't that be easier? Then you wouldn't have to worry about getting home so early."

"I have to be home for Judy anyway, but she wouldn't be home until later. So I guess it's okay with me. Do you want to stay at Uncle Tim's tonight, Dan?"

"Sure," I answered. I liked to stay with him and Auntie Loo because they had a roll-away bed that slid into the wall, and Uncle Tim would push it while I was lying in it. Judy and I used to stay with them together, but she was older now and had dances to attend. "I get to sleep in the roll-away."

"Hurry and get your pajamas, robe and toothbrush," my mother said.

"Okay," I said as I walked into the living room to get my pajamas that I kept folded on top of the blanket in the left arm of the hide-a-bed. I found them and walked back through the kitchen toward the bedroom closet to get my robe. I found it on its hanger, took it off and walked into the bathroom where I took my toothbrush off the rack inside the medicine cabinet door. I had everything I needed to spend the night at Uncle Tim's. "I'm all ready," I announced as I walked back into the kitchen, carrying my pajamas, robe and toothbrush.

"Let me get you a sack for your stuff," my mother said, opening the bottom drawer next to the cupboard where Judy and I kept the bowling pins and where I kept my baseball glove. "Everything will be easier to carry now," she added, putting my things into the sack. "There. You're all set."

"Tell Judy I'll talk to her tomorrow. I want to hear all about the dance and if she danced with anyone like Tom Welch or Scooter Johnson."

"I'll tell her. But you'd better be going now. You don't want to be late."

"Are you sure you can't talk George into going to the game?" Uncle Tim asked as he opened the kitchen door.

"I don't think so," my mother answered. "He wants to see the 1954 model cars. We'll have fun. You two enjoy the game."

"We will," I said as Uncle Tim held the door open for me. "I'll see you tomorrow," I added as I walked out into the chilled fall twilight.

"Have a good time tonight, Anne," Uncle Tim said, holding the door open. "I'll bring Dan home in the morning."

"Thanks, Tim. It's nice having you around."

"It's no problem. He likes to listen to me," Uncle Tim said, laughing. "I'll see you tomorrow," he added, following me out the door.

"Goodbye. See you tomorrow, Dan," my mother said, closing the door behind us.

I turned and waved to her standing behind the kitchen door and then followed Uncle Tim to his gray, 1948 Plymouth coupe, waiting for us at the end of the long driveway that led to our white, three room house.

XXI

❀

*U*ncle Tim opened the passenger side door for me, and I slid onto the seat as he closed the door and walked around the front of the car to the driver's side. I remember how small I felt and how big he looked as he sat behind the steering wheel and started the car. I can remember thinking he had to be the biggest man in the world, but when you're nine and you have an Uncle Tim, you should feel that way. I feel the same today, although he doesn't look as big anymore, and I don't feel so small sitting in the front seat of his car. Thanks to Brother Kelley, I'm beginning to understand such phenomena more clearly now.

"Ready to go?" Uncle Tim asked as he shifted the car into reverse.

"I'm ready," I answered as I watched him engage the clutch and shift gears.

"Okay," he said, letting out the clutch and gently accelerating as he backed out of the long driveway toward Aberdeen Street. He pulled out of the driveway and turned to the right up Aberdeen, straightened out the car, shifted into first, and headed toward Texas Avenue—two blocks west of my house. As we turned right on Texas, I studied the wood grandstand of Clark Park that stood empty now, temporarily giving way to Naranche Stadium and football.

"Why can't they play in Clark Park?" I asked as we drove along Texas Avenue parallel to the left field fence.

"Sometimes they do play football in Clark Park," Uncle Tim answered. "You know about the University of Montana Grizzlies and the Montana State College Bobcats, don't you?"

"Sure. I think I like the Bobcats better."

"Well, I've watched them play at Clark Park on a Saturday afternoon, but Butte High and Central always play at Naranche Stadium because of the lights."

"I wished they played in Clark Park. I like to sit in the grandstand."

"You also like to sit in the dugout," Uncle Tim added, smiling, as he turned left onto Wall Street and drove behind the Clark Park grandstand. I was nine years old now, but the grandstand's majesty hadn't faded with the years. Clark Park was home to me.

"I know," I said, smiling in return and seeing Uncle Tim limping across the snow-covered infield dragging his walking cast. "Sometimes I can't think of any place else to go."

"How about going back to school?" he asked, still smiling as we continued driving past the grandstand.

"Sometimes I'd rather sit in the dugout than go to school."

"There are worse places to sit, I suppose," he said as he turned right on Florence Avenue and headed north toward Grand Avenue.

"Do you think I'll be able to play in Clark Park like my dad did?"

"I hope so, Dan. I don't see any reason why not. Unless it burns down."

"Clark Park never will burn down, will it?"

"I don't think so. Not Clark Park. It'll be there waiting for you."

"That makes me feel better," I said as he turned left onto Grand and toward Harrison Avenue.

Maybe every city can claim to be a city of lights, but not every one can boast of a Hill bathed in light that you can observe from any point on The Flat to the south. From the western slope of The Hill and Big Butte, our cone-shaped mountain left over from some ancient volcanic action at least partly responsible for the mineral deposits left in "The Richest Hill on Earth," to the eastern slope and the Leonard Mine—as well as the attached communities of Meaderville, McQueen, and East Butte—The Hill, in 1953, was alive with light. Even today, approaching Butte from the south on US Highway 10, you drive over Harding Way across the Continental Divide and gradually descend through the dark night, following switchback after switchback, until a clearing in the mountain pines finally affords you a clear line of sight to the lights of the Mining City glistening below on the valley floor.

To this day I've never been able to understand how George Lewis ever could refer to the city waiting behind those lights as "Hungry Hill" or "Hell's Kitchen." If the light of Heaven isn't as bright as the light of Butte, visible from that promontory point on Harding Way, then I don't want anything to do with Heaven. If Butte is an expression of Hell's Kitchen, then I'll sit at its table anytime. I don't see how anyone could go hungry in Butte, unless he had to live on the West Side. If you had to live on the West Side, I doubt if you'd even notice the lights. I wonder if Macbeth would have? Shakespeare would have and Brother Kelley has, and, probably unlike Uncle Tim and even my mother, both of them could even explain their attraction. Still, they've all noticed the lights.

However, one thing bothers me today, now that I think about it. Brother Kelley, Uncle Tim and my mother always lived with those lights, but if you look at The Hill from The Flat today, or if you look at it from that same Harding Way switchback, you see the lights only until your eyes reach the eastern slope and confront the black hole of the Anaconda Company's Berkeley Pit. You can call it progress if you want to, but The Hill is darker today than it ever was in its mining past. Resembling a monster with an insatiable appetite that seems determined to devour everything in sight, The Pit, begun in 1955, keeps growing and swallowing gallus frames. It might be impressive in its own right, but I like the gallus frames better. You can see their lights rising above, and illuminating, The Hill, but you can't see the lights of the ore trucks crawling their way up the steep slopes of The Pit. You only can hear the constant, and foreboding, rumble of their engines. I wish we could journey into space and leave The Hill alone. I'd feel better. But the lights have to signify something. And we have to discover their secret to give ourselves the chance to continue on with honor and dignity.

That's what Brother Kelley says and he doesn't lie. He says that if you live in Butte with the Berkeley Pit, you can't help confronting the fact that Macbeth might be right. He believes in symbols, and he says The Pit symbolizes profound changes occurring in the very structure of life. I never thought much about symbols before because words always seemed to make more sense. But now I'm beginning to see that symbols possess a certain power that words don't. The gallus frames have power, for example. Uncle Tim's nose has power. The crucifix has power. I can't explain it with words yet, but I can see courage and love in those symbols. Life has to be more than "a tale told by an idiot full of sound and fury signifying nothing," even if Clark Park burned down and even if the Berkeley Pit swallows up the entire Hill and even if John Glenn and the explorers who will follow don't find any next world anywhere in space. Clark Park was made of wood, and we can't stop The Pit because the Anaconda Company wouldn't stand for it. And we can't stop ourselves from exploring space, either. Macbeth's life may have been meaningless, but neither mine nor anyone else's has to be just because we live with Berkeley Pits and space explorers. I'm not going to give up that easily. I'd hate to think that Uncle Tim endured those broken noses in vain.

If it were possible, he would have prevented Clark Park from burning down. And when he assured me it wouldn't, I believed him. I trusted him, and his assurance made me feel better as he turned right onto Harrison Avenue, The Flat's main north-south thoroughfare, for the trip up The Hill to Naranche Stadium. I turned my attention from the wood grandstand of Clark Park to the black, iron gallus frames that came into clear view as we headed north toward the Northern Pacific Railroad viaduct where Harrison Avenue eased to the left and became Front Street, running parallel to the base of The Hill.

"Did you build the gallus frames?" I asked.

"No, not all of them," Uncle Tim answered. "But I wish I had, and I even feel as though I did sometimes. I've lived next to the Mountain Con's gallus frame for so long I feel like I built it. But I did build the Kelley. You can see its lights up there on the east side of The Hill above Dublin Gulch. Do you see it?" he asked, pointing in its direction.

"I think so. Did you build it all by yourself?"

"I had a little help from a few other iron workers," Uncle Tim answered with a smile. "But I walked almost all its iron and drove in my share of rivets."

"Weren't you afraid to climb that high?"

"I wasn't afraid, but I was cautious. I like to walk the iron, but I try not to show off. I've seen men show off and pay for it. The gallus frames are unforgiving, and you have to respect anything you happen to be working on. But sometimes I can't resist showing off just a little, I guess," he added, smiling again. "But I don't enjoy falling off gallus frames, and I don't enjoy having to walk through the falling snow, dragging my cast behind me."

"I'd like to build something as big as a gallus frame someday. What do you mean when you call them 'monuments to eternity?'" I asked as he drove underneath the Northern Pacific viaduct, up the gradual incline, and headed west on Front Street.

"They're monuments because they stand so tall and proud and dignified—just as individual people should," he answered. "And they're monuments to eternity because they're made of iron and they will last," he concluded, stealing a quick glance up The Hill.

"I'd like to be a monument to eternity like a gallus frame. Can individual people stand that tall and proud?"

"I hope so," Uncle Tim answered, stopping for the red light at the corner of Front and Utah. "I know Butte people can because the gallus frames are in their blood."

"Can you recognize all the mines by the gallus frames even at night?" I asked as the light turned green and Uncle Tim turned right onto Utah Street and headed Uptown, closer to Naranche Stadium.

"Sure I can," he answered. "I know all the mines because I've climbed all the gallus frames."

"Do you have to climb them to get to know them? Do you have to climb the gallus frames to recognize them and their mines?" I asked as he continued north on Utah towards Uptown.

"No," Uncle Tim answered, blessing himself as he drove past St Joseph's Church on our left. "You don't have to climb them to get to know them. You just have to live with them and be proud of them. I know many men who climb them but don't know them. They'd rather live someplace else. But not me. I don't want to live anywhere else. I've always wanted to know the gallus frames."

"I want to know them just like you do."

"You will if you want to. Just be patient," Uncle Tim said as he drove over the Utah Street railroad tracks and past the warehouses that lined either side of the rails. "You have a lot of time to learn them" he added as we drove past the point where Arizona Street meets Utah alongside the Silver Bow Homes housing development built by the WPA during the depression. And then I saw the lights of Naranche Stadium.

"There are the lights! There's Naranche Stadium!" I exclaimed, pointing out the driver's side of the car to the illuminated stadium beckoning to us just two blocks west of Arizona Street.

"Yes, there it is. The home of the Butte High Bulldogs. Pretty impressive, right?" he asked as he drove past the stadium and stopped for the red light at the corner of Arizona and Mercury Street.

"It sure is. Look at all the lights. It looks just like day light. Where are we going to park?"

"We'll drive to Main Street and then walk a couple of blocks down The Hill to the stadium. We have plenty of time," Uncle Tim answered as the light turned green and he turned left on Mercury and headed toward Main.

I just stared out the car window marveling at the lights that lit up the stadium, Butte High School and what seemed like all of Main Street. Scooter Johnson hadn't run 60 yards for a touchdown yet, and for a moment I almost switched my allegiance to Butte High, simply on the strength of the lights' power. Magic filled the air as Uncle Tim found a parking place on South Main Street, one block down from the Park Street intersection and just two blocks above Naranche Stadium. We stepped out of the car, locked and closed the doors, and headed toward the stadium.

You didn't need a calendar to tell you that Clark Park summer evenings had passed. I didn't feel the biting cold associated with the ballpark's skating rink in the winter when the pot-bellied stove in the hothouse, which doubled as the baseball clubhouse in the summer, offered warmth and comfort. No one ever seemed to mind the winter cold of the skating rink as long as the hothouse beckoned, and now no one seemed to mind the fall chill in the air as long as Naranche Stadium 's lights shined. I can remember seeing hundreds of people walking down Main Street and filing into the stadium through its northwest entrance on South Main. Everyone appeared to be welcoming the fall darkness, even though some seemed overly protected against the autumn air. Their ear muffs, scarves and winter coats were more appropriate for the skating rink than for the Butte-Central game to be contested on a chilly, but far from bitter, autumn evening.

I wasn't disappointed when Uncle Tim and I walked through the gate and into the stadium, and both of us were captured by the magic created by the bright lights and accompanying feel and smell of fall in the air. He didn't find himself in Naranche Stadium because he felt obligated to take me somewhere. He wanted to be there in response to his own will, and I was fortunate enough to have the opportunity to join him. I found it comforting to know that you could be 29 and still be allowed to feel the magic. Uncle Tim understood high school football, but the boys dressed in maroon and white—and warming up under the shadow of the east goal posts—and the boys dressed in purple and white—and warming up under the shadow of the west goal posts—were neither boys nor men. They were football players, school colors glistening under the bright lights, magically freed from the constraints of everyday time. No wonder people willingly filed into Naranche Stadium—with most of them wearing only adequate protection against the fall chill in the air.

Uncle Tim and I walked through the northwest gate on South Main and, following our senses, immediately headed for the concession stand located just inside the gate and along the north wall above the top row of spectator seats. He reached into his left back pocket, found his wallet, took out a dollar bill, bought me a cup of hot chocolate and himself a cup of coffee and scanned the rows of wood benches looking for his iron worker friends. His eyes lit up when he spotted one of them waving, and we made our way to our seats just a few rows above Central's north side, maroon and white student cheering section. To this day I've never tasted a better cup of hot chocolate, and I'll bet anything that Uncle Tim would say he's never tasted a better cup of coffee, either. His nose may have been broken, but he still could smell. And when his friend, holding the brown paper bag, reached over and poured something from the bottle inside into his coffee, Uncle Tim broke into a broad smile as the steam lifted the pungent aroma of coffee and brandy within range of his scarred, Irish nose.

XXII

I think we were experiencing what Brother Kelley refers to as ritual. He says that ritual involves much more than doing something according to an established pattern or simply out of habit. He says that human beings have a dual, rather than singular, nature and that ritual feeds our spiritual side just as our regular, everyday food feeds our physical, or sensual, side. And we are responsible for feeding our spiritual nature. He also says that if what he teaches has no practical application in the real world of experience, he's wasting our time. Therefore, he always encourages us to test what he says outside the walls of his classroom to determine whether or not he's telling the truth. He never lies on purpose, but he wants us to tell him if we can't find any experiential evidence in the practical world to support his conclusions.

So far, I haven't uncovered any lies, and when I test his ideas about ritual, I always think of Uncle Tim, as he sipped his coffee at the Butte-Central game in 1953. Judging from his unforgettable smile, that cup of coffee did more for his spiritual nature than it did for his sensual nature and he knew it. Unlike Brother Kelley, he just couldn't explain the magic which, as far as I can see, represents the only difference between them. Brother Kelley can explain what Uncle Tim can feel, and he can smile at that one difference, which explains his humility. I'm more than willing to listen to, and trust, Brother Kelley because he doesn't lie.

He says we all have the capacity to create ritual and that we need it to feed our spiritual nature which then complements our sensual nature, creating the necessary balance between the pair of opposites.

He makes great sense to me because we obviously have a dual nature, and just as obviously we can't afford to ignore the well-being of either side of our humanity. But he says that love and affirmation of the monstrous nature of life are prerequisites for ritual and that a sensual experience can be exciting but not satisfying. And he says that as long as human beings have the capacity to create ritual, life never can be meaningless—whether we live as kings or paupers or whether we live on the West Side or in Dublin Gulch under the protective shadow of the Kelley gallus frame. He says even kings need ritual because even they can't afford to ignore their spiritual nature. In fact, he says kings may need ritual more than the rest of us because of the enormous social pressures that accompany the role.

It's too bad Macbeth never had a teacher like Brother Kelley. He doesn't make any accommodating promises, and after listening to him it's hard to believe that life is "a tale told by an idiot full of sound and fury signifying nothing." He says that pain and death are natural parts of life and that an individual has the capacity to triumph over both of them. He inspires me because, without telling any lies, he celebrates the greatness an individual human being can attain. He proves to us that, without feeling sorry for ourselves, we're equipped to triumph in the "absurd world" we have to experience. I know he's right because look at the crucifix, look at the gallus frames, look at my mother, look at my dad and look at Uncle Tim's nose. All those monuments to eternity inspire me because they remind me of my capacity to triumph over pain and death. Brother Kelley isn't simply spouting something he learned in college that he feels obligated to tell us because he wants us to pass tests. He lives and believes what he says and uses everyday examples from life in Butte that all of us can understand, if we want to.

You can tell he loves Butte because it's clear that he learned about love and ritual before he went to college and before he joined the Irish Christian Brothers. But Brother Kelley must be unique because the other Brothers neither talk nor carry themselves as he does. But he says we have to know ourselves in depth. If we don't, we easily can think we have to acquire an impressive title to be somebody. And if we accept that conclusion, we just as easily can walk the path of Macbeth. I want to avoid that path because I don't want to live in despair, and I want to enjoy life without having to live on the West Side as George has to. If I can't change George, then I hope he never makes it to the West Side. He won't be as likable if he does. I don't think Brother Kelley's teaching is obscure and overly complicated. For example, when I examine my life in the "ugliest city in the continental United States," I can see that I've already experienced ritual. And if that's the case, I can continue to create it without anyone's help. Then I can live with honor and humility by acknowledging that the world of experience is the same for all of us, regardless of where we live or what titles we acquire. Brother Kelley makes me feel like I'm made of iron and like I can stand tall and proud in quiet triumph over pain and death—just like the black, iron gallus frames that decorate The Hill.

After listening to him I feel as inspired as I do when I come out of confession restored to the state of sanctifying grace. And being in that state has to describe Uncle Tim and me that night at Naranche Stadium more than nine years ago. His smile surpassed any one I've ever seen on any penitent who just finished his penance following confession. When you love, therefore, you must be in the state of sanctifying grace. If that's the case, why don't we live for love and seek to remain in that state? It sure beats living in the state of mortal sin. But sometimes I think you have to experience mortal sin before you can experience sanctifying grace. But if committing mortal sin indicates that you hate God, then going to confession must restore you to loving God, which explains the feeling of being in the state of sanctifying grace. It's a state of love.

It's hard to avoid mortal sin and still be a boy struggling to become a man. But I don't commit mortal sin because I hate God. I know that for a fact. I've French kissed before, for example, but how could anyone be sent to Hell for French kissing? Even if you kissed just to get turned on, how could something like that result in you being sent to Hell? It doesn't make sense, but there has to be something to the concepts of sin and mortal sin. Based on what Brother Kelley says and based on my own experience with life, I think we deserve to experience Hell—whatever it may be—only if we refuse to live our capacity for love. It seems to me that if you live that capacity with devotion and commitment, you not only create ritual that feeds your spiritual nature, but also you never fall out of the state of sanctifying grace—even if you French kiss.

Brother Kelley also says we can experience ritual without having to explain it. He says it's quiet and works like magic, which explains why he can smile when we refer to the Mass as the magic show. He says the Mass has the power to awaken our capacity for love if we participate and listen. He must be telling the truth because even the majesty created by the bright lights of Naranche Stadium can't compare to the majesty of the Mass. I could go to Mass, and to a baseball game, every day because, like baseball, it's quiet. Baseball is magic, like the Mass, because if you listen and allow yourself to participate, you can find a lot to love. But if you take the lights and the bands and the cheerleaders and the colors away from football, you aren't left with much to love. Grunts and groans, along with the clashing of shoulder pads and helmets, aren't sounds that touch the soul. But the chime of the altar bell and the crack of the bat are sounds that have that power. I never tire of either of them.

Even if the magic of football can't match that of the Mass and baseball, my experience has convinced me of one fact. A dream was born for a nine-year-old boy caught up in the magic of the Butte-Central football game that night in September of 1953—a dream that couldn't have been born without it. When Bobby 'Scooter' Johnson took a handoff from Tom Welch on his own 40 yard line and slanted off left tackle into the Butte High secondary and then angled for the south sideline to speed 60 yards for the only touchdown of the game, I responded with deafening shouts of "Go, Scooter, Go!" and was immediately given to dreams of gridiron glory wearing the maroon and white of Butte Central and sprinting through the defense of the hated rival, the Butte High Bulldogs, for touchdown after touchdown, as the Maroons ground the Bulldogs into the dust of Naranche Stadium.

But the dream born that night didn't stop at gridiron glory. And I didn't come to Central because I was a Catholic and Catholic boys went to Central because their parents felt responsible for sending them to Catholic schools. My mother would have sent me to Central when I left the eighth grade at the new junior high because she was a woman who wanted to do her duty to the Church and to me. She hadn't sent me to a Catholic grade school, but she would have sent me to the Catholic high school. Maybe I would have wanted to go to Central even if I hadn't been part of the magic that fateful night in

Naranche Stadium. After all, I was a loyal and obedient Catholic. But
I played football for Emerson in the grade school league, and we even
played for the City Championship in Naranche Stadium four years
after Central beat Butte High 6-0—losing by that same score. I did
play in Naranche Stadium as the star running back for the blue and
gold. Also, my friends on that team, if they dreamed at all, dreamed
of purple and white, not of maroon and white. After a year at the
new junior high I would have been faced with a tough dilemma.

I was loyal to my religion because its majesty had captured my
heart, and my sister was going to Central and I was loyal to my
family. But, on the other hand, I would have been going to school
with my friends for eight years, and I was loyal to them. Plus I could
be loyal to Butte High and still be loyal to my religion and to my
family. I wouldn't have given up the Church just because I went to
Butte High, and I wouldn't have deserted my family, either. I would
have faced a tough decision, and I don't know what I would have
done. I don't even know if I would have had a choice. If I'd have gone
to Central simply in obedience to some church rule, I don't know
if I could have been loyal to its colors. But I never had to face any
dilemma. The thought of going to Butte High never once crossed my
mind after that night in Naranche Stadium—no matter how strong
my friendships with my public school classmates might have been.

I didn't know anyone when I took the entrance exam at Central.
In fact, I was scared stiff because as strange as it may sound, we public
school students were afraid of our Catholic counterparts. They swore
and fought more than we did. But still I went, and no one had to
force me, even if it meant leaving my friends at the junior high and
starting all over again with guys who had strong parish identities. I
attended St. Ann's Church, but I really didn't belong to St. Ann's or
any other parish. I belonged to Emerson and wore its blue and gold
without wishing it was maroon and white. I lived completely outside
the parish life and the Catholic school atmosphere. I didn't belong to
anything, but still I went. However, thanks to Brother Kelley and his
teaching, I understand that I wasn't anyone special.

I wasn't some special person of uncommon courage who decided
to go to Central against all odds. But I was obedient. I was the same
person, the same boy, who sat in the dugout at Clark Park on a snowy
day in the late fall of 1950, disobedient to my teacher and even to

my mother. Still, I went to Central out of obedience. My mother wanted me to go to Central, and Uncle Tim wanted me to wear the maroon and white he never wore. But I didn't go to Central out of obedience to either one, or both, of them—no matter how obvious it may appear. After listening to Brother Kelley for almost a year, I think I understand that I went to Central for the same reason I sat in the dugout that day almost 12 years ago. I went to the dugout and I went to Central out of obedience to the power of love.

XXIII

I can see more clearly now. For example, I can see how Macbeth easily could be right. Life can be "a tale told by an idiot full of sound and fury signifying nothing." It's a matter of obedience. Macbeth despaired at the end of his life, not at its beginning. As long as he was slitting the enemy "from the nave to the chaps," motivated by his commitment to duty and obedience to his king, he didn't complain about the nothingness of life. Macbeth's original path isn't easy because its rewards aren't as immediate and as glamorous as we'd like them to be. He could have become the Thane of Cawdor because of his devotion to duty, but he couldn't have been named king as long as Duncan and his sons lived. If he would have held fast to his original path of duty and obedience, he would have lived a life of honor and dignity, but given the chance to choose between the path which offered the promise of ultimate rewards and that which offered the promise of immediate rewards, he chose the immediate. That tragic choice eventually led him to despair. Macbeth's despair can affect anyone because discovering and adhering to the path of duty and obedience to the power of love isn't easy. But life is meaningless only if, for whatever reason, we never walk on—or if we leave—that obedient path. If we stick to it, life always is an adventure. But once we depart from it, the adventure fades and the senseless sound and fury eventually comes to signify nothing.

So, where does this leave me at the age of 17 with explorers venturing into space where Heaven, the home of the souls of the faithful departed, is supposed to be? Before 1962 17-year-olds weren't burdened with such a question because no one had ventured into space—in person—to test the existence of something we've always obediently believed. But we're exploring space in earnest now, and I'm glad because I like the adventure of it all. But what if the explorers don't find anything? How can you believe in something if you can't find any proof that it exists? If Heaven, as we've always conceived it, doesn't exist, then neither does Hell. And if there is no home for the souls of the faithful departed, or for those of the unfaithfully departed, then the time spent between birth and death has to be meaningless. If you live to get to Heaven only to discover there is no such place, what do you live for? Maybe the older generations never will have to ask such questions, but you can't be 17 in 1962, with space exploration under way in earnest, and avoid them. Times have changed. Even Butte is changing.

No 17-year-old before my generation had to face the reality of the Berkeley Pit. I can't count on the wheels atop the gallus frames turning forever as 17-year-olds before The Pit at least thought they could. What do you do when you're 17 and facing the end of such a formative era? I know you can't be afraid because you're from Butte and Butte boys have courage. But do you just forget Butte and thoughtlessly embrace a new era of sound and fury without the promising and foreboding presence of Heaven and Hell? No, you don't take that path because boys from Butte are loyal. Then what do you do if the space explorers and the earth explorers, mining the shafts of The Hill, never find any next world either up there or down there? I think you learn from everyday life and from 'Macbeth' that you can experience Heaven and Hell while you live because Macbeth had to experience Hell. And he chose it for himself. No one sent him there. He could have chosen to experience Heaven, but he couldn't find his courage. He had no monuments to eternity to inspire him.

But if you've been lucky enough to experience Butte, you've been lucky enough to experience Heaven. And so that you don't forget the Mining City, you make its gallus frames, its people of the mines, its ballpark and its Garden Spot of the Rockies monuments to eternity and vow, out of loyalty to them, never to stray from the path they illuminate. That's what you do when you're 17 and living in Butte, Montana, in 1962 with men exploring space and with an open pit mine swallowing up gallus frames as it eats its way westward toward the lights of Big Butte. You make that vow, and you continue with your story about Butte, Central, Julie Shaw and the power of love.

My dreams of enduring love began in the first grade when I caught sight of Sandra Potter. Dreams of gridiron glory come and go, but dreams of enduring love never die. My dream of such love with Sandra never lasted beyond the third grade, if that long, but the dream itself still hasn't died. My friends always accuse me of wearing my heart on my sleeve, and they, especially my best friend, Dave Jacobsen, think I'm crazy. Sometimes, I have to agree, but I never can seem to help myself. When I fall in love, it's always totally, never halfway. I don't hold anything back when the thunderbolt strikes, which explains why I listened very carefully when Brother Kelley explained the power of love. Like everyone else, I laughed at what he said—but only on the outside. I didn't laugh on the inside, however, because I had experienced love's power at the age of six with Sandra Potter, and I was experiencing it now, at the age of 17, with Julie Shaw.

When I catch sight of my beloved, my heart jumps to my throat and beats a thousand times a minute. I always keep it to myself, of course, but I believe in what Brother Kelley says about the power of love. And I can't help thinking of how glorious it would be if the feeling ever were mutual. A union between two people united by love could withstand anything. I don't think I'm crazy. I think everyone else is, although I always hesitate to say so.

I first discovered Julie Shaw in the second half of my junior year, when I was 16 and she was a sophomore and 15. With the emergence of puberty, I grew more confident in the pursuit of my beloved and didn't love from quite the same distance as I had before. During the second semester of my junior year, my friend, Paul Brennan, and I would make our nightly trek to Centerville and Walkerville—at the very top of The Hill past the Lexington mine—in hope of catching sight of Julie and Patty Rossini who was the object of his desires. Dave Jacobsen, Jake to us, thought both of us were crazy, but he focused primarily on me because I never expressed any desire to outgrow my obedience and show the girls who was boss, as Jake did and still does. Besides, it's hard to be the boss when you look 13. But I have to admire Jake's honesty. And honest or not, girls must be attracted to guys who show them who's boss because Jake always has enjoyed better luck than either Paul or I.

Still, our mutual interest in love, if from different perspectives, and my pursuit of Julie Shaw has united us these past four years—especially the last year and a half. During this time I never was alone in my pursuit, and I always seemed to be making the least progress. But I wouldn't give up, even though Paul, who had been my closest ally throughout the pursuit, began telling me I was crazy. I dated other girls, but in my eyes no one ever approached Julie Shaw. I was convinced that no other pursuer could match my devotion to her, and I knew that if I ever had the opportunity to show her, she would see. Then no one else would have a chance.

I'd never had a date with her. In fact, I'd never even taken her home from a dance, although I had danced with her countless times. But I'll never forget that Friday just two weeks ago when I decided I had to be bold. I wouldn't be content just to dance with her. This time I'd take her home as well. I arrived at school well before eight that morning, put my books in my locker in senior hall on the third floor, kept my coat on and walked down the stairs to the main study hall to find Jake and Paul. I wanted to see if they were interested in going to eight o'clock Mass next door at St. Pat's.

XXIV

*I*f you don't bring loyalty and love with you to Central, you certainly find it worthy of both once you get here. The building itself, reflecting the solid, ornate, red brick design common to established schools, has the power to inspire. I attended the new junior high for a year, but, architecturally, it lacked the majesty of Emerson which looks likes Central and even Butte High. All three schools rise at least two stories—three for Central counting the basement floor—and all three appear warm and welcoming with their architectural grandeur. The junior high, being brand new, proved to be impressively functional in its modern, campus style, but I never felt attached to it. The school lacked the warmth and personality I was accustomed to. Butte High houses over 2,000 boys and girls to Central's 400 boys, but Central owns one, great advantage over its public counterpart—and maybe over any other school anywhere. Central has its study hall.

With classrooms framing either end, Central's study hall covers the entire north side of the first floor, above the basement level, and serves as the center of student life. We gather there before school starts, conduct our pep rallies there, stage our wrestling matches there, hold our dances—or mixers—there, celebrate our retreat Masses there, and, finally, we study—or pretend to study or find ways not to study—there under the watchful gaze of one of the Irish Christian Brothers. I'm telling this story in 1962 and we're exploring space, but in the study hall at Central we still have inkwells in desks that sit in straight rows attached to long, wooden runners that allow them to be moved in sections to clear the area for a dance or a wrestling match. You can sit in one of these desks and read the history of the school, if you aren't interested in reading the history of the United States or of the world. Central's history is inscribed on almost every desk, and you can read names and dates reaching back to the 1920s. Just reading one of the desks can inspire me, and I feel honored to be a part of Central's storied past.

And if the desks aren't enough, pictures of every graduating class from 1922 to 1961—soon to be followed by the class of 1962—decorate the study hall walls. Maybe you can miss the history etched in the desks because some of the tops have been sanded down, obscuring the dates and names, but you can't miss the history recorded on the walls. You can feel Central's commanding presence in the study hall, and I don't think the school could have the same affect without it.

In addition to preserving its proud heritage, the study hall is the center of Central's warmth. Steam radiators line the walls underneath the windows looking across the vacant lot behind the Brothers' house toward Galena Street and the rear entrance to Girls' Central. Comforting steam heat and the opportunity to watch the girls emerge from their mysterious environs combine to give Central a warmth that no school anywhere in the country can match. I spotted Jake and Paul standing by the windows, enjoying the view, as I entered the study hall through the doors near the classroom at the east end and headed across the floor. I walked between the rows of ordered desks and the front stage, where we enact our pep rally skits and celebrate Mass during retreats—drawn toward the warmth of the steam heat, the mystery of Girls' Central and, especially, that of Julie Shaw.

I found Jake leaning against one of the radiators striking the classic pose of the senior letterman that he was. You have to be a senior and a letterman to lean with your back against the radiator, elbows extended behind and resting on the wood protection covering the iron coils, facing the expanse of the study hall and not the Galena Street entrance to Girls' Central. In keeping with his image as a senior letterman and boss, Jake stood there as if he no longer noticed the mysterious presence of Girls' Central across the street. When he wants to, and not before, he acknowledges its presence with a shrug, accompanied by his famous groan—as if he's stooping beneath his senior letterman dignity.

Jake manages to get away with such behavior because he's acting as he thinks he's supposed to act, and his thick beard creates the impression of being grown up. So, Jake simply acts the way a grown up, senior letterman is supposed to act. He can make you laugh, but he looks confident wearing his maroon letter sweater with the white, block BC stitched on the left pocket and the three white stripes circling the left arm. He won the letter that neither Paul nor I ever have, and he wears his sweater practically. The letter sweater helps to win the favor of the girls anxiously waiting across the street at Girls' Central.

Paul and I are seniors, too, but we aren't lettermen. And as I walked across the study hall, I found him leaning on the wood cover of the iron radiator, elbows supporting the classic pose of the senior non-letterman, staring longingly in the direction of Girls' Central across Galena Street. I know that pose well because I think I've worn out a spot in front of one of the radiators this year, and I wouldn't be surprised if Brother Kelley erects a statue of me to mark the spot after I leave. He smiles and takes note of my position every morning when he enters the study hall through the door that leads to and from the Brothers' house, and, humorously, he never lets me forget it. He understands us, and I don't think anyone ever could fool him.

Unlike Paul and me Jake looked like he should be standing with his back toward Girls' Central. At five ten he isn't any taller than either one of us, but he looks older. He lettered in wrestling, and he has the broad shoulders and thick chest to prove it, creating the appearance of masculine readiness that seems beyond his 17 years. His high forehead only contributes to that appearance, and his solid, distinguished Butte nose, sculpted jaw and heavily whiskered face combine to create a sense of rugged masculinity that you expect of someone in total control of his world—someone like Uncle Tim, for example. But Jake's only 17 years old.

There's no mistaking Paul's 17 years, just as there's no mistaking mine. Our masculinity still is emerging, and recent growing spurts have pushed both of us up to five ten, as the rest of our appearance struggles to catch up. All three of us wear flat tops, or crew cuts, but Paul and I don't look like Jake. His hair pushed back from his forehead and temples a couple of years ago, helping to create his mature appearance. In contrast, Paul's black hair and my light brown shade is just beginning to recede from our foreheads and temples, leaving a noticeable trace of whiskers along both sideburns near our ears. I like to rub my hands along these sideburns against the grain. I can use my Gillette razor now, too, and I like to hear the blade scrape through the whiskers. It's a new, welcomed sound for me, but Jake's a veteran by now.

Paul's smooth and even flat top emphasizes his prominent, high cheekbones, but his face—like mine—remains young. A high bridge and sharp angles give his nose a definite Butte distinction. In fact, if you took the three of us and lined us up side by side—given Jake's wide nostrils, Paul's high bridge, and my Roman antiquity—you'd see three classic Butte profiles. I guess the girls would say that Jake's handsome and athletic because the letter sweater, alone, isn't enough for them—whether they attend Girls' Central or Butte High. But Paul and I are athletic, too. I easily can look like I belong on a pitcher's mound, and sometimes I think I could do better than 'Rainbow' Ralph Terry. Mazeroski never would have hit that home run off me. And Paul just as easily looks like he belongs on a basketball court. The girls must find us somewhat handsome, I guess—or at least lately so—because we've enjoyed some success with Girls' Central and even with Butte High. But letter sweaters do seem to make a difference—along with being able to look like the boss.

Still, a distinct difference separates the three of us. Jake's the most adult looking 17-year-old I know. He's a picture of adolescent maturity. And Paul and I are the most, or at least among the most, immature 17-year-olds I know. We're pictures of adolescent vulnerability, and we can't even wear letter sweaters to hide it. We wear the same denims, the same white socks, the same V-neck sweaters, the same black—or brown—oxfords and the same hair style, but basically we're studies in contrast. However, in spite of that contrast, or maybe even because of it, the three of us are friends and the alliance is strong. Besides, in matters concerning affairs of the heart, we wouldn't have any experienced authority to consult if Jake looked as vulnerable as Paul and I. And, more often than not, our conversations center around such affairs. Today would prove to be no exception as I walked across the study hall and assumed my position next to Paul Brennan, who already was staring, across Galena Street, at the mysterious presence of Girls' Central.

XXV

"Do you guys want to go to Mass?" I asked, looking out the window and leaning my elbows on the radiator's solid wood cover.

"I can see you do," Jake answered. "You're still wearing your jacket like you're in a hurry or something. Can't you at least say hello first before you ask us if we want to go to Mass? What's on your mind?" he asked, turning around to look out the window just in time to see the first of the girls leave their school and begin their walk down the alley and past our back door on their way to St. Pat's and eight o'clock Mass.

Sometimes I'd rather watch the girls walk down the alley than go to Mass. They rarely look up, but they know we're watching and they like it. If they don't, they just have to walk half a block west on Galena and then south one block on Washington to get to the church. Walking down the alley between St. Pat's and Boys' Central isn't that much of a short cut. But the girls like to be seen, which is fine with me. I like to watch.

"I just want to go to Mass this morning," I answered.

"But why this morning?" Paul asked. "Why not yesterday or any other day this week?"

"Come on, you can tell us," Jake said. "We're your friends. Remember?"

"Jake, there's Lori," I said, pointing to the Galena Street doors of Girls' Central.

"So, what am I supposed to do? Jump for joy? I see her all the time."

"Why isn't she wearing your letter sweater?" Paul asked.

"Because I want to wear it. Why should she wear it?"

"If it were my sweater and if I were going with her, I'd have her wear it," I said.

"I know you would," Jake said, "and you'd never let her out of your sight, either. You wouldn't even go out with the guys."

"I'm not that bad, Jake. But if I were going with a girl like Lori, I'd definitely pay more attention to her."

"So would I," Paul joined in. "You're pretty lucky, Jake."

"What does luck have to do with it? Maybe if the two of you paid more attention to me, you'd have someone to go with. Did you ever think of that?"

"I've thought about it," I answered, "but I can't treat girls like you do. If I were going with Lori, I'd have to pay more attention to her."

"Why? Who told you that?"

"No one," I answered. "That's just what you do when you go with someone."

"That's right," Paul offered, still looking out the window. "Don't you want to go to Mass because Lori will be there?"

"No," Jake answered, "because if I go, I'll have to walk her back to school."

"You mean you don't want to walk her back to school?" I asked in disbelief.

"That's right. Unlike you, it's not something I live for. Lori has no trouble finding her own way back to Girls' Central."

"But don't you ever worry about someone else taking her out?" Paul asked.

"Who's going to take her out? I've been going with her for two years now. Besides, she wouldn't go out with anyone else."

"Aren't you taking a lot for granted, Jake?" I asked.

"No. I'm just showing her who's boss."

"Hey, Dan, look!" Paul broke in. "Here comes Julie."

At the mention of her name, I knew I was done for. I could feel my blood rush to my face and my heart jump to my throat as it started to beat at least a thousand times a minute. I looked out the window toward where Paul was pointing, and sure enough, there she was just about to step off the sidewalk onto Galena Street. I didn't have to see her face very clearly because whenever I thought of her, I could see it as you can see someone's face in a dream. The Everly

Brothers' song, 'Dream,' is no joke. Whenever I wanted Julie, all I had to do was dream, and there she was. Only this wasn't a dream. She was walking across Galena Street on her way to Mass at St. Pat's.

I could see her black hair glistening in the morning sunlight, and she was wearing a short, white jacket that covered her white blouse and the blue straps of her uniform jumper. The visible blue of her skirt reached to the top of her knees, revealing what I thought to be the most beautiful legs in the universe. She was wearing black flats along with her tan colored nylons, and I watched her cross the street and head for the alley running behind our school.

"Now I get it!" Jake exclaimed, looking me in the eye. "Now I see why you want to go to Mass. Aren't you ever going to get her out of your mind? She doesn't care if she sees you in church or anywhere else. You're crazy. She loves having all you idiots drool over her, and you're simply another one of 'em. Why don't you leave her alone and make her come to you? If she wants to, she will. Why do you have to chase her?"

"First of all, I'm no idiot, and I don't drool over her," I answered in my defense as I watched Julie walk down the alley in full view of everyone watching out the windows. "And I don't chase her."

"Don't chase her? I'd like to know what else you call it. What do you call riding up to Centerville every night just to see her, if you're lucky? What do you call it, Brennan?"

"I don't know if I'd call it chasing, Jake," Paul answered, stammering.

"That's because you're almost as stuck on Patty Rossini as Kristich is on Julie Shaw. Only you know that Rossini could care less about you. Our friend here hasn't learned that lesson about his Julie yet."

"Maybe so, Jake, but you watch. Patty will care some day. She'll come to me some day."

"Maybe Julie never will come to me," I said. "But if she doesn't care now, it's because she doesn't really know me."

"Doesn't know you? Who are you trying to kid?" Jake asked. "You dance every slow dance you can with her just so you can smell her perfume and get turned on, and you call her on the phone every night and pant at the sound of her voice, just like all the other fools who call her. And you can say she doesn't know you? If you ask me, I'd say that she knows you better than you know yourself. And if she cared about you, she wouldn't dangle you on a string like she does everyone else."

"I'm not asking you, Jake," I angrily announced. "Maybe other guys dance with Julie just to get turned on, but I don't. I'm interested in her. And if she doesn't understand that, it's because she doesn't know me, even though I do talk to her on the phone very night. But I call her because I want to talk to her. I don't call to get a date just so I can tell everyone that I got a date with Julie Shaw so that I then can brag about what I got off her. I want to go out with her, and I don't care if I get anything. I just want to go out with her. Do you understand?"

"Settle down," Jake answered, turning back toward the study hall. "I didn't mean to get you so excited. It's not that big a deal."

"It is to me."

"You still haven't told us why you're determined to go to Mass this morning," Paul said as we watched Julie disappear behind the school. "If we're going to go, we better get started. It's almost eight o'clock."

"I talked to Julie on the phone last night because I wanted to see if she was going to the dance tonight, and towards the end of our conversation . . ."

"Two hours later," Jake broke in, famous groan and all.

"Towards the end of our conversation, 45 minutes later," I continued, turning to stare at Jake as he groaned again and turned away, shaking his head, "I asked her if she was going to Mass tomorrow. She said she was planning on it, and I told her I'd see her there."

"You're not going to walk her back to school, are you?" Paul asked in total disbelief.

"If you are," Jake said, "I'll go just to see the spectacle."

"Of course I'm not going to walk her back to school. I'm not going with her, so I don't have that right. But if I were, I'd gladly walk her back every day. For now, however, I just told he I'd see her after Mass, that's all. But maybe tonight will be a different story."

"What's so special about tonight?" Jake asked, looking me in the eye once again.

"I'm going to take her home from the dance tonight if it kills me. Tonight's the night."

"Sure it is," Jake said warily.

"I'm serious, Jake. This is it. I'm going to take her home. I'll make sure I get to her before anyone else has a chance."

"Are you going to wait for her outside the school?" Paul asked.

"Outside the school?" Jake asked sarcastically. "He'll have to stake out her house to even have a prayer."

"I have it all figured out. Just wait and see. I'll take her home. But now I'm going to go to Mass, because I told her I'd see her after church. Are you guys coming or not?"

"I'll go, I guess," Paul answered. "It'll be worth the time just to watch you."

"You should talk," I told him. "You'd faint if Patty came up to you and said 'hi' after Mass."

"Not quite. Even I'm not as bad as you are. I'll go and take my chances."

"I know one of you would faint," Jake said. "I'll go just to show the two of you how it's done. I'll even walk Lori back to school, even if I have to go against my principles."

"That's generous of you, Jake," I said with a smile. "I'm sure you'll make Lori's day. Are we ready then?"

"Just let me get my jacket from my locker," Paul said. "I'll meet you by the back door. Wait for me there," he added, walking away from the warmth of the radiators.

"Okay," I said. "But don't waste any time. I don't like to be too late. Come on, Jake, let's go," I added, motioning toward the study hall exit.

"I'm coming," he groaned, walking away from the radiators and the view of Galena Street and Girls' Central.

We walked across the study hall between the rows of desks and the stage and out the middle exit into the main hallway just in front of our school chapel with its white votive candles, secure in their red vases, glowing in the darkness. I stopped briefly in front of the chapel and then turned right to follow Jake down the hall toward the stairs that led to the back door of the school, just across the alley from St. Pat's.

We didn't have to wait long for Paul, and the three of us walked out the back door together across the alley and up the sidewalk that led to St. Pat's front porch steps. With their arms folded across their breasts or with their missals cradled against their bodies with their left arms, several girls in their navy blue uniforms, some dressed in sweaters and some in light, spring jackets, joined us in the walk up the stairs. Neither Jake nor Paul nor I carried a missal, but after Mass Jake would be carrying Lori's in his left hand as he held her left hand in his right hand for the walk north on Washington to Park Street and then east for half a block to the more secluded entrance to Girls' Central.

I've taken that walk a few times, but for some reason I haven't had the chance to take it as often I would have liked, which explains why I listen carefully when Ricky Nelson sings about the streets of 'Lonesome Town.' I've been there and I've tried to forget on those streets, as the song suggests, but I've never been completely successful. But the pain I've experienced has to be a natural part of life that results from answering the call to love. I can see that pain in all my monuments to eternity because you can't achieve that status if, somehow, you've escaped the pain. But I see triumph as well in those monuments. In fact, I don't see how anyone can experience triumph without first accepting the pain. For example, Macbeth's attempt to escape the pain led to his despair. So, I guess I'm better off for having walked the streets of 'Lonesome Town,' and I probably haven't walked them for the last time, either. After all, you can't be afraid and still remain loyal to the triumphant, black, iron gallus frames that stand tall and proud and dignified on the slopes, and atop the crest, of The Richest Hill on Earth.

XXVI

Walking into St. Pat's reminds me of walking into Clark Park. When you passed through that left field gate, you left the world of Aberdeen Streets behind and entered one of majesty, enchantment and magic. I never tired of walking into Clark Park or into St. Pat's. So, I pulled open the heavy brass door that guarded the church's southern, or Mercury Street, entrance, and Jake, Paul and I followed four girls into the vestibule. The girls found the holy water, made the sign of the cross and walked up the center aisle to find their pew. Jake, Paul and I found the same holy water, made the same sign of the cross, but walked toward the right side aisle, away from the center of the church, to find our pew. When you make the sign of the cross with fingers dipped in holy water, you know you're in church, and you can feel the silent reverence which, in turn, gives the magic a chance to work.

You never get tired of that silent reverence, and it's a welcomed relief from a noisy study hall filled with a few hundred boys enjoying the time before the eight-thirty bell summons them to monastic silence. But no bells ring at St. Pat's. When you make the sign of the cross, you don't need any bell to signal you to be silent. And when you entered Clark Park through the left field gate, you didn't need any ballpark announcer to tell you to be impressed. St. Pat's commands, and Clark Park commanded, respect and reverence—just as do the gallus frames, my dad, Uncle Tim and his nose, my mother, Brother Kelley and Butte itself.

Jake, Paul and I walked down the right side aisle and found a spot to our liking, not quite in the middle of the section. We genuflected on our right knees and moved into the pew—Jake first, then Paul and then me. We knelt down, made the sign of the cross again, and scanned the pews in the center section where most of the girls were sitting. Most of the people in church were students, but a good portion of them were women who were regulars, with a smattering of working men who could come to eight o'clock Mass on their way to work. As I prayed before Mass, I looked for familiar faces and for anyone else I cared to see.

Like most of the boys at Central, I'm not pious. Such boys always carry missals and sit in the center section past the middle. I never desired that identity, although I do own a missal that I like to take to Mass on Sunday. But I wouldn't be caught dead at eight o'clock Mass at St. Pat's carrying a missal and sitting in the center section past the middle. I only want to carry the missal belonging to the girl I'm walking back to school. I don't trust piety and want no part of it. You can't be a child of the gallus frames, be true to them, and be pious at the same time.

If I have no desire to be pious, I do want to be religious, just like my monuments to eternity. Pious people are loud while religious people are quiet. Brother Kelley told us that William Faulkner, whom he calls the greatest American writer of them all, says that the truth is quiet, that it doesn't have to be loud because it will last. People in Butte normally might not read the likes of Faulkner, but they do listen to the gallus frames, baseball and the Mass. If Faulkner's telling the truth, the gallus frames, baseball and the Mass are expressions of the truth. And, unlike Brother Hollohan, for example, Brother Kelley is quiet. Come to think of it, Brother Hollohan has to be loud to make us afraid of him, but Brother Kelley never has to be to make us respect him.

Like my monuments to eternity, I try to keep the rules, even if I don't always succeed like the pious boys who never seem normal. I try to keep the rules because I want to be obedient like those same monuments. But they've broken the rules themselves, which explains why they understand when someone else breaks them. However, they never break the rule of the gallus frames. They always listen to and obey their song of loyalty and love, which is all the gallus frames expect out of people. That's one rule you can't break. Macbeth did and look what happened. He had to have committed mortal sin which means that the sins associated with religious people must be venial in nature. The pious guys I know, as well as the pious Brothers, don't act like any monuments to eternity I listen to. Maybe they avoid venial sins by obeying the rules, but, on the other hand, they certainly don't act like they're obedient to the love song of the gallus frames.

Monsignor Riley hadn't emerged from the sacristy yet as Jake, Paul and I made the sign of the cross again and sat back in our pew. I like eight o'clock Mass because Monsignor Riley never preaches a sermon, and he can say Mass faster than any priest alive. He has to be quick because school starts at eight thirty-five, and if you walk a girl back to Girls' Central, you need some time to make it back to Boys' Central before first period. But even though he has to hurry, I don't think he has to mumble quite as much as he does. When I listen to Monsignor Riley, I can hear some Latin, but sometimes I can't recognize the other sounds. On the whole, however, his mumbling doesn't effect the Latin majesty of the Mass which has little to do with any words, especially the English words of the sermon.

I try to listen to sermons on Sunday, but I'm always more interested in the Mass itself and the majesty of the church with its statues, stained glass windows, votive candles and stations of the cross. I don't see any enchantment or feel any magic in the words of the priest. Sometimes you can come across a priest who's an accomplished speaker, but I always have a hard time understanding his message. And then oftentimes the priests talk about money. I don't understand what money has to do with religion.

But I can understand the church as an enchanted place housing the statues, the altar, the tabernacle, the Blessed Sacrament and—maybe most important of all—the crucifix. If the crucifix isn't a deserving monument to eternity, then nothing is. Anyone who can't see pain in the crucifix has to be blind. I'm only 17, and I can see it, just as I can see pain in the gallus frames, my dad, Uncle Tim and his nose, Brother Kelley, my mother, baseball and in Butte. But if you keep looking and if you study any monument to eternity, you eventually see the triumph. And the crucifix is quiet. Maybe William Faulkner is right. Maybe the crucifix doesn't have to be loud because it's the truth and will last. I looked over the majesty of the church, with its crucifix suspended above the altar, and just as the altar boy quietly rang the sacristy bell, I finally spotted Julie Shaw, in all her splendor, sitting in the center pew to the right of the main aisle. Everyone stood as Monsignor Riley, dressed in his gold vestments and tasseled, purple cap, emerged from the sacristy and walked to the foot of the altar. He removed his cap and gave it to the altar boy, bowed and began to mumble—sometimes even in Latin. My eyes focused on Julie's splendor and then on the majesty of the crucifix, rendering the words insignificant.

In the silence and solitude of the church I only could hear the Latin mumblings and intonations of Monsignor Riley and the Latin responses of the altar boy as he knelt to the right of Monsignor Riley and recited the Confiteor. I like that prayer because it's a part of the Mass, but reading it in English is similar to reading Shakespeare. The language is majestic, but you have to think about it to understand. I don't associate any magic with the Confiteor when I read it in English and start to think about sin. I can't see what a monument to eternity has to confess that could be so awful. How can a person obedient to the call of love offend anyone?

When I don't have to read the Confiteor in English, I can listen to the Latin sounds and pray in my own way. I don't know what Jake and Paul did with their silence as Monsignor Riley continued with Mass, but I prayed during mine and I'm not ashamed to admit it. I prayed quietly to the Almighty God of the Confiteor to help me with Julie Shaw. I was convinced she was the girl for me, and I sought some help for her to recognize the same. I'd be true to her no matter what, and if she could see my loyalty, she'd respond with her own and we'd be united in love. I watched Julie stand, sit and kneel, and when I listened to Monsignor Riley's Latin mumblings and watched his movements on the altar, without reading any English translation of his words, I didn't have to think about sin. I believe in the Mass, but I question the priests and their words. What if the space explorers don't find God Almighty up there in space?

I also thought about the story of Christ because it reminded me of 'Macbeth' or vice-versa. The Temptation in the Desert with Christ and Satan reminds me of the temptation in 'Macbeth' with him and the witches. When you think about it, if the space explorers don't find any God in their travels, how can any Satan exist in his Kingdom of Hell? Then you have to ask if the Temptation in the Desert really happened. But Brother Kelley says that something doesn't have to have happened to be true, like Chaucer and 'The Canterbury Tales.' He doesn't have to be describing an actual pilgrimage to be telling the truth. As Judy once said, and as Uncle Tim always proves, you have to use your imagination to make a story the truth.

I still find the idea about temptation to be a little confusing, but I can't help thinking about it nonetheless. I know my mother's faced a similar temptation with George Lewis. She could have married him by now, but she hasn't, even if marriage, in appearance at the very least, would have made her life easier. Christ didn't obey Satan, either, but Macbeth obeyed the witches. My mother's life isn't easy and I know she can feel awfully frustrated at times, but she never has given me the impression that "life is a tale told by an idiot full of sound and fury signifying nothing." If George's life weren't so amusing, I don't think it would signify anything. It appears that Macbeth could have been equivalent to Christ if he hadn't obeyed the witches. And, to me, Christ's story celebrates courage and love. He found his courage but Macbeth didn't, even though he could slit the enemy "from the nave to the chaps."

From what I can understand, Christ must be religious and not pious. Otherwise, he wouldn't keep the company of sinners, unless he's a crusader who wants to show off his piety. And if Christ is religious, my mother must have chosen to be religious in contrast to Macbeth who chose a different path, which explains his tragedy. As far as I can see then, being religious is synonymous with being obedient to love, and living that level of obedience makes any individual a monument to eternity or, as Brother Kelley would say, a hero—whether or not the individual is aware of the achievement. The process is interesting and not so complicated when you stop to think about it. Furthermore and whether or not the individual realizes it, I think a religious person—a monument to eternity, a hero—is more influenced by the story of Christ than by the words of the priest. And the Mass must present the celebration of that story. An individual, therefore, can live the story of Christ and not even know it, and Macbeth chose not to live that story. I, for one, don't want to make that same mistake. I didn't know if Julie wanted to live in obedience to love, but I hoped so. Anyway, I prayed to that effect, but I don't think anyone can coerce an individual into living that obedience. You have to decide it for yourself.

When I think about the Mass, I realize I like the consecration and the ringing of the altar bell the best of all. I can't imagine the Mass without the chime of the altar bell any more than I can imagine baseball without the crack of the bat. Only the Benediction of the Blessed Sacrament, celebrated at the end of one of our school year's silent retreats when we all sing 'Holy God We Praise Thy Name' and 'Tantum Ergo,' can match the majesty of the consecration. I have no idea what 'Tantum Ergo' means, but it has to have something to do with magic because I have the worst voice in the history of voices. I wouldn't touch the 'Ave Maria,' for example, but my eyes can tear up when someone sings it properly.

No one wants to sing at the consecration, but when the bells ring and the priest elevates the host, you can't help listening. I don't see how a church could exist without the Mass. That altar celebration is far more powerful than any pulpit oration, with the exception of those a retreat master can deliver concerning the reality of Hell. The retreat exercise itself can create the appropriate mood, and when the retreat master delivers his talk about the fires of Hell, I listen. But if the space explorers don't discover any Heaven amidst the expanse of space, what happens to all those retreat talks about the majestic pain, darkness and stench of Hell? The subterranean darkness of Hell is more than a match for the celestial light of Heaven, and, whatever those images ultimately turn out to signify, I hope I always can choose the celestial light over the subterranean darkness.

Holy Communion follows the consecration, and if the Host isn't an example of an enchanted object, there is no such thing. I remember the Sisters at St. Ann's telling us that our teeth would fall out if we dared to touch the consecrated Host with them. I can smile at the Sisters' directive now because I no longer believe it, but, nonetheless, I learned to recognize the Host as a sacred object. I chew cookies all right, but I'll never chew the Host. How can you chew a consecrated, enchanted object? No wonder we refer to the Mass as the magic show. Can you think of a better way to describe the Holy Sacrifice of the Mass?

Usually, when I hear the chime of the altar bell and when I hear the priest say "Domine non sum dignus," signaling the end of the long Canon of the Mass, I feel like going to communion to receive the Blessed Sacrament—but not at eight o'clock Mass at St. Pat's with the girls, and Julie Shaw especially, in attendance. When Monsignor Riley turned to the congregation and said "Domine non sum dignus" in clear Latin, the girls headed for communion and the boys headed for the front porch to wait for them to emerge from the enchanted world of the crucifix into the everyday world of slag heaps and gallus frames. If the magic hadn't worked by then, it wasn't going to work anyway.

When I heard Monsignor Riley's Latin intonation, I looked at my watch and smiled. It read eight-fifteen as usual. You can count on him saying "Domine non sum dignus" at eight-fifteen just as you can count on the mine whistles blowing at four-thirty to signal the end of the day shift. I poked Jake and Paul, pointed to the time, and they smiled in recognition as we stood up, genuflected and began to make our way toward the heavy brass doors guarding the entrance to the church. I led the way to the holy water just inside the vestibule, dipped my right forefinger and middle finger and made the sign of the cross as I walked toward the doors and waited for Jake and Paul. They found the water, blessed themselves, and now that we all were properly anointed, I pushed open a brass door and walked out of the church and into the Friday morning, spring sunshine. I continued across the front porch to assume the standard pose of a Butte Central boy who leans back and rests his elbows on the marble slab that runs the length of the ten foot concrete wall facing Mercury Street. His right leg is slightly bent at the knee as he awaits the end of Mass and the emergence of the Butte Central girls into the bright, spring sunlight.

XXVII

" **N**obody can say Mass as fast as Monsignor Riley," I said as the three of us joined the crowd lined up against the concrete wall. "Do you think he pronounces all the words or does he just mumble? Have you ever thought about it?"

"I thought you were thinking about Julie," Jake answered, "and not about whether or not Monsignor Riley mumbles or speaks Latin."

"I think about it, I suppose," Paul said. "Sometimes I can't make out what he's saying. I think he wants to get through the Mass as quickly as possible."

"He probably has other things to do," Jake added, shifting his feet and his weight from his left leg to his right leg. "But why should you care in the first place?"

"I just think it's interesting, but I don't think it makes any difference whether or not he mumbles. He's still saying the Mass, and his approach to it simply is part of his charm."

"How can Monsignor Riley have charm?" Jake asked. "Besides, I thought you only were interested in Julie's charm."

"He can have charm," I answered, "but not like Julie. Priests have different personalities. For example, say that Brother Kelley and Brother Hollohan were priests. Would you want to go to confession to Father Hollohan?"

"You wouldn't get me near that guy," Jake answered emphatically.

"Me either," Paul said. "He'd have the shortest line in the history of confession lines. I'd go to him only if I had no choice, and then I'd probably lie, commit a sacrilege and be in real trouble."

"Now what about Father Kelley?" I asked.

"I don't know him like you two do," Jake answered, "but from what you say about him and from what I can see and hear myself, I'd go to confession to him. He's not like Hollohan."

"I wouldn't think twice about going to him," Paul said. "He'd have the longest line in the history of confession lines. He understands and wouldn't be interested in using penance to punish. Brother Hollohan, or Father Hollohan, really would lay it on. Everyone would be afraid of him."

"See, that's why I like to watch priests say Mass. I like to study the different personalities. Some priests are more interested in showing off than in saying Mass. At least Monsignor Riley isn't a show off. He's just a man who's probably said a million Masses and realizes that if the power of the Mass completely depends on the personality of the priest, we're all in trouble anyway. He perfectly fits the eight o'clock Mass because people are in a hurry. It's all very interesting," I said, standing up straight as I realized that Monsignor Riley had to be approaching the end by now. He didn't waste any time cleaning the chalice and the patent, either.

"I thought you only were interested in girls and love and Julie," Jake said.

"That's true, but I think I'm interested in individuals in general. You have to admit that we're fascinating creatures."

"Speaking of fascinating," Paul said, "did you spot Julie in church?"

"How could I miss her? She belongs in church."

"I've heard everything now," Jake groaned. "You'd think we were talking about the Blessed Virgin Mary. She definitely belongs in church, but Julie Shaw's a different story. I can think of many adjectives to describe her, but blessed virgin doesn't apply. You're unbelievable."

"Julie belongs in church because she matches its beauty and majesty. Doesn't she, Paul?" I asked in search of an ally.

"I guess so, if you look at it that way," he stammered in response.

"One of these days you'd better decide to join the real world," Jake said, looking directly at me. "You've been listening to too many Buddy Holly and Ricky Nelson records. Julie is Julie Shaw from

Centerville. She isn't the Blessed Virgin Mary, and she isn't Peggy Sue or Mary Lou, either. If you understood that difference, she wouldn't be able to make such a fool out of you."

"She doesn't make a fool out of me, and I live in the real world, Jake. And maybe Buddy Holly and Ricky Nelson aren't as meaningless as you might think. Maybe you ought to listen to them sometime. If I act foolish, it isn't because of Julie Shaw."

"You're in a class by yourself, Buddy," Jake said, shaking his head and smiling. "I can't believe it."

"Why don't you two settle down a little?" Paul broke in. "Mass is over and it's time to watch. And for you, Jake, it's time to walk. Are you ready?"

"Real funny, Brennan. Sure, I'm ready. You guys just watch. I'll show you the proper technique," he added as the heavy brass opened and first of the girls emerged from the majesty of the church.

I no longer was leaning against the concrete wall. Instead, I was standing as straight as I could, shifting my weight from my left leg to my right leg and back again. I kept my hands in my pockets because I didn't know what else to do with them as I waited for the inevitable moment when Julie would emerge from the church. Whenever I knew I was going to see her, no matter the circumstances, the same anxious feeling came over me. It wasn't easy for me to ask her to dance, for example. I had to work up my courage and gradually ease my way across the study hall floor. Even when I was determined to act with supreme confidence, my determination eroded when I faced the moment of truth.

Lori Santini, Jake's steady girlfriend for the past couple of years, stepped out onto the porch before Julie. When Paul and I saw her, we nudged Jake, and he sprung into action with the style of a guy in total command. He walked a few steps to the middle of the porch and met Lori. She stopped and waved hello to Paul and me before she handed Jake her missal which he took in his left hand, as if he didn't want anyone to notice he was carrying it. Paul and I returned Lori's smile, and my attention, momentarily, was diverted from thoughts of Julie as I watched Lori and Jake join hands and walk toward the steps leading to the Washington Street side of St. Pat's. He didn't smile nor did he say anything as they walked down the steps hand in hand. They reached the bottom step, still walking in silence, turned right and disappeared as they walked north on Washington toward Park Street as part of the daily parade of steady couples.

"You can count on Jake not smiling just as you can count on Monsignor Riley saying 'Domine non sum dignus' at eight-fifteen every morning," I said. "He's priceless," I added, leaning against the concrete wall of the porch once again and supporting myself with my elbows.

"You're right there," Paul said. "Jake's in charge, and, remember, he's never been without a steady girl."

"At least he seems to be in charge," I said, watching the heavy brass doors.

"We'll have to take that comment up another day," Paul said. "Look, here comes Julie."

He was right. I saw her in all her majesty, walking through the doorway and looking directly at me as I leaned against the concrete wall with my hands thrust in my pockets. I've never seen the Blessed Virgin Mary, but I can tell the difference between such a vision and the sight of Julie Shaw. Julie, and not the Blessed Virgin Mary, walked up to me with her brown eyes sparkling and her black hair shining in the morning sunlight. And her smile, enhanced by her slightly rouged cheeks, illuminated her face in an earthly majesty that rivaled any Heavenly expression of the same. She was no vision. She was as real to me as Lori was to Jake, and her smile was meant for me. I felt my heart leap to my throat and begin to beat a thousand times a minute, and it didn't slow down at all when I heard her soft, feminine voice.

"Hi, Dan," she seemed to sing. "You said you'd see me at church this morning."

"That's right," I said between heartbeats. "You always can count on me. Are you going to the dance tonight?"

"Yes," she answered, smiling. "Are you?"

"I think so," I answered as Paul listened and tried not to laugh.

"I hope I get a chance to dance with you. Make sure you ask me. Okay?" she asked as she started to walk away toward the stairs that led to the alley running behind Boys' Central.

"I'll see you tonight for sure. And I'll ask you to dance. You can count on that."

"Okay. I'll be looking forward to it," she said, still smiling. "I'll see you tonight. Goodbye, Dan. Goodbye, Paul."

"Goodbye, Julie," Paul replied.

"Goodbye, Julie," I said. "I'll be looking for you tonight," I added as she waved and headed down the stairs toward the alley, arms folded across her breasts. I watched her uniform skirt sway to the rhythm of her walk, and I couldn't help noticing her nylon-tanned legs that didn't belong to any heavenly vision of anything. Julie's a vision of earthly majesty, and if we don't find any heavenly majesty in space where we've always thought it to be, we have nothing else. And without love I don't see how majesty of any kind can exist—no matter where it lives.

"I'll take her home tonight if it kills me," I said. "I have to. I have to give her the chance to know me. It's not enough to talk to her on the phone or to dance with her once or twice. I have to be with her. She says I'm her favorite person to talk to on the phone. Just think how much better it'll be when we're actually together. Isn't that right?"

"I don't know," Paul answered. "You're hooked worse than I ever have been. But Jake's right, you know. Taking her home tonight is going to be a real challenge. You're not the only guy with that idea. You'd better ask her before she even has a chance to get on the dance floor or you'll miss your chance."

"I have it all figured out," I said as we started to walk towards the steps leading back to Central. "It all depends on if Jake picks me up a little early tonight. But you know him. He's never been on time in his life. How can I expect him to be early?"

"Listen," Paul said, walking down the steps, "if Jake knows you're going to take Julie home tonight after all your previous threats, if he knows tonight's the night, he'll pick you up early. He won't want to miss the show. You know Jake. He'll watch every move you make."

"I know he will," I said smiling, as we reached the school's back door. "He always parks the car in perfect position, just in case I work up enough courage to kiss my date goodnight. He's had more than a few laughs at my expense. I'm not as smooth as he is, but at least I keep him entertained."

"That's for sure. He'd like nothing better than to go park with you and Julie in the back seat. What would you do then?" Paul asked as we pulled open the heavy oak door and walked into the school and up the stairs towards our third floor lockers.

"What!" I exclaimed, stopping halfway up the stairs to the main floor. "I can't park with Julie on the first date. You don't park with any girl on the first date, unless you're just interested in seeing what you can get. I've been there, but this is different. Even Jake has to realize that. He wouldn't go park under these circumstances. Would he?"

"I think he'd be tempted just to give you the chance to show Julie who's boss," Paul answered as we continued up the stairs.

"I'll have to speak to him about that. Unless he wants a dead body on his hands, he'd better not go park. My heart wouldn't stop at my throat. It would break completely clear."

"What?" Paul asked.

"Never mind," I answered as I worked the combination lock attached to my locker. "I'll talk to him. He can park with Lori, if he wants to, after they take Julie and me home. What about you? Are you going to take anyone home tonight?"

"I don't know," Paul answered as we reached into our lockers to get our books. "I might try to take Patty home, but I'm not sure. She hasn't had much time for me lately. I'll have to wait and see. Do you have all your books?"

"I'm ready. Let's go downstairs to watch the fortunates sprint back from Girls' Central. Just once, I'd like to see Jake actually sprint."

"That'll be the day. Don't hold your breath," Paul added laughing, as we slammed our lockers shut and headed down the stairs for the study hall before we had to answer the bell that, until lunch time, called us to monastic silence.

XXVIII

The guys who walk their girls back to Girls' Central have to make it back to school before the first bell rings at eight-thirty to avoid being late, which doesn't seem too serious until you realize that an International Child Beater stands by the door, brandishing his leather strap, waiting to greet any late arrivals. If Brother Williams, or a Brother of similar temperament, has that duty, the punishment's not too severe—as long as you don't try to take advantage of the situation. If Brother Kelley has that duty, you have little to worry about, unless you arrogantly flaunt your disrespect for the rules. He wouldn't hit anyone, but he has little tolerance for arrogance. But you're in big trouble if you confront Brother Hollohan because he's always looking for an excuse to unleash his leather strap. Jake never has any problem because he's never stayed long enough at Girls' Central to give himself the chance to be late. However, whenever I've taken the journey from St. Pat's to Girls' Central, I've had to sprint across Park and down Idaho to beat the bell. I've always made it, but I've pushed my luck a couple of times.

Paul and I walked down the steps to the main floor and looked down the stairs to the basement level to see who was standing guard. We saw Brother Williams, nodded to each other, and walked into the study hall and across the floor—between the rows of desks and the front stage—to the same iron radiators featuring the wood covers. The study hall was more crowded now and noisier as well. It's not easy to keep 400 boys quiet, no matter how much history lives in the room. But when the bell rings at eight-thirty, the school day begins, and having been called to silence, we obey. The Brothers can't expect us to take their vows of poverty and chastity, but they can, and do, expect us to share their vow of obedience.

To some extent we obey out of fear. Only a fool enjoys being hit on the palms of his hand with a leather strap wielded by someone skilled in, and sometimes delighted by, the practice. We don't call the Irish Christian Brothers the International Child Beaters for nothing. Still, you can't leave Central without getting the leather, as we refer to it. But you have to be careful about whom you disobey. Brother Williams, or a Brother sharing his attitude, likes students and punishes with compassion. He believes our best interests are served by obedience, and he uses the leather strap as a legitimate means to achieve that end.

But Brother Hollohan is a different story. He doesn't like students, and, if for some reason, you pick him to disobey, you have to expect big trouble. I didn't exactly pick him, but I was unlucky enough to bounce an orange off his leg one lunch period when I was playing catch with Paul in the senior hallway. I knew I shouldn't have been playing catch with an orange in the first place, but the offense hardly called for me to be beaten within an inch of my life. If it weren't for men like Brother Williams and Brother Kelley, I'd go to Butte High in a minute, not caring at all about the virtue of obedience. Brother Hollohan shouldn't be a Brother. I can understand the need for obedience and I respect it as a virtue, but if it's beaten into you by the likes of him, you'll never acquire it. Brother Kelley, on the other hand, is completely different. You want to obey him. But the bell calling us to monastic silence hadn't rung yet for the 400 boys assembled in the study hall as Paul and I leaned on the wood cover of one of the iron radiators and waited for the sprinters to dash across Galena Street in their race to beat the bell and to avoid the leather.

As usual, we looked out the window in the direction of the corner of Galena and Idaho and noticed Jake strolling across the street with time to spare. In keeping with his character, he didn't look up, but I wasn't fooled. He knew that we and the other guys were watching. He stood at the same radiators long enough to know how many eyes would be focused on him. I don't know of a girl alive who could make Jake run down Idaho Street, but I can't act like him. I've tried, only to find that it's not natural for me.

"Look at Jake," I said to Paul, pointing toward the window. "Do you think he'll ever run down Idaho Street?"

"He wouldn't run down Idaho if he walked Kim Novak or Natalie Wood back to Girls' Central after Mass. He'd just say goodbye, drop them off and casually walk back to school as if nothing had happened. He's amazing."

"If I walked Natalie Wood back to Girls' Central, someone would have to drag me back to school. But I'd probably faint on the porch of the church before I ever assumed the position to make the missal exchange," I added, laughing.

"I'm sure you would. If you freeze at the sight of Julie Shaw, I'd hate to see what you'd do when confronted with Natalie Wood," Paul said, still looking out the window as Jake disappeared from sight. "Here they come," he added as the first sprinter appeared, followed closely by the others. "I wonder if they really have trouble leaving their girls or if they just enjoy being watched as they sprint down Idaho."

"I'm sure it's a combination of both. Being aware of the crowd is part of the fun," I answered, speaking from experience as the last of the sprinters dashed across Galena and headed for the front door of the school. "Let's go to class. The bell's going to ring any second now. I think they all made it back safely today."

"I think you're right. We won't hear the crack of the leather today."

"At least not for this act of disobedience," I said as we walked across the study hall between the rows of desks and the front stage. We reached the doors nearest the east stairway when the bell rang, calling us to silence. We obeyed and walked up the stairs to the third floor and to physics class in the first classroom on the right at the top of the stairs. Jake's placement on a different academic track, what the school referred to as 4-B as opposed to 4-A, spared him from the more scientific classes. I wouldn't see him until lunch, but it didn't matter. I couldn't talk to him before then anyway.

I try to be a curious listener and I might be in 4-A, but physics doesn't make much sense to me. It's interesting, with all those pulleys and formulas, but I can't always figure out the calculations. Still, someone has to able to meet the challenge because we've managed to send men into space. As I said before, I like the adventure of it all, but I can't help thinking about the results of space exploration. What if the explorers don't find any next world out there? What if we land men on the moon and find it uninhabitable? What do we do then? The moon is mysterious now, along with Heaven and Hell, but what happens when the mystery is unmasked?

Maybe we've asked these questions in the past, but we haven't had to face them head on before. And as Brother Kelley says, we have to want to know the truth. We can't be afraid. But what if the truth tells us we can't live on the moon, and what if it tells us there is no celestial Heaven nor any subterranean Hell? Do we give up? I don't think so because only cowards give up. Instead, I think we try to live right now in life just the way we experience it. I think the mystery lives right here, and I think it has something to do with the creative power of love. I think the power of love is more interesting than the craters of the moon, and we just have to live our individual capacity for it, even if we can't explain it. I think that mystery lives in the gallus frames and the crucifix. I even think it lives in Central. I don't see why we can't study this earthly mystery and the mystery of space at the same time just to keep contemporary life in balance.

I listened in physics and chemistry, all the time thinking of the night's dance and the mystery of love and Julie Shaw, and finally made it to solid geometry—the last class before lunch. I like Brother Martin, but solid geometry is beyond me and I always breathe a sigh of relief when the bell rings, calling me to lunch. I'm never the last student out of Brother Martin's class, and I didn't waste any time on this day, either. In fact, I left the classroom more quickly than usual because I wanted to get a seat with Jake at lunch. I had to tell him that he couldn't go park with Julie and me in the back seat. I was counting on being with Julie even before I asked her home, but I was confident that tonight would be the night. I hurried out of the third floor classroom, found my locker, dropped off my books, grabbed my lunch, slammed the locker door shut and headed for the stairway at the west end of the school, taking care not to run. We aren't allowed to run in the halls, and Central is an obedient school.

Carrying my lunch sack, I made it down the stairs as fast as I could, bought a carton of milk in the lunch room just to the left of the darker, more mysterious chapel and walked across the hall toward the study hall that now served as the cafeteria for 400 boys.

We didn't have to obey any rule of silence during lunch, except during retreat days when we couldn't talk inside the building at any time. I looked forward to those three days every year, although I did manage to whisper to Jake and Paul every now and then. At the end of a three-day, silent retreat, I always felt like I did after confession or like Uncle Tim had to feel when he smelled that coffee at the Butte-Central game in 1953. I know sanctifying grace has to be real because I've experienced it. It's a mystery, but either we get it from some outside source or we awaken it ourselves.

But this Friday wasn't a retreat day, and the study hall was noisy, if not loud. I couldn't see Jake or Paul anywhere so I found a desk toward the front of the third row and sat down to wait for them. I just started to open my lunch sack when I spotted Jake walking into our study hall cafeteria. He looked around, found me and started to walk over to the desk. Usually, we sat two to a desk during lunch, and I moved over to make room for him as he slid in next to me.

XXIX

"Three more periods to go, Buddy," he said as he sat down. "Do you think you'll make it?"

"Real funny, Jake," I said. "But I wouldn't mind being able to sing like Buddy Holly."

"But he's dead. Remember?"

"I know, but his songs aren't. Not yet anyway."

"That's for sure. Not with you around."

"Do you ever listen to those songs?" I asked.

"Sure, I listen to them, but not like you do. No one listens to them like you do. They're only songs, you know."

"I know. But some songs are better than others."

"They're all the same to me," Jake said, unwrapping his sandwiches. "I just dance to them. You have to dance to something."

"Don't you ever listen to them while you're dancing with Lori?" I asked, reaching into my lunch sack for my fried egg sandwiches.

"I don't pay that much attention to them. I just dance with her."

"You mean you never listen to 'To Know Him is to Love Him' when you dance with Lori?" I asked, taking a bite of my sandwich as Paul showed up and moved into the seat next to us.

"What are you two talking about?" he asked, opening his lunch sack.

"Songs," I answered. "I was just asking Jake if he listens to songs like 'To Know Him is to Love Him' when he dances with Lori."

"And," Jake said, "I was about to say that I don't pay much attention to it because it's only a song."

"You're crazy, Jake," I said. "How can you not listen to that song? It's a classic. How about you, Brenns?"

"I don't know. I don't see anyone swooning over me. Lori swoons over Jake, and he never listens to the song."

"Maybe so, but that's no reason not to believe in it."

"Believe in it?" Jake asked. "You mean you believe in that song?"

"Sure," I answered, finishing half of my first fried egg sandwich. "You have to believe in something."

"I can agree with that," Jake said. "But a song? Believe in a song? No wonder you act so crazy. Even Brennan doesn't belong in your class, and he's bad enough. And you call me crazy."

"Maybe I am crazy, but someday you'll find out. Maybe we're supposed to believe in songs. Did you ever think of that?" I asked, biting into the other half of my sandwich as Paul listened intently. "Maybe we'd all be better off if we took songs more seriously."

"What about Julie?" Jake asked. "Do you think she believes in songs?"

"I don't know," I answered, finishing the second half of my first sandwich. "What do you think, Brenns?"

"How should I know?" he answered, biting into his tuna fish sandwich. "You know her better than I do. You're the one who talks to her on the phone every night."

"I'll bet you anything she doesn't believe in them," Jake said. "And I'll bet you anything she doesn't care about anyone who does, which explains why I think you're crazy for chasing her all over town. And if you take her home tonight, we'll go park, and then we'll find out who believes what," he added, biting into his second peanut butter and jelly sandwich.

"I don't chase her all over town. And don't go park. I'm going to take her home tonight, and if I had my own car, I'd take her home myself."

"That I'd like to see," Jake laughed. "You and Julie all alone? I can't believe it."

"I would. I'd take her home myself if I could."

"Even I don't believe that," Paul said, finishing half of his second sandwich.

"It's the truth. But I have to go with you, Jake. Just don't go park. You don't park with a girl on the first date."

"Okay, okay. Don't get excited. I won't go park. But you didn't answer my question. Do you think Julie believes in songs?"

"Well," I answered, taking the final bite of my second fried egg sandwich, "to tell the truth, I think she does."

"You're crazy," Jake replied.

"But I think she might be afraid to live them."

"Do you think she likes fried egg sandwiches?" Paul asked.

"Why do you ask that?"

"Because," Jake answered, "you have two of them every Friday."

"I like the smell of them in the morning when my mother's frying the eggs. Because of that smell I look forward to eating them at lunch. Fridays and fried eggs go together. I don't want anything else. I count on them," I said, squeezing my paper sack into a ball.

"I still think you're crazy," Jake said. "I don't know why peanut butter and jelly can't be as good as fried egg just once. Don't you get tired of them?"

"No. How can you get tired of something so significant? Besides, the fried egg's not important. I don't see why tuna fish or peanut butter and jelly can't be of equal significance. I just like fried egg with Durkees."

"Well," Jake said, "you're going to end up with egg on your face tonight. You'll be lucky if you even have a chance to ask Julie home."

"That's why I want you to come early tonight. Do you think you could manage to pick me up at eight-thirty?"

"Eight-thirty? Do you want to be here to help move the desks or something?"

"I just want to be here early so that I can get to Julie before anyone else has the chance. Can you pick me up at eight-thirty?"

"For this occasion I'll be there. Do you want me to pick you up, too?" Jake asked, looking at Paul.

"No. Not tonight. I'll take my dad's car. I don't want Dan to miss his big chance because of me."

"Who are you going to take home?" Jake asked.

"I don't know. I'd like to take Patty home, but I doubt it. I'll just have to see what happens."

"You're welcome to come with us, you know. The more the merrier. With four people in the back seat, Julie would have to sit closer to Buddy Holly here. Maybe you could sing a little 'Peggy Sue' in her ear."

"You guys are real funny. I'm glad the bell's about to ring because then I won't have to listen to either of you until school's out. Who knows? Maybe I'll have the last laugh. I'll take her home. You wait and see."

"We'll wait and we'll see," Jake said as the three of us stood up at the same time. "We'd better go upstairs and get our books."

"Three more periods to go and we're free again," Paul said as we dropped our lunch sacks in the garbage can beside the main study hall entrance and walked out into the hallway still noisy with the sound of voices.

"Wait 'till you guys see me in action," I said as we started to walk up the stairs to the third floor. "Nothing but courage tonight. Julie won't know what hit her," I added, stopping at my locker.

"Maybe," Jake said, laughing, "but you always look like you've been hit. Try to control yourself tonight," he continued, walking past me to his locker several feet down the hall. "I don't want you to faint in the back seat of my car."

"Then don't go park," Paul joined in—just as the bell rang, calling us to silence one more time.

XXX

I lived from bell to bell in the afternoon, just as I had in the morning. I try to concentrate in school, but sometimes I find it almost impossible—even in Brother Kelley's class. But at least he understands. I can be pretty exhausted by the time I get to his class at the end of the week, but, then, so can he, which makes me feel better. He always has something to teach and never sits at his desk, after assigning us work to do while we sit at our desks. I can't say I was looking forward to his class, exactly, but when the bell rang summoning us to sixth period, I still went more willingly than grudgingly. After all, it was Brother Kelley's class as well as sixth period on a Friday—the Friday of the dance.

He looked tired as I walked into his classroom at the west end of the study hall on the school's main floor, and white chalk dust, even more than usual, covered his black cassock. He liked to use the blackboard, and after writing a key word, he'd start to explain the idea he had in mind. Before you knew it, the chalk dust would fly, and the entire blackboard would be covered with arrows and circles that somehow related to the main idea he wrote on the board in the first place. Some of my classmates paid more attention to how Brother Kelley taught—to his style—than they did to what he was trying to teach. At first I belonged in that category because I'd never experienced a teacher like him at Central, the junior high or at Emerson. I'd heard about him, of course, but even then I wasn't fully prepared. No one can prepare anyone for Brother Kelley. You have to experience him for yourself. He's demanding, but he's everyone's teacher. I've never known him to play favorites.

He's not an exceptionally big man, but he never has to resort to using his leather strap to scare us into listening to him. Instead, he reminds us of our duty as students to listen—from the heart, as he says, and not merely with the ears. During his 15 years of teaching he says he's come across many students who couldn't read or write very well, but that he's yet to come across a student incapable of listening. If you listen with the heart, he says, you'll do your duty. And if performance of duty doesn't motivate us, we're all in trouble because it's our responsibility to be men of duty, just like the men and women who built The Richest Hill on Earth. I don't know about anyone else, but his talk of duty inspires me. All my monuments to eternity, including Brother Kelley, are individuals devoted to duty. I listen to, and trust, him because he lives what he teaches. He says Chaucer shows us that you have to practice before you preach. He says we'll understand if we listen and that all of us can live what we understand, even if we can't explain it.

He says that some of us may be able to explain someday, if we want to, but duty only calls us to live the essence of the individual heart. He says we can't mistake the inability to explain what we know for the inability to live it. He says conditions that once supported life are changing now, and he points to the Berkeley Pit as an example. So, we have to know on purpose, or consciously, what we once lived accidentally, or unconsciously, from now on if we are to live with the same honor and courage and dignity and humility and love that marked the lives of men and women before The Pit started to eat the gallus frames. He says it only takes courage to live what you know and what you understand in your heart and that all of us are equal when it comes to courage. He says we just have to be individuals authentically interested in duty to discover its sacrificial demands. And he says it's tragic, like Macbeth, when we don't live our individual capacity for courage. Tragedy doesn't apply only to kings, which explains why we should pay attention to Macbeth whether we live in Dublin Gulch, on the West Side, in Floral Park or in the shadow of Clark Park.

Given their opposition, it's hard to believe that Brother Kelley and Brother Hollohan can live in the same house. Brother Hollohan can use Brother Kelley's words, but I never believe him because I can see that he doesn't practice before he preaches. He isn't honest, and he wears a permanent scowl on his face as if he's constantly angry at something or someone. Brother Kelley doesn't wear a perpetual smile and he's been known to raise his voice in anger more than once, but, unlike Brother Hollohan, he never takes his anger out on his students. As far as I can see, I think Brother Kelley is angry only because he cares about us. Unlike Brother Hollohan, once again, I think he's earned the right to talk about the creative power of love. And Brother Kelley believes in obedience whereas Brother Hollohan only resents and hates it. He'd be happier if he weren't a Brother, and I don't know why he ever entered the order. He's not dedicated to anything, and, besides, he almost too handsome to be a Brother.

Brother Kelley's handsome as well, if you can use such a term in reference to Irish Christian Brothers who aren't supposed to be aware of such things. But he's almost six feet tall, which makes him an inch or two shorter than Brother Hollohan, and I'd say he weighs about 160 pounds, although the cassock he wears can hide his weight. With his broad shoulders, Brother Hollohan looks huskier, even though Brother Kelley looks more masculine, in the manner of Uncle Tim. But then he comes from Dublin Gulch and has nothing to prove. Brother Hollohan is more vain about his appearance, as reflected in his perfectly trimmed, black, crew-cut hair, and, to verify his manhood, he wears his leather—which he is quick to use—strapped to his right side like a Western gunslinger. But I wouldn't trust him under any circumstances because his black cassock never—and I mean never—is covered by white chalk dust.

Brother Kelley has to be close to 40, like Uncle Tim, but he still looks as young as Brother Hollohan who's only been teaching for ten years. He doesn't wear his hair in the flat top style favored by Brother Hollohan, but his eyes are forever alert. You can't fool Brother Kelley. On the other hand, Brother Hollohan's so busy being angry that sometimes his eyes don't see anything. He's mean, but you can fool him. Brother Kelley, however, sees everything, and he only has to focus his eyes on students to keep them in line. He doesn't need a leather strap holstered on his side. His eyes mean business. Wrinkles that are beginning to form around them, to match those already fixed around the corners of his mouth, look natural, but Brother Hollohan's similar set developed as a result of the constant scowl that dominates his face. Brother Kelley's nose reminds me of Uncle Tim's, though its bridge doesn't show as many bumps and scars.

Brother Hollohan likes to hit, but even a quick glance at his nose can tell anyone that he's never been hit himself. No wonder I don't trust him.

I don't trust his smooth, white hands either. He might like to use his leather, but I'm convinced he'd offer a dead fish to anyone who had to shake hands with him. Brother Kelley's hands might not be a big as Brother Hollohan's, but they look more trustworthy. The thumb and forefinger of his right hand look permanently discolored from years of chalk dust working its way into the skin, and his veins bulge prominently on the back of either hand. Brother Hollohan's long fingers look like they were made to grip a leather strap, and he makes good use of them. He can swing a leather with unmatched power and authority, as well as with unmatched enjoyment. Brother Kelley's fingers, not quite as long but thicker, can just as easily grip a leather or a miner's muck stick as they can a piece of chalk or a copy of 'Macbeth.' His copy of Shakespeare's play sat open on the top of his desk, and he was erasing the blackboard when I walked into his classroom for sixth period and found my seat in the middle of the second row nearest the door.

Paul walked into the room shortly after I did and found his seat in the next row directly across from me. Brother Kelley didn't use an alphabetical seating chart, which meant we could sit wherever we wanted as long as we sat in the same seat all year. Paul and I might sit next to each other, but we never talk. In fact, nobody talks in Brother Kelley's classroom. Among other things, his deep and dignified voice, that reminds me of the ballpark announcer's from my days at Clark Park, commands attention. With his commanding presence, he doesn't have to rely on enforcing rules to preserve classroom decorum. Paul and I acknowledged each other and watched Brother Kelley try to brush the chalk dust off his cassock, only to make it worse.

"Takes a real genius to brush off chalk dust with hands covered with it," he said, laughing at himself.

We all laughed with him, but none of us said anything in return.

"Everyone excited about 'Macbeth?'" he asked. "I would be if I were you, sitting in sixth period on Friday before a spring dance. Under those conditions I couldn't get the play out of my mind."

We all laughed but none of us knew what to say in response. Brother Kelley always made himself available and he always was ready to talk, but if you ever approached him, you had to be ready for serious conversation. He had a lot to say, and if you were sincere, he was just as willing to listen. He doesn't like students who like to hear themselves talk, and while he's friendly, he's not exactly a friend. I think he'd describe himself as being wise. He's always serious about teaching, even during the last period on a Friday before a spring dance, and he proved to be true to form on this particular Friday as the prospect of a date with Julie Shaw dominated my thoughts. He never failed to give us the opportunity to learn, and he's the only teacher in the school who could take my mind off Julie Shaw for 50 minutes during that last period of that Friday before that spring dance.

I listened to him talk about Macbeth and Duncan, the king Macbeth eventually murdered, or I should say I listened to him explain the connection between Macbeth and Duncan. He explained rather than talked, and he says if you have nothing to explain, you have nothing to teach. He always tells us that as long as he's willing to explain, he has the right to expect us to be willing to understand in return. He won't allow us simply to memorize what he says because he can't encourage an unwillingness to think nor can he encourage a willingness to have someone think for us. He says the men and women who built Butte weren't slaves and that we shouldn't be, either. We should be free like Butte is free. He makes sense to me, and his expectations don't discriminate in any way. I was more than willing to try to understand as he explained the relationship between Macbeth and Duncan.

He pointed out how nature turned upside down after Macbeth killed Duncan, which he found interesting because even though Duncan is king, his murder wouldn't be enough to create such chaos. Then he asked us why, and none of us knew what to say. If we think we know how to answer one of his questions, we're usually afraid to speak up—not because we're afraid of Brother Kelley but because we still lack confidence. However, he understands and doesn't force us to say anything. He always tells us not to be afraid and reminds us that anything we say or ask in honesty is worth hearing and answering. But still, we usually wait for him to answer his own question. Invariably, his answer—which sometimes is the answer I have I mind as well—always sounds more interesting. He answered this particular question about Duncan by saying that he wasn't a great king.

He said that Duncan, unlike Macbeth, lacked the personal majesty to match that of the role. Then he asked if we all understood, and we all nodded yes. I don't know if the rest of the class really understood, but I at least thought I did. If Macbeth didn't have the majesty Brother Kelley had in mind, he couldn't "slit the enemy from the nave to the chaps." Brother Kelley said that on the basis of that majesty Macbeth, more so than Duncan, deserved to become king. He exhibited the necessary majesty to rule as a commanding presence. He said the combination of loyalty and fear he would have inspired would have ensured him a long and heroic reign. He said Macbeth didn't have to be king to be heroic. Instead, he would have brought heroism to the throne.

He also said that if Duncan were such a great king, he never would have given Macbeth the opportunity to kill him in the first place. But he was blinded by the majesty of his role and lost sight of the real world. No wonder, he said, we aren't horrified by Macbeth's murder of Duncan. The murder isn't the tragedy. The real tragedy involved Macbeth choosing the path of immediate, temporary rewards over that of ultimate, eternal rewards. Then he said it was similar to choosing the comfort of a West Side mansion to escape the shadow of the gallus frames. When he mentioned the West Side and the gallus frames, everything made sense because he made the essence of the play current and applicable to Butte and my experience. You listen with your heart to something that real and immediate. Brother Kelley didn't want any of us to follow Macbeth's path. He taught with compassion and love and didn't want any of us to live in misery.

He made 'Macbeth' real, and he said we could live in a West Side mansion with honor and dignity and courage and humility as long as we never lost sight of the gallus frames. But we can't choose the mansion over those virtues because if we do, we'll eventually agree with Macbeth and conclude that life's "a tale told by an idiot full of sound and fury signifying nothing." Then he said that was the truth, and the bell rang—only nobody jumped up to leave. If anyone can touch your heart, Brother Kelley can. I'm going to miss him, but I know I'm stronger because of him. He hasn't given me courage as much as he's made me aware of that potential which lives within me. He laughed when nobody moved, shrugged his shoulders, lifted his hands, holding his palms upward and said: "See, there's the bell that summons Duncan to Heaven or to Hell." We all laughed and began to get up and leave the classroom.

"Are you coming?" Paul asked, getting up out of his desk.

"Yes, but I want to ask Brother Kelley a question first."

"What do you want to ask? Don't you understand what he was talking about?"

"I understand. That's why I want to ask him a question."

"What's the question?"

"I want to ask him something about the Garden of Eden Story."

"You're going to take Julie home from the dance tonight, and you want to ask Brother Kelley a question about the Garden of Eden story. Jake's right. You have to be crazy."

"It won't take long. Are you going right home now?" I asked.

"I think so," Paul answered.

"I'll see you at the dance tonight then. Are you coming early?"

"Of course. I have to see you and your plan in action. I wouldn't miss the opportunity."

"I won't disappoint you. See you tonight."

"Okay. See you later," Paul said as he walked out the door, leaving me alone with Brother Kelley.

I'd been wanting to ask him about the Garden of Eden story all year because it had been on my mind ever since my sophomore year when Brother Williams told me that it really happened and that if Eve would have avoided eating the apple, my dad wouldn't have died. I respected Brother Williams, but his answer continued to trouble me. I studied my experience as Brother Kelley said, and I had come to realize that life was more complicated than Brother Williams' answer would lead anyone to believe. But he was a good man who wasn't purposely trying to lie to me. I had a hard time believing him because, as I've said, I couldn't dislike Eve no matter how hard I tried. And believe me I did try because I wanted my dad alive rather than dead.

To further complicate matters, I found I had to admire Eve when I thought about the story because she wasn't afraid and she had courage. In fact, I admired her far more than I did Adam and even more than I admired God—and that really scared me. I had to see what Brother Kelley would say because he has a different way of looking at stories. I was sure, I thought, that the Garden of Eden story didn't happen, but I didn't want to think it was a lie. People like my mother, for example, seemed to be as admirable as Eve. The Garden of Eden story appeared to be every bit as real as 'Macbeth,' when I saw it in light of Brother Kelley's teaching. But the dilemma was, and still is, confusing. I had to ask him.

"Brother Kelley," I said, approaching his desk, "can I ask you a question?"

"Sure, Dan," he answered, looking me directly in the eye. "Go ahead."

"Brother Kelley," I said, without averting my eyes, "did the Garden of Eden story really happen?"

"Do you mean is it historical fact?"

"Yes, that's what I mean."

"You ask honest questions, Dan. I like to see that, but what if I say no? Will you believe me?"

"Only if the evidence is on your side."

"Good for you," Brother Kelley said, smiling. "Always trust the evidence. Never simply trust the man because the man can lie, even if he doesn't realize it. Now, let's examine the evidence. Okay?"

"Okay," I answered.

"Do you think there ever was a time when snakes could talk?"

"No, I don't think so."

"Do you think there was a time in history, before Eve ate the apple, when individuals didn't die?"

"I don't think so. It doesn't make sense."

"Have you ever heard of anthropology and archeology?"

"Yes."

"Well," Brother Kelley continued, "those scientists have discovered bones that have to be older that what Adam and Eve could have been at the time of the Garden."

"So the story isn't a record of historical fact?"

"The evidence says it isn't," he answered as his eyes lit up. "But that doesn't mean it hasn't happened and can't continue to happen."

"What do you mean?"

"Dan," he answered, with his eyes alive with wonder and looking directly at me, "the Garden of Eden story is supposed to happen all the time. That's why it's the truth. Think of 'Macbeth.' That story can, and does, happen all the time right here in Butte, Montana. Only it's more tragic when it happens here. Still, such an example helps to explain how the Garden of Eden story is the truth. The Eden story can happen all the time. Just study your experience in Butte, and you'll discover it for yourself. You have to want to know, and then you have to have the courage to think. When you discover evidence of the Eden story happening in the real world of your own experience with life, you'll discover a faith that nothing can destroy. But before you can discover that faith, you have to ask your question. Do you understand?"

"I think so," I answered.

"Just think, Dan, and trust experience and reason. If the Garden of Eden story doesn't happen, we never can grow up. So don't be afraid. Okay?"

"I won't be afraid," I said, smiling. "I'm from Butte, and Butte boys aren't afraid."

"Now you're talking," he said, putting his right arm around my shoulders and walking toward the door.

I'll never forget that moment when he put is arm around my shoulders. I didn't know what to say when we reached the doorway. I felt as though I had experienced the beatific vision and sanctifying grace, both at the same time.

"Thanks, Brother Kelley," I managed to say as he dropped his arm and turned to lock his door.

"You're welcome, Dan. Are you sure you understand?"

"I think so."

"And you won't be afraid?"

"I won't be afraid."

"Good. I don't think you will be," he said, turning away from his classroom door. "Are you going to the dance tonight?"

"Yes."

"Enjoy yourself," he said, standing next to his door with his books cupped in his left hand.

"I will," I said as he turned to walk into the study hall toward the door that led to the Brothers' house. "Thanks again," I added before I turned to walk up the stairs to my third floor locker.

"You're welcome, Dan," he replied, stopping by the study hall entrance and turning to look back at me. Then he turned to his left and headed across the room.

I watched him walk across the floor and through the doorway leading to the Brothers' house, and then I turned and walked up the stairs to the third floor. My heart pounded in anticipation of the coming dance, and I knew, now, that I was better off for living in obedience to love—even if I had to disobey Jake, the expert in affairs of the heart and my best friend.

XXXI

*B*y the time I made it to my locker everyone else had left school, but I didn't feel deserted. The combination of having talked to Brother Kelley and of anticipating taking Julie home from the dance more than kept me occupied. I just had to remember to talk to Jake later on the phone just to make sure he wouldn't forget to pick me up early for the dance.

I wasn't in any hurry to get home because I had lost my bowling and shuffleboard partner so I took my time and stopped for a coke at Woolworth's dime store on Park Street, hoping that I might catch Julie. I had my cherry coke, although Julie was nowhere in sight, and decided to hitch-hike home rather than take the bus. I walked east on Park Street and began to thumb a ride at the corner of Park and Arizona that marked the eastern boundary of Uptown. Before long, I managed to hitch a ride from a woman who had been shopping at Hennesey's, Butte's celebrated department store, and now was heading home to The Flat. She lived on its southern fringes further out on Harrison Avenue than I did, but she dropped me off at the corner of Harrison and George Street, just a block from the western edge of Clark Park and about four blocks from my house on Aberdeen Street. I thanked her for the ride, stepped out of the car and walked with the green light across Harrison Avenue toward the park and home.

I knew my mother wouldn't be home for dinner. She had told me in the morning that she and George were going out for fish and chips after work, and she asked if I wanted to go along. I said I'd rather stay home and fix some macaroni and cheese or some spaghetti with

Chef Boyardee's mushroom sauce. I had come to like my time at home, and I don't remember ever being lonely once I got used to being alone. In fact, much of the time I'd rather be alone, and, as it is with all monuments to eternity, my mother doesn't have to be in the house to be a presence. I try not to abuse her trust in me, and I've promised myself and all my monuments to eternity, whether or not they realize it, that I'll always be loyal to the gallus frames and Clark Park and Aberdeen Street. To live otherwise would be to commit mortal sin and, like Macbeth, to fall out of the state of sanctifying grace. If you remain in that state, life never is a "tale told by an idiot full of sound and fury signifying nothing." But if you choose to leave the state of sanctifying grace, you have to face the nothingness eventually.

Almost five years have passed since Clark Park burned down, and every time I walk through the park, I have to stop and think of what used to be. It troubles me to think that boys and girls are growing up in Butte, and will continue to grow up in the Mining City, without knowing Clark Park. But it was made of wood and had to go sometime, just as my dad had to, I suppose. Still, I worry about boys and girls in Butte who don't, and won't, have the chance to sit in the grandstand and listen to the resonant voice of the ballpark announcer presenting the starting lineups.

Brother Kelley's right. Conditions that once supported life are changing. Clark Park has burned down, and if anything supported life in Butte, it was that ballpark. The Berkeley Pit's eating way the gallus frames on The Hill, and they've supported life in Butte just as much as Clark Park did. Before we know it, only the Columbia Gardens will be left, and they'll last only as long as the gallus frames do. At one time we could think that the gallus frames would last forever, but not any more. Brother Kelley's right again. We have to start living on purpose now. We can't live by accident anymore. We have to think to preserve the honor and courage and dignity and humility that lived along with all that supported life. Times always change, but not so drastically as these. Clark Park has burned down; the Berkeley Pit's swallowing up the gallus frames and we're exploring space. I can't help thinking that the changes I'm experiencing go far beyond the surface, and I understand Julie Shaw's purple bow much better now.

I walked through the park, following the usual path that took me through the middle of the baseball diamond that boys and girls before me had carved out of the hardy grass. The snow was almost completely gone now, and the puddles, that just a few days ago flooded home plate and all the bases, had almost dried up. In a matter of days the diamond would be playable once again, just as it has been as long as I can remember. But for the past five years boys and girls played baseball without the imposing ballpark grandstand to feed their imagination. I hope they can continue to play baseball with the appropriate wonder and awe without Clark Park to remind them, but I'm not sure. If it doesn't come naturally, they have to be taught to love baseball to play it with honor and dignity. Brother Kelley remembers Clark Park, and he would teach baseball accordingly. But then I'm sure he believes in the mysterious power of love.

The walk up Aberdeen Street was quiet and not nearly as fearful as the walk I took more than 11 years before in the snow with Uncle Tim dragging his walking cast. I don't think Brother Hollohan could scare me as thoroughly as I was scared that night. But Uncle Tim proved himself to be more in line with Brother Kelley than with Brother Hollohan. He faced a tough choice, and I thought for sure he'd whip me for my act of disobedience. But he didn't, and I'm glad. If he had, I don't think he'd qualify to be a monument to eternity. He wouldn't have proven himself worthy of the honor.

I reached the long, narrow sidewalk that split the basepath between first and second base and noticed the familiar lake that had formed between the house and the garage at the back end of the two lots. The snow was almost completely gone, but enough remained under the neighbor's hedge, bordering our driveway, to create sufficient runoff to form the lake. At least I could walk, safely, down the long sidewalk without having to contend with the large lake that formed in front of the house when the spring thaw first arrived. My dad's black, spiked baseball shoes are too small for me now, but if they weren't, I'd still put them on just to hear the clatter of the spikes on the hard concrete. Next to the crack of the bat and the chime of the altar bell, I don't think I've heard a more inspiring sound.

My mother always locked the kitchen door, but she always left a key hanging on a nail between it and the storm door. I found the key on the same nail, smiled, opened the door and stepped into the kitchen.

Judy had been gone since 1957 when she went to school to become a teacher, so I've had the house to myself for the past five years. As a result, I've come to know it intimately—especially the kitchen that served as both a bowling alley and shuffleboard arena. If Clark Park and the gallus frames and the Columbia Gardens supported, and still support, life in Butte, this kitchen supported, and supports, my life in the house. I can't keep coming back here forever, and I haven't played shuffleboard with potted meat cans for quite some time, although I have to admit that I still bowl a few frames every now and then. The kitchen is a shrine, just like the tabernacle that houses the Blessed Sacrament. I think we need such shrines, along with altars, to remind us of the mystery of love. Brother Kelley's classroom is a shrine, too. Come to think of it, Butte is a city of shrines. I don't want to, and never will, forget any of its sacred objects no matter what choices I may have to face. If the Garden of Eden story can happen all the time, then so can the Temptation in the Desert. I'm glad I'm growing up in the sacred city of Butte, Montana, because I'll be able to recognize the Temptation in the Desert when I see it. Butte has prepared me and I'll be ready for it.

I found my boots in the bedroom closet, walked back into the kitchen, and found the garage key in the lazy-Susan dish sitting on top of the refrigerator. Then I grabbed the bailing pan out from underneath the sink and walked outside to the garage to get the bucket. In late spring I didn't have to battle a steady stream of water fed by the melting snow covering the driveway and the expansive lawn. The basement had survived one more thaw, and it could breathe easily now—until next spring's runoff would threaten it once again. Only then I wouldn't be here to defend it. My mother would have to face the next threat on her own.

I filled the bucket a few times, and the lake receded. Every year I manage to take a little more gravel with the water, and the lake bed grows deeper. Over the years I've dumped a lot of gravel down the alley, along with the water, and I can't help noticing the hole I've left, reminding me of the Berkeley Pit. When the Anaconda Company first started digging it in 1955, you hardly noticed the change in The Hill, but after seven years, The Pit's no longer just another mine on the east end of The Hill. Instead, it is the east end and threatens the entire Hill. My mother can bail out the water that seemingly threatens her basement, but I don't know who, or what, will stop the progress of The Pit.

I took the bucket back into the garage, locked the door, and walked back into the house to get ready for dinner. I put the garage key and the bailing pan back where they belonged and returned the boots to the bedroom closet. I decided to have spaghetti with Chef Boyardee's mushroom sauce, and as I was boiling the water and heating up the sauce, I couldn't help thinking about the pork chop sandwich I would have tonight after the dance when I was with Julie. As long as I can have a pork chop sandwich immediately after midnight on a Saturday morning, I never want to eat meat on Friday. Maybe no one deserves to go to Hell for breaking that rule, but obeying it certainly improves the taste of the Saturday morning pork chop.

And as long as it's a rule, I think you have to obey it. As I said earlier, I've committed mortal sins, as defined by the Church, but I've never eaten meat on Friday and never will. Sometimes you can't avoid other mortal sins without being pious, but I can't think of an excuse for purposefully eating meat on Friday. I'm home alone all the time on Fridays, and no one ever would know if I fixed myself a bologna sandwich or fried a hamburger. But I can't do it. It's not right. But if the Church suddenly said I could eat meat on Friday, I'd be the first to break out the bologna and the hamburger. There's more to obedience than meets the eye, and I know Brother Kelley would agree.

I fixed the spaghetti and tried to eat it as neatly as I could, without dribbling the sauce all over my chin and down the front of my shirt. I could have broken the noodles in half before I put them in the water or I could have cut them on my plate, but I chose to do neither. I like to put the spaghetti in whole because I like to watch the individual noodles slide off the side of the pan into the boiling water. And once I transfer the finished product to my plate, I like to roll it up on my fork. It's easy to eat fast when you're alone, but if you can slow down, the food tastes better. Sometimes how you do something is more important than the end result, and it's not simply a matter of being polite. For example, how Uncle Tim shaved was more important to him than actually cutting his beard. No wonder I pay attention to how I shave—now that I've developed a trace of whiskers.

I finished my spaghetti and glass of milk, picked up the dishes from the kitchen table, the pots and pans from the stove and put them on the kitchen counter next to the sink. I opened the cupboard doors under the sink and found the dish rack, the plastic dishpan and the detergent. I placed the dish rack across the left side of the sink, put the dish pan in the sink near the drain and squirted some detergent into the blue, plastic pan now filling up with hot water. I washed the dishes with the cloth dish rag, placed them in the dish rack, rinsed them with hot water and then dried them with the clean dish towel that was hanging on its rack to the right of the cupboard that held our bowling pins, my dad's last baseball glove and my first, my current Duke Snider model—although I hate the Dodgers—and the two pairs of black, steel spiked baseball shoes—my own and my dad's. I put the dishes, pots and silverware in the proper cupboards and drawers, cleaned and put the dish rack and dish pan back underneath the sink, rinsed it, wiped off the counter top and the kitchen table with the dish rag, dried both with the dish towel, placed the dish rag over the side of the plastic dish pan, hung the dish towel on the rack to the right of the all-purpose cupboard, pushed my chair flush with the table and moved the centerpiece back to the middle where it belonged. Then I reached for the telephone, and dialed Jake's number.

"Jake?" I asked as I heard someone pick up the phone on the other end.

"Who else?" he answered. "What's going on?"

"Not much. I just finished eating and doing the dishes. Before that I had to bail out the water that had collected between the house and the garage."

"You do have that problem, I remember. Lots of fun, no doubt."

"It's not that bad," I said. "This is my last spring of bailing, but I'll probably miss it because it signals the end of winter."

"You're crazy," Jake said. "Haven't you ever heard of a calendar?"

"Of course, but you don't need one to tell you winter's over when you have a lake forming between your house and garage. When bailing season begins, winter's over."

"You are crazy. Your mother must not be home tonight."

"No, not yet. She went out to dinner with George."

"Are they ever going to get married?"

"I don't know. I don't think they could get along if they did. I'm sure George thinks they could, but not my mother. She's more discriminate."

"Then why does she go out with him every night?"

"Because she loves him, I think, but not with the love she associates with marriage. George doesn't see any difference, but they wouldn't get along if they decided to get married. Maybe the situation will change after I leave. Maybe they'll get married then, but I doubt it."

"I like George," Jake said. "He always manages to make me laugh."

"I know what you mean. But he has some strange ideas, too. I like him, but I don't always believe him. He doesn't make as much sense as Brother Kelley."

"Speaking of him" Jake said, "where were you after school? I didn't see you."

"Didn't Brenns tell you?"

"I didn't see him, either."

"I had to see Brother Kelley after school."

"Why?"

"I had to ask him a question."

"What question?"

"I wanted to ask him about the Garden of Eden story."

"You've got to be kidding! What does that story have to do with Julie Shaw and the dance tonight? I thought you were all hot and bothered about taking her home."

"I am going to take her home. But you don't know Brother Kelley."

"He must be something if he can get your mind off Julie. I can't do that no matter what I say. Are you sure you're still going to take her home?"

"Of course. Tonight's the night. No doubt about it."

"Still, I'll believe it when I see it. Do you think Julie listens to the Garden of Eden story?"

"I don't know. But if she does, I hope she isn't afraid to live it."

"You're crazy. First the songs and now the Garden of Eden story. Maybe after tonight you'll get all this out of your system and join the real world. What time do you want me to pick you up?"

"Eight-thirty," I answered. "And don't be late tonight. I have to be there early."

"I'll be on time. Don't worry. I have to see this to believe it. At least I can say this about you. You're never dull."

"Thanks, Jake. I'll see you at eight-thirty. Be on time. Okay?"

"No problem. Get ready to go park," he said, hanging up the phone before I had a chance to respond, although I could imagine the laughter being heard throughout Floral Park.

Finally, I hung up the phone and looked out the kitchen window as I thought about Julie and the Garden of Eden. I wondered what Eden could be if it wasn't an historical place. It must have something to do with the mystery of love, I thought. If two people are obedient to the power of love, I continued, maybe, with their union, they can create paradise. Reveling in my thoughts of creating paradise with Julie Shaw, I gazed wistfully out the kitchen door window. Then I saw George's 1962 red Plymouth turn off Aberdeen Street and into the long driveway leading to our house.

XXXII

George stopped the car and I watched as my mother got out, closed the passenger side door and started to walk toward the house. He hesitated for a minute, waiting for my mother to clear the driveway, and then slowly began to back out. I watched as he steered his Plymouth onto Aberdeen Street, straightened it out, and headed it in the direction of Clark Park and his house across The Flat to the west. As he headed down Aberdeen, my mother reached the concrete stoop leading to the kitchen door, and, turning the doorknob, I pulled the door open for her.

"Hi," she said, wiping her feet on the rug lying in front of the door.

"Hi," I replied. "How were the fish and chips?"

"Pretty good. We just went out to the Donnabelle."

"You went to the Donnabelle? That's where Jake and I and the rest of the guys like to hang out. You could have gone someplace much more comfortable. And you could have avoided Harrison Avenue in the process."

"I know," my mother answered, laughing as she walked into her bedroom. "But you now George. He likes drive-ins."

"I know. But does he have to take you to a drive-in for fish and chips on a Friday after work?"

"They have the best fish in town."

"Did you eat in the car?"

"No," my mother answered from her bedroom. "Even George doesn't go that far. We might drink a cup of coffee in the car at night, but we like to go inside and sit at the counter when we order something like fish and chips. Does that make you feel better?" she asked with a laugh.

"A little bit. Do you listen to Buddy Holly and Ricky Nelson and Elvis Presley while you drink your coffee and eat your fish and chips?" I asked, smiling, as my mother walked back into the kitchen wearing her light blue house coat and matching, blue slippers.

"There, I feel much more comfortable now," she said, letting out a sigh of relief. "What did you ask?"

"If you and George listened to Buddy Holly and Ricky Nelson and Elvis Presley while you drink your coffee and eat your fish and chips."

"No," she said, smiling, and pulling up a chair at the kitchen table. "We have our own music from our era. So we don't really listen to yours. But some of the songs you kids listen to aren't so different. Some of them aren't as original as you might think."

"What do you mean?" I asked, sitting down across the table from her.

"Your dad's and my favorite song was 'My Happiness.'"

"Connie Francis sings that."

"But she's not the first. That was our song," she added, still smiling.

"Did you dance to it at the Boobnega?"

"Sometimes. But your dad usually was too busy keeping the boys from other neighborhoods out of the Boobnega to pay much attention to dancing. Mainly, we danced to 'My Happiness' at the Gardens. But that was our song wherever we went."

"I never had the chance to dance to it at the Boobnega, but I'm sure I have at the Gardens at a prom. Do those old time dance bands play 'My Happiness?'"

"What do you mean those old time dance bands? I grew up on those bands."

"I know, but I'm not as good a dancer as you are. I like to dance and listen to the songs, but I don't dance very well to the music you grew up with. I like to waltz, for example, but I don't think I'm as good as you and Dad were. We dance a little differently today."

"Maybe at your school mixers you do, but I like to help chaperone your proms. I've recognized 'My Happiness' on those occasions at the Gardens, and kids today can dance pretty well when the proper band is playing. Songs like 'My Happiness' don't belong just to your generation. They belong to mine, too."

"I guess you're right," I said. "Do you and George have a song?"

"We like to dance and George is a good dancer, but we don't have a song like your dad and I did."

"Is that why you don't get married?"

"I suppose it has something to do with it. But speaking of songs, what do you have planned for tonight?"

"Jake and I are going to the dance at school."

"What time does it start?"

"Nine o'clock."

"Knowing Dave," my mother said, laughing—she never called him Jake and he always was Dave to her—"the two of you will be late, as usual."

"Not tonight," I said. "He's going to pick me up at eight-thirty."

"Why so early tonight?"

"Because I want to get there before the dance starts for once."

"But you've never wanted to be early before."

"I know, but this is different," I said as I felt the blood rush to my cheeks.

"What's so different tonight?"

"You know Julie Shaw?"

"You mean the girl from Centerville, from Missoula Avenue, whom you talk to on the phone all the time?"

"Yes, she's the one."

"I know her mother. She always comes up to the courthouse. Julie's father died not too long ago, I think."

"Well, I'm going to take her home from the dance tonight."

"That's nice, but why do you have to leave here at eight-thirty if the dance doesn't start until nine o'clock?"

"Because I'm not the only one who'd like to take her home, and I want to beat everyone else there so that I can ask her first."

"I don't know if I like to sound of this," my mother said, looking me in the eye. "Do you know what you're doing? She must do something to have so many boys after her. Why doesn't she settle with one for a while? Why not you? You seem to be loyal to her. Or why not someone else? I'm not so sure I'd trust a girl who has so many boys after her, if I were you. What does she think?"

"I don't think she really knows me. I don't think she understands that it's like 'My Happiness' with me. I guess I have to find out if it can be the same with her. So, I'm going to take her home, even though Jake thinks I'm crazy."

"Sometimes I think he's crazy," my mother said, laughing. "Both of you probably are crazy in your own, separate ways."

"If being crazy means believing in songs like 'My Happiness,' then I don't mind it because that means people like you and Dad were crazy. But if being crazy means thinking that it isn't adult to believe in songs, then I don't want any part of it. I guess I want to find out if Julie is crazy like I am."

"Dan, I'll tell you something. She's either crazy or afraid. Many girls are afraid of crazy people like you and would rather have crazy people like Dave. They think they'll be more secure. You can't do anything about that, but you can tell the difference if you're patient. So pay attention tonight and don't be fooled."

"I won't be fooled. I'll be able to tell."

"That's good. Did you get something to eat?"

"Yes. I fixed some spaghetti with mushroom sauce after I bailed out the water that had collected between the house and the garage."

"I see you did the dishes," my mother said, looking at the sink.

"I always do the dishes."

"Don't be too hasty. You aren't that good."

"Well, I do them most of the time."

"That's more like it. But if you're going to leave by eight-thirty, you'd better get ready. George and I are going dancing at the Elks tonight, and I have to get in the bathroom, too, so don't waste any time."

"Okay," I said, getting up from my chair at the kitchen table. "I won't take long. I just have to shave."

"You're right," my mother said, smiling. "That won't take too long."

"You have to admit that I look older than I did last year," I replied, stopping and turning around in the bedroom archway. "I'll be a man like Uncle Tim one of these days."

"Go get ready," she said, laughing. "And don't forget what I told you."

"I won't," I said as I turned and walked toward the bathroom at the back end of the house next to the alley and far removed from the heat registers on either side of the kitchen wall.

I closed the bathroom door behind me and looked at my face reflected in the long, narrow medicine cabinet mirror. I had the beginnings of a beard all right, but it hadn't grown thick and heavy yet. I opened the medicine cabinet door, reached in with both hands, picked up my Gillette razor and can of Gillette Foamy shaving cream and placed them on the small, square shelf just to the left of the sink and above the clothes hamper that sat against the wall across from the bathtub. I turned on the hot water, reached over and grabbed a washrag draped over the lion-claw tub and placed it under the stream. The steam rose from the sink when I picked up the soaking washrag, rung it out and gently pressed it to my face to soften my whiskers, just as I had seen Uncle Tim do so many times. I folded the washrag and placed it on the edge of the sink next to the hot water faucet, put in the drain plug and reached for a towel hanging on one of the holders to the right of the sink and just above the bathtub. I took it off its holder and wiped the steam off the mirror on the medicine cabinet door. I could see my face clearly once again, and I reached for the Gillette Foamy on the shelf, picked it up and squirted some into the palm of my left hand. I turned off the hot water faucet, wiped the steam away from the mirror once again and applied the shaving cream, with my right hand, to the shaveable—and unshaveable—areas of my face. I rinsed my hands in the hot water that had collected in the sink and reached for my Gillette with my right hand. I took the towel in my left hand and wiped the steam off the mirror for the third time, and, beginning with my right sideburn, started to shave.

I listened to the Gillette blue blade cut through the whiskers as I pulled the razor down the right side of my face, and I thought of what my mother had said about either being crazy or afraid. Julie had to be one or the other because if not, she wouldn't talk to me the way she did. I just hoped she was crazy as I switched to the left side of my face and continued to listen as the Gillette sliced through my fresh beard. I gently shaved the foamy from my beardless areas just to be safe, ran some more hot water on the washrag and applied the heat to my face again.

I can see why Uncle Tim paid attention to how he shaved. Sometimes I think I'd like to prolong it, just as I would a baseball game. But I had finished so I dried my face with the towel, put the razor and the shaving cream back in the medicine cabinet on the bottom shelf, draped the washrag over the edge of the bathtub and reached for my bottle of Old Spice after shave, sitting on the top shelf above my razor and can of Foamy. I shook a few drops of Old Spice into my left hand, rubbed both hands together, and patted the after shave into my skin in imitation of Uncle Tim's method. I put the Old Spice back into the medicine cabinet, closed the door, examined my whiskered sideburns and smooth chin, neck and upper lip and decided that I was ready for the dance. I just had to brush my flat top, change my clothes and wait for Jake.

I turned, opened the bathroom door, and walked to the closet to find a fresh shirt and a clean pair of denims. I found my tan denims and my light blue, short-sleeved, Penney's Towncraft shirt with the button-down collar and changed into them, laying my school shirt and school denims across my mother's bed. I sat on the bench to the left of her bed next to the closet, took off the white socks I had worn to school, got up and walked over to the dresser sitting against the bedroom's west wall and chose a clean pair to wear to the dance. I walked back to the bench, sat down and slipped on the clean socks. I stood up and stepped into my brown loafers, picked up my school clothes, walked into the bathroom, put them into the hamper, walked back out into the bedroom and into the closet, grabbed my dark green, lightweight jacket, took one last look in the mirror nailed to the inside of the closet door and decided I had done my best. I was ready for the dance, convinced I wasn't afraid—and just as convinced I had to be crazy.

"Well, I'm ready to go," I announced as I walked back out into the kitchen. "I just have to wait for Jake. I hope he's on time for once."

"What are you going to do after the dance, provided you're lucky enough to take Julie home?" my mother asked, still seated at the kitchen table.

"I want to get a pork chop first of all and then take a ride out to the Donnabelle to see what's going on. After that we'll take Julie up The Hill and home. But I have to have a pork chop. Did you eat them when you were young?"

"Yes, I did. Only we used to ride the street car Uptown. We didn't have cars to drive. I still can smell the pork chop sandwiches. They've been a part of Butte as long as I can remember."

"Even longer than the Donnabelle's fish and chips?" I asked, smiling

"Much longer," my mother answered. "There's no comparison. By the way, what time are you going to be home from this date?"

"I should be home around one-thirty. The dance ends at midnight, and Julie probably will have to home by one o'clock. I'm sure Jake'll take me home before he takes Lori home. But if I don't get my date with Julie for some reason, I'll probably come home with Paul. Either way, I should be home by one-thirty at the latest. If I'm going to be any later, I'll call you," I added as I looked out the kitchen door window and spied the lights of Jake's 1958 Chevy Impala as he pulled into the long driveway. "Jake's here, and he's actually on time. I can't believe it. He must not want to miss any of the fun."

"Have a good time," my mother said, getting up from the kitchen table, "and be careful. Remember what I said and don't be home late."

"I will. And If I'm going to be too late, I'll call you. Have a good time at the Elks," I added, opening the kitchen door.

"I will," she said.

"Goodbye," I said as I stepped out the door.

"Goodbye," she replied as I closed the door and walked to Jake's Impala, idling patiently in the driveway in front of our empty garage.

XXXIII

"Tonight's the big night," Jake said as I opened the passenger side door and slid onto the front seat.

"This is it," I replied confidently. "Are you ready?"

"What do I have to be ready for? If you've seen one dance, you've seen them all," he answered as he backed the Impala out of the driveway and headed it west on Aberdeen Street in the direction of Clark Park.

"You're crazy, Jake. You're just trying to act tough. You know every dance isn't the same."

"They always play the same songs, and the same people always dance the same way. Everything's the same. So what's the big deal?"

"You have to listen to the songs. They make the dance," I said as he turned right on Texas Avenue and drove parallel to what used to be the ballpark's left field fence. "You have to let the songs work."

"What are you talking about?" he asked as he turned left onto the wide expanse of Wall Street that once accommodated the cars and buses that brought the fans to the Clark Park grandstand. "What do you mean you have to let the songs work?"

"You have to listen to them."

"You already said that," Jake replied as he drove down Wall toward Florence Avenue at the western boundary of Clark Park. "But how do you let the songs work?"

"You have to listen to the story the singer creates."

"That world isn't real. I'd rather listen to the real world and not some fake world created by a singer."

"If you'd let yourself listen to the songs, you wouldn't feel that way," I said as he turned right on Florence and headed for Grand Avenue, the main east-west thoroughfare of The Flat. "I'm not so sure you're as tough as you let on. Why do you have the radio turned on?" I asked, smiling.

'I'll turn it off," he answered, reaching over to turn the knob that cut off Elvis Presley in the middle of 'Are You Lonesome Tonight.'

"Haven't you ever been that lonesome?" I asked as he turned left onto Grand Avenue toward the intersection with Harrison Avenue, the main north-south artery of The Flat.

"No, because I've never had any trouble finding a girlfriend. If I acted like you, maybe I'd be lonesome all the time. Just like you are."

"Come on, Jake. I'm not lonesome all the time. That's not what I mean, and that's not what the song means."

"Then what does it mean?" he asked, stopping for the red light at the corner of Grand and Harrison. "What's so special about it?"

"It's a love song, Jake."

"So what? What's so special about another love song?" he asked as he turned right with the green light and headed north on Harrison Avenue toward The Hill and toward the lights of the gallus frames and the darkness of the Berkeley Pit.

"I've experienced this one, Jake, and that helps give the song its power," I answered as he drove up Harrison past the new Civic Center and underneath the Northern Pacific Railroad viaduct to Front Street that marked the southern boundary of The Hill.

"What power?"

"I don't know what you call it, but I know it's real. You can feel it working if you just listen.

"Come on, Buddy," he said, likening me, once more, to Buddy Holly. "It's just a song. Don't get too excited."

"But it's the truth, Jake," I said as he drove along Front Street toward the light at its intersection with Utah.

"How can a song be the truth? It's just something that someone makes up. That's all. Then somebody records it and people buy it. Then the singer makes money. It doesn't have anything to do with the truth."

"But 'Are You Lonesome Tonight' really happens which makes it the truth. Nothing else matters. The Elvis Presley singing the song is different from the one making the money."

"You're crazy," he said, stopping for the red light at the corner of Front and Utah.

"Maybe, but if I am now, I have the feeling I always will be."

"Why?" Jake asked, turning right with the green light onto Utah and heading up The Hill closer to the gallus frame lights and the Berkeley Pit darkness.

"Because I can't help it, and because I want to be crazy."

"What do you mean by that comment?" he asked as we continued our climb up Utah.

"I want to be crazy because everyone I admire is crazy. And I want to be like the people I admire. My dad was crazy because my mother told me they had their own song. Do you know what it was?"

"What song?" Jake asked quietly, blessing himself as we drove past St. Joseph's Church on the left-hand side of the street just south of the Utah Street railroad tracks and warehouses.

"You know Connie Francis, don't you?"

"Of course I do," he answered as the Impala bumped its way across the first of Utah Street's railroad tracks. "Do you think I'm an idiot?"

"No," I answered as Utah smoothed out again and as the Impala climbed The Hill. "But I wasn't sure if you were aware of who sings what."

"I know Connie Francis," he said as we drove through the intersection where Arizona Street, also running perpendicular to Front Street, meets and takes over from Utah Street adjacent to the last row of the WPA's Silver Bow Homes and just two blocks east of Butte High School and Naranche Stadium. I could see the stadium standing empty in the spring twilight, with no bright lights calling it to life.

"She sings 'My Happiness,' my mother and dad's favorite song. They believed in it. It was their song, and they tried to live it. My Uncle Tim believes in songs, too. I know because he used to sing to me when I was younger, and he still will today if I ask him to. He likes to sing about Ivan Skavinsky Skavar."

"Who's he?" Jake asked as he pulled up to the red light at the corner of Arizona and Mercury Street, just two blocks south of Park Street and the center of Uptown life and closer still to the gallus frame lights that now dominated the Berkeley Pit darkness as Uptown buildings obscured the east side of The Hill.

"I don't know. I never heard of him before, but it doesn't make any difference. Whenever Uncle Tim sings about him, his eyes light up and a smile crosses his face. Brother Kelley is the same way. He doesn't sing about Ivan Skavinsky Skavar, but he does talk about 'Macbeth' which is made up, like a song. But Brother Kelley says that 'Macbeth' can happen all the time right here in Butte, and we can see for ourselves if we just pay attention. If it happens, it's the truth."

"That's just Brother Kelley talking," Jake replied, turning left with the green light onto Mercury and heading west away from the darkness of The Pit toward Big Butte, our volcanic mountain cone and home to the decorative Big M—representing the Montana School of Mines—whose brightly lit boulders frame the western edge of The Hill in contrast to the eastern darkness.

"No, it isn't, Jake," I said as we drove past the remnants of Butte's red light district, or what Uncle Tim referred to as "The Green Gates of Education." The district isn't as active as it once was, but we still can point to The Dumas, The Missoula Rooms, The Empire and 14 South Wyoming or Blonde Edna's. Butte's pious citizens hate the whorehouses, but Brother Kelley says we have worse things to get upset about, and I think he's right. "Brother Kelley knows what he's talking about," I continued, "and he can prove what he says. Besides, I've experienced 'Are You Lonesome Tonight.' I know it's not a lie. Uncle Tim calls the gallus frames monuments to eternity, and I think individuals can live as such monuments if they want to or even if they're unaware of their stature. Uncle Tim may not think of himself as a monument, but I think he is just as I think my dad is, my mother is and Brother Kelley is. I even think baseball and Butte, itself, are monuments to eternity. And whether or not they know it, I want to be what I admire in my monuments."

'You're crazy," Jake said as he drove through the intersection of Mercury and Wyoming with 14 South standing watch one half block to the north. "But like I said before, you're never dull," he added as he steered the Impala toward the light at the corner of Mercury and South Main Street.

"If you have to be crazy to be a monument to eternity, then I guess I'll be crazy," I said as Jake slowed down for the red light at the South Main intersection.

"How can you refer to someone, or to yourself, as a monument?" he asked, stopping for the red light. "It sounds pretty arrogant to me. I've heard you expound on many topics, but I've never heard you talk about monuments to eternity before. Does Brother Kelley talk about them, too?"

"He talks about heroes, but I think the terms are equivalent," I answered, looking out the passenger window at the Silver Dollar Bar sitting on the northwestern corner of the intersection and across the street from Pork Chop John's. Butte's Negroes patronize the Silver Dollar, and even though they once organized a baseball team called the Colored Giants and played in the Montana State League—before the days of the Copper League of my memory—their numbers have decreased over the years. I've read all about the Colored Giants in my dad's scrap book where he kept newspaper clippings of the games he played against them. And Uncle Tim likes to tell stories about Lefty Kingman and the home runs he used to hit, just like Lou Gehrig. I've always wanted to visit the Silver Dollar, but I'd only go with someone who had earned his place. I looked across the street at Pork Chop John's and didn't see any line forming. Saturday morning, now just a little more than three hours away, would change that scene.

"You're telling me you want to be a hero?" Jake asked as he drove the Impala through the green light, past Pork Chop John's and closer to Central and the study hall, soon to be transformed into a dance hall. "I've heard everything now. You have to be crazy."

"I think you have to be crazy to be a hero or a monument to eternity. It's a requirement. I think we're destined to be monuments to eternity, to be heroes. Brother Kelley is trying to teach us that potential, but I want you to keep this conversation between you and me. I'm not ready to sound like a fool. Okay?"

"Okay. I couldn't repeat what you've said even if I wanted to," he said as he drove through the green light at the intersection of Mercury and Montana Street, the north-south artery that feeds the west end of Uptown and marks the western boundary of Centerville. "I've never heard anything like it. But I do have one serious question," he said as Central and the study hall lights came into clear view directly ahead.

"What's that?"

"Do you really think Julie Shaw's crazy, according to your understanding of the word?" he asked as he angle parked the Impala on the West Mercury side of the school.

"I don't know," I answered as we both stepped out of the car, locked the doors and pushed them closed, "but I'm going to find out tonight. As my mother said, she's either crazy or afraid," I concluded as we walked from the car to the Idaho Street entrance to Central and the dance.

XXXIV

❀

$\mathcal{A}$s I expected, the study hall was brightly lit, but when the music started, the lights would dim, and its transformation into a dance hall would be complete. I would dance with Julie in an enchanted world that celebrated, whether or not anyone realized it, the mystery of love and an individual's service to it. Maybe this world isn't real in reference to Jake's sense of reality, but I think our capacity to live in service to love is real. Shakespeare had to believe that or else he wouldn't have written 'Macbeth,' and Brother Kelley has to believe it as well. Otherwise, he wouldn't teach with the same commitment and compassion.

"Do you think you have enough time to spring into action?" Jake asked as we paused in front of the doors before going inside.

"I think so," I answered. "We're 15 minutes early."

"I see Brennan's made it," he said, pointing to his dad's white Chrysler. "I wonder how long he's been here."

"There's only one way to find out," I said as I stepped in front of Jake, pulled open the solid oak door, and walked inside.

"That'll be 45 cents, boys," Brother Williams said as soon as the door closed behind us.

"Okay," I said, reaching into my pocket to find some change. "Are you going to give us a free dance before we graduate?" I asked, handing him the money.

"If you behave yourselves, we'll let you have a prom. But it won't be free," he answered, accepting the money.

"Is Brother Kelley going to be here tonight?" I asked.

"Not tonight, Dan. It's not his turn. I think he went home to visit his parents. You're here early tonight, Dave," Brother Williams said as Jake handed him his 45 cents. "It's not like you."

"It's his fault," Jake said, pointing to me. "He wanted to be early."

"Well, whoever's at fault, it's nice to see you here. Just walk up the steps, turn to your right, and you'll find the dance hall. It looks like a study hall, but don't mind the desks," he said, laughing at his joke.

"They won't get in the way tonight," I said as I heard Jake groan.

"Just walk up the steps, will you?" he asked. "Don't mind Buddy here, Brother. He's crazy," Jake added, pushing me up the stairs toward the second floor study hall.

The two classrooms at the top of the stairs serve as coat rooms on dance nights, and I led to way to the boys' coatroom at the top of the staircase and to the right. I left my jacket on top of one of the desks and joined Jake who, dressed in his letterman's sweater, was still standing in the main hallway.

"Brenns must be inside," I said. "He's not in the coat room."

"I've never been to a dance this early," Jake said. "I hope Lori doesn't come too soon."

"Why?" I asked as we walked toward the doorway that led into the study hall.

"Because I'll have to dance with her longer than usual. I don't want her to get the wrong idea," he added as we entered the study hall.

"This is your chance to be a little crazy, Jake," I said as we spotted Paul walking toward us.

The study hall desks, firmly attached to their wooden runners, had been moved away from the center of the room toward the walls which meant you had to climb over at least seven rows if you wanted to get to the radiators sitting underneath the windows looking across Galena to Girls' Central. When I was a freshman, I went to all the dances, but I rarely danced. Not too many girls were interested in dancing with freshmen boys who looked like they belonged in the sixth grade. Still, I listened to the songs that fed my dreams. And because I had some friends in the same boat and because we all carried some money in our pockets, I could sit in one of the desks and play poker while I listened and dreamed. But as a 17—year-old senior I had graduated from the desks, and I knew there could be "no hesitatin'" tonight.

"All right, what's the plan?" Paul asked without saying hello to either of us.

"At least you could say hello first," Jake answered before I had a chance to say anything.

"Excuse me," Paul laughed. "Hi, Jake. What's the plan tonight, Dan?"

"I'm going to ask Julie to dance before anyone else can get to her, and I'm going to ask her home right away. That's the plan."

"Are you going to keep her on the dance floor all night?" Paul asked.

"I will if she wants to stay out there."

"Don't hold your breath," Jake said. "She has to spread herself around so she can make fools out of everyone. I'm not so sure it's worth being crazy."

"What does that mean?" Paul asked.

"Nothing," Jake answered. "Just something we were talking about on the way up here. It's no big deal. You two can stand here by the door if you want to, but I'm going to join the rest of the guys across the floor where we belong. We're a little to close to the entrance for comfort. Lori will find me too easily over here. Good luck, Buddy. Let me know how things turn out."

"Thanks, Jake. See you later," I said as he walked across the floor. It was just about nine o'clock, and a number of girls had made their way into the study hall that was about to become enchanted as 'Bouncing Billy' Venture, the local radio personality from KXLF, prepared the records.

"How are you going to get to her first?" Paul asked.

"I'm going to stand right here by these doors where I can see the top of the stairs and the girls' coat room. From this position I'll be able to see her come out of the room. She has to cross the hallway to come through this doorway, and when she does, I'm going to ask her to dance."

"No matter what the song?"

"No matter what the song."

"Even if it's a fast song?"

"As soon as she comes through the doorway, I'll be ready, no matter what," I answered as the light flickered and the girls stole a few glances at the boys gathered across what now had become a dance floor.

"Well, good luck. I think it's time I joined the rest of the guys. Let me know what happens."

"I will," I said. "See you later."

"Don't chicken out," he added, walking away and leaving me alone with my perfect view of the stairs and the entrance to the girls' coatroom.

"Don't worry," I said as the lights dimmed and 'Bouncing Billy' announced that he would begin "with a little tune by the late Buddy Holly entitled 'Oh Boy!'"

I think I've always believed in songs, and, with the exception of 'The Ballad of Davy Crockett,' my first favorite had to be 'The Tennessee Waltz' by Patti Page. I remember dancing with Linda Drusich to that song at our eighth grade hayride. Judy had to teach me how to dance beforehand, but I'll never forget that song and the moonlit wagon ride through the foothills and valleys of the southwestern Montana mountains. Even though I never danced with Linda again and never had a date with her, that particular dance provided me with the first of many enchanted moments created by listening to, and believing in, the songs.

Marked by such moments, how can life be a "tale told by an idiot full of sound and fury signifying nothing?" Life isn't one, continuous enchanted moment by any means—I wouldn't call my dad's death an enchanted moment, for example, nor can I consider the time spent in 'Lonesome Town' to be enchanted—but at the same time it's not all pain. If you only acknowledge the pain, life can seem pretty worthless, and if you only acknowledge enchanted moments, life can appear too rosy. It seems to be that truth lies somewhere in between, and we join Macbeth only if we live either extreme. George, for example, searches for one, continuous enchanted moment. If he were to succeed, he'd be miserable, but he'll never realize his goal. I wish he could see the humor in his quest.

I remember being offended by Elvis Presley at first because he seemed so contrary to singers like Patti Page, and his songs seemed to have little, if anything, in common with the likes of 'Tennessee Waltz.' In fact, I liked Pat Boone, initially, more than I liked Elvis, but I grew tired of him and his white bucks. He didn't seem to belong in Butte, and, besides, I eventually decided he was too pious. Then, I listened to Elvis and 'Heartbreak Hotel' and discovered it to be a faster version of 'Lonesome Town.' Both songs acknowledge the pain of a broken heart. But you can't experience either 'Heartbreak Hotel' and 'Lonesome Town' if you avoid living in service to love. You have to spend some time staring at the walls of 'Heartbreak Hotel' and some time walking the streets of 'Lonesome Town' to experience authentic enchanted moments. Acknowledging the crucifix, no one can tell me that Christ would fail to understand either song. And neither Elvis Presley nor Ricky Nelson sings of the virtues of piety.

I think 'Don't be Cruel' and 'Hello, Mary Lou' are their best songs, and whoever has seen Mary Lou—and said goodbye to his heart as a result—has to be an expression of the true heart that Elvis identifies. If Mary Lou's heart is equally true, she and the guy who sees her will live in service to love where neither will be cruel to the other. How do I know 'Hello Mary Lou' is true? I just have to substitute Julie for her name to be the guy Ricky Nelson is singing about.

If that means I have a true heart, I can't be alone. That heart has to be the essence of us all. Christ has to be an expression of a true heart, doesn't he? And the Pharisees, who have little, or no, regard for the majesty of love, are cruel to his heart that's true. Then, why can't individual human beings share Christ's true heart? Maybe the Mass is more a celebration of love than a reminder of sin. Maybe the Mass really is a love song. But I know one thing for sure. The songs of Elvis Presley and Ricky Nelson are more closely related to the crucifix than are the sermons of the priests. Their songs are monuments to eternity, but I can't say the same for priests' sermons. They talk too much about sin and not enough about love. Also, like any monument to eternity, I think Christ would be crazy today. So, how can I be wrong for wanting to be crazy? How can you ever experience the state of mortal sin if you live in service to love?

Julie hadn't walked up the stairs yet, but I never took my eyes off them as Buddy Holly's voice filled the dance hall. I watched the stairs and listened to the song as the dance floor remained empty. No one liked to be the first couple on the floor, but it only takes one steady couple to get the dance started. I kept watch on the stairs and thought about Buddy Holly and 'Oh Boy!' Sometimes I think he's the greatest of them all, which explains why Jake likes to refer to me as Buddy.

'Bouncing Billy' wasn't aware of the significance of his first selection, but I was as I listened to Buddy sing about "no hesitatin'." It seemed that all my life I'd been waiting, just like the guy in Buddy Holly's song, and I knew that if Julie could be with me tonight, the world certainly would see that she was meant for me. If Buddy Holly isn't singing about a heart that's true, I don't know what he's singing about. I don't know if anyone else in the dance hall listened to his song, but I did. Buddy Holly made it up, of course, just as Shakespeare made up 'Macbeth,' but I was living 'Oh Boy!' right then and there. The song was alive. I hadn't, and haven't, lived 'Macbeth,' but I'm beginning to understand how people can live that tragedy without even realizing it. Brother Kelley's right. Stories can happen all the time, and a song is like a story. When you're living a song, you can't help being a believer.

Billy followed up Buddy Holly with The Crests and 'Sixteen Candles' which proved to be slow enough to coax several of the steady couples to the dance floor, including Jake and Lori. I wished Julie would emerge out of the coat room because I believed 'Sixteen Candles,' too. That many candles can make a lot of light, but their light never could shine as bright as that reflected in Julie's eyes—and the eyes set the heart in motion. Ricky Nelson, or whomever he's singing about, had to see Mary Lou before he could say goodbye to his heart, and I had to see Julie before I could do the same. If our eyes saw each other the same way, the resulting love would live forever. I'd never be cruel to her true heart, and I hoped she wasn't afraid.

But because Julie still hadn't walked up the stairs, I had to be content listening to The Crests and watching the other couples on the dance floor, without taking my eyes off the staircase for very long. Jake surprised me by dancing with Lori so soon. It wasn't like him, and I thought for sure he'd make her wait longer than the second dance. He took Lori for granted at times, although I put her in the same league with Julie in matters of female charm and enchantment, but he certainly looked content tonight. He had his right arm placed securely around her waist, and her right arm joined his left behind his back in a hammer lock position. Her left arm enclosed his shoulders, and her left hand rested on the back of his neck. Given the circumstances even Jake had to listen to 'Sixteen Candles.'

With regard to dancing form, Jake and Lori were representative of all steady couples. You don't park with a girl on the first date nor do you assume the hammer lock position on the first dance. In compliance with standard form you hold the girl's right hand in your left hand and extend your arm, slightly bent at the elbow. Sometimes the girl places her hand on your right shoulder so that she can protect herself and push you away if you take liberties and rest your right arm too far around her waist. I've been pushed away a few times, but only pious girls push you away all the time. If you're lucky, the girl puts her left arm around your right shoulder so that you can get your right arm around her waist a little further and inch closer to her. Only if Julie and I were to become a steady couple, could I look forward to assuming the hammer lock position.

From my vantage point just inside the study hall doorway, I could keep my eyes on the stairs and listen to Billy Venture's songs at the same time. It's hard not to notice him because he doesn't call himself 'Bouncing Billy' for nothing. He's convinced that he's more important than the records he spins. No wonder I don't trust disc jockeys and their contrived nicknames. But I didn't think of 'Bouncing Billy' for long because just as he announced 'Tallahassee Lassie' by Freddie Cannon, I saw Julie walk up the stairs, reach the top, and turn left into the girls' coat room.

My heart began to pound in anticipation as I realized she had arrived and there could be no "hesitatin." If there were, this dance would turn out to be no different from the others. I'd dance with Julie, but someone else would take her home, without any guarantee that her date lived up to his true heart. I kept my eyes glued to the coat room as my heart pounded in my chest just as it does, believe it or not, whenever I listen to the Yankees on the radio or watch them on television. I didn't think I'd survive the seventh game of the 1960 World Series. I was working some trigonometry problems while the game was being piped to all the classrooms over the school intercom system, but I couldn't concentrate no matter how hard I tried. And when Mazeroski hit 'Rainbow Ralph's' hanging curve, or whatever pitch, over Forbes' Field left field wall, I broke my pencil in half in agonized disbelief. My heart pounded throughout that game, and now it was pounding every bit as hard, maybe harder, as I waited for Julie to emerge from the coat room. Then I saw her, and my pounding heart jumped to my throat just as Freddie Cannon was singing about his "Tallahassee Lassie down in FLA." But for me it was 'Hello, Julie, Goodbye Heart' all over again. Ricky Nelson doesn't lie. And I saw Julie Shaw, not the Blessed Virgin Mary.

She stopped just outside the coat room door, and I struggled to catch my breath and to control my pounding heart. Maybe the pounding heart is related to being crazy, but whatever it's related to or whatever it means, I know it doesn't signify "a tale told by an idiot full of sound and fury signifying nothing." Life, just as we experience it with dances in high school study halls, can signify everything. The songs help because they can awaken our capacity for love, but if you don't need the Columbia Gardens, you don't even need the songs. If Macbeth didn't have to live in a palace to make life signify something, we don't have to dance at the Columbia Gardens to make the event signify something. In fact, if we rely on palaces and mountain garden spots to provide us with significant moments, we could be in serious trouble because, like Clark Park, the Gardens is made of wood. The singers create an enchanted world with their songs, and you have to recognize and pay attention to it, even if it isn't part of Jake's reality. Regardless of what he says, the mystery of love, complete with anguish and rapture, is real. Maybe the anguish of 'Heartbreak Hotel' awaited me, but I wasn't afraid. I was enchanted by love and the sight of Julie Shaw.

XXXV

She was radiant with light, and her black hair glistened in contrast with the slight, pink blush of her cheeks. Her lightly freckled Irish nose and soft, inviting lips bathed in the light of her face, and even long, dark eyelashes couldn't hide the sparkle of her alluring, brown eyes. As she turned her head to greet her girlfriends standing in the main hallway, I noticed that her hair looked slightly different than usual. Then I saw the purple bow, neatly pinned just above her right ear, that provided the finishing touch and completed the enchanting picture of her face. Her pastel colored, cotton blouse complemented both the purple bow and her dark, pleated skirt that hung slightly above her knees. I watched her body move back and forth to the rhythm of the conversation, and her skirt swayed from side to side as if she were moving gracefully around the dance floor. I couldn't hear her voice, but that didn't matter. I'd heard it enough times on the telephone to imagine its pleasing resonance.

She ended her conversation and started to walk across the hall just as I heard Billy Venture say that he was going "to slow it down just a little bit with some belly rubbin' music from Ricky Nelson called 'Lonesome Town.'" I hated to hear Ricky's song reduced to that level, but I guess that's the difference between Billy Venture and me. I can't tolerate the desecration of anything I hold sacred, and I wasn't going to ask Julie to dance just to "rub bellies." The 'Bouncing Billy' Ventures of the world can make my blood boil. What represents mere "belly rubbin' music" to them can be seen as sacred truth to some of us. I'm not pious, but I'm not a blasphemer, either. I can smile at the thought of 'Lonesome Town,' but only because I've learned to respect the reality it expresses.

I watched Julie walk across the hall and looked from side to side and behind me to see if anyone posed a threat to my plan. As far as I could see, the coast was clear, but I wasn't about to take any chances. My heart felt like it was going to burst as I moved closer to the doorway and as Julie made her way across the hall. I positioned myself as closely as I could to the study hall entrance, and she stepped across the threshold just as Ricky Nelson began to sing about his city for broken-hearted lovers. But before his words had a chance to register with either of us, I stepped in front of her and asked her to dance.

"Would you like to dance, Julie?" I asked just as she stepped inside the door.

"What?" she asked in surprise, looking at me but not recognizing either my voice or my presence.

"Would you like to dance?" I asked again as my heart continued to pound in my chest.

"Oh, Dan," she said. "Hi, you startled me. Sure, I'd love to dance."

Acting as calmly as I could, I reached down and took her left hand in my right hand, and led her away from the doorway. Ricky had just begun to sing about the broken hearts in Lonesome Town when we reached the dance floor, and my heart hadn't quieted down at all as I placed my right arm around her waist and felt her left hand reach around my right shoulder. Feeling relieved and encouraged now, I held her right hand in my left hand, but not in the hammer lock position associated with the steady couples. I could feel the closeness of her body as we danced to the haunting strains of Ricky Nelson's lament.

My heart continued to pound in my chest, as well as in my throat, and before I had the chance to say anything, Ricky was singing about learning to forget in Lonesome Town's streets of regret. I knew I had to dance with her again, and I didn't want her to get the impression that I was willing to take her back to the girls' side of the dance hall after just one dance. Besides, I had to ask her now while I had the chance. If I didn't, I'd be in deep trouble. As Ricky concluded his song, I removed my right arm from around her waist, as she took her left arm from around my shoulder, and I let go of her right hand with my left hand. But as my heart pounded even harder, I felt her left hand meet my right hand. I clasped her fingers in mine and asked her if she'd like to dance again. She said she'd love to, and at least now I had some breathing room. Still, my heart continued to pound as I stood on the dance floor holding Julie's hand in mine as Billy Venture sounded off between songs.

"That didn't take long, did it?" I asked, trying to catch my breath.

"What didn't take long?" Julie asked.

"The song, 'Lonesome Town.'"

"Oh, no," she said, smiling, as my eyes caught hers and my heart jumped to my throat. "It's a pretty short song."

"Do you like it?" I asked, trying to control my pounding heart.

"It's sad, but I like Ricky Nelson."

"I do, too. I like him and Buddy Holly best of all, I think."

"I know. I talk to you almost every night on the phone. Remember?"

"That's right," I stammered. "You sure look nice tonight, Julie," I said, changing the subject.

"Thanks, Dan. You look nice, too."

"I like the bow in your hair. I don't think I've seen it before."

"Thank you. I've had it for quite a while. I just don't wear it very often."

"It goes with your hair. And I like the smell of it, too. Did you put perfume on it?" I asked, shuffling my feet.

"No," she laughed. "I try to keep the perfume on my neck, behind my ears."

"Well," I said, managing a smile, "it sure smells good, wherever you wear it. Do you have any plans for after the dance?" I asked before I had a chance to think of what to say next.

"No, not really. I guess I'll go home with the girls after it's over."

My heart, which had since returned to my chest, jumped back to my throat in anticipation of what I had to say next. I had waited for a year, and, remembering Brother Kelley's words about the courage of boys from Butte, I couldn't be afraid. I wanted to understand the nature of life one way or the other, but confronting, without fear, Macbeth's despair over the apparent meaninglessness of life was nothing like this. I tried to swallow my heart as I asked her the question I had dreamed of.

"Would you like to go home with me?" I asked.

"Sure, Dan. I'd love to," she answered as her eyes met mine.

"That'll be nice," I said, without taking my eyes off hers as I felt my heart return to my chest at the same time that Billy Venture announced that The Platters would be next up with 'Harbor Lights.' It made no difference to me that Butte was a land-locked city of gallus frames and slag heaps, and it made no difference that an obnoxious show-off with a contrived nickname was playing the songs. I just thanked 'Bouncing Billy' for deciding "to slow it down one more time."

I had danced slow dances with Julie before, but this time I was going to take her home after the dance. I felt proud of myself for going through with my plan, and I felt secure in the fact that, at least for tonight, someone else would be disappointed at not being able to take Julie home. I had my right arm around her waist and I could feel her left arm around my right shoulder again, but this time I was more relaxed. I was living an enchanted moment that had to signify something, and I didn't do anything to break the magic spell. I just asked Julie the name of her perfume and she answered: "Faberge." I'm not so sure that brand of perfume should be legal. When you're crazy as Jake says I am, it only makes you crazier.

The Platters went on singing about harbor lights, and I held Julie as close as I could, without being too forward, and delighted in the smell of her perfume that seemed to live in the purple bow. We danced by Jake and Lori, but I didn't pay any attention to them, much to Jake's disgust. I could see him groan, but it didn't matter to me. I could have buried myself in Julie's black hair and smelled that purple bow forever. But The Platters stopped singing, and Julie took her arm from around my shoulder. I removed my arm from around her waist and found her left hand with my right hand as the music stopped and the sound of voices returned to the dance hall.

"I'd better go back now, Dan," she said as the boys began to walk the girls back to their side of the dance hall, leaving the steady couples to occupy the floor. When those couples didn't dance, they always found a seat in one of the desks that were pushed against the back wall and clustered underneath the windows facing the Galena Street entrance to Girls' Central. I would have preferred to stay on the dance floor or to sit in one of the desks, but Julie and I were far from being a steady couple.

"Okay," I replied as I held her hand in mine and started walking toward the girls gathered in front, and to the right, of the stage. "But don't forget who's taking you home," I said smiling, as I found her group of girlfriends.

"I won't," she said with a laugh. "I'll save the last dance for you."

With her last comment she had provided me with all the proof I needed to know that she at least listened to the songs. I laughed in response and let go of her hand as she turned to talk to her friends while Billy Venture decided to "speed it up a little now with Joey Dee and The Starlighters and 'Shout.'" I like the twist, but Joey Dee is a far cry from Elvis Presley or Ricky Nelson or Buddy Holly. I knew Jake wouldn't be doing the twist as I walked around the edge of the dance floor looking for him and Lori.

"Why aren't you out there twistin' with Julie?" he asked as I found him safely settled with Lori, sitting in a desk close to the windows that looked toward Galena Street.

"She had to get back to her friends," I answered, sitting sideways in the desk in front of them.

"She must not have had much to say to them," he said, nodding his head in the direction of the dance floor. "She didn't waste any time finding someone else to dance with."

"I don't care," I said, smiling broadly. "I did it. I'm taking her home, and she's saving the last dance for me. There was no 'hesitatin' tonight. You should have been there. I thought I was going to faint. But I asked her, and she said she'd love to go home with me. Then we danced to 'Harbor Lights,' and I could smell her perfume. She wears Faberge'. I swear its fragrance settled in the purple bow pinned to her hair. I'll never forget it as long as I live. If there's no Faberge' in Heaven, I want no part of that celestial city. Jake, I think I've just experienced paradise."

"You're crazy," he groaned.

"I don't think he's so crazy," Lori said. "Are you two coming home with us tonight, Dan?"

"Who else could put up with him?" Jake asked before I had a chance to answer Lori's question. "When you're as crazy as he is, you have to have someone to look after you, and no one looks after him better than I do."

"But why is he so crazy?" Lori asked. "He doesn't look crazy to me."

"He's crazy because he believes in the songs he listens to. He's crazy because he thinks they're real, because he thinks they're the truth. That's what it means to be crazy, and Buddy Holly the second here is the craziest guy I know. Brennan is almost as bad, but at least he's beginning to see the light."

"Maybe you're the one who doesn't see the light, Jake," I said in my own defense. "Maybe you have to be crazy to see the light. Did you ever think of that?"

"What kind of light are you talking about?" he asked.

"I think monuments to eternity have seen the light."

"What's a monument to eternity?" Lori asked.

"Don't ask that question, Lori," Jake groaned. "We'll be here all night. If he starts talking about that subject, he'll forget to take Julie home."

"Nothing will make me forget to take her home. But you should think about light and what it can mean. I think we all should. You should have Brother Kelley. He talks about the Light of the World. When I think about that light and listen to the songs, I can't help thinking that people like Buddy Holly, whether or not they realize it, sing about the same thing Brother Kelley explains in English class."

"Do you really think about those things?" Lori asked as Jake groaned once again.

"Yes. I can't help it sometimes, especially when I dance with Julie."

"Come on, Buddy," Jake said. "You're talking about Julie Shaw and not the Blessed Virgin Mary. Maybe Mary is the Light of the World, but Julie Shaw certainly isn't. If she were, she'd be as true to you as you are to her. You have to leave your dream world of Ricky Nelson and Buddy Holly. Wake up, and join the rest of us in the real world."

"I don't live in a dream world, Jake. I live in this world with its gallus frames and slag heaps. I just listen to the dream world of Ricky Nelson and Buddy Holly. I don't think anyone should consider it a lie just because it's made up. We should listen to it and let the magic work."

"Come on, Lori, let's go dance," Jake said with a groan. "He'll find out tonight what's real and what isn't. We'll go park."

"Jake, you can't go park!" I exclaimed, slamming my fist down on the desk. "You can't do that."

"Do you think your Blessed Virgin Julie never has parked before?"

"That's not the point. I don't care if she's parked before, and I'm sure she has. I'm no idiot. But you don't park with a girl on the first date. You just don't. Okay?" I asked, looking up at him and Lori from my seat in the desk.

"Take it easy. I won't. Don't worry. I'll meet you after the dance."

"We'll have fun, Dan," Lori said with her cheeks blushed. "I'm looking forward to it. And if you don't mind me saying so, I hope Julie realizes how lucky she is," she added as Jake groaned one more time.

"Thanks, Lori. I don't mind you saying that."

"That's enough. I can't take any more. Let's go dance and listen to the dream world," Jake concluded as he led Lori to the dance floor where, as befitting a steady couple, they naturally assumed the hammer lock position.

XXXVI

"*D*id you ask her?" Paul asked as he sat down in the desk vacated by Jake and Lori.

"I sure did."

"Did she say yes?"

"Of course. How could she turn me down?" I asked with a smile on my face. "Lori says that she hopes Julie understands how lucky she is."

"That's the last thing you needed to hear," Paul said, laughing, "but there's probably some truth to it. I'm not so sure that the rest of the guys who chase Julie—excuse me, I know you don't like to be accused of chasing her—really care about her as you do."

"Maybe not. The sight of her is enough to make my heart jump to my throat and pound a thousand times a minute."

"You're calm now."

"I know, but wait until the end of the dance. Wait until I sit in Jake's back seat with her. She'll be able to hear my heart pounding, and I won't be able to do anything about it. Have you experienced such a phenomenon?"

"Not quite to the degree you have. But I'm not as crazy as you are. You're in a class by yourself."

"Maybe so, but I hope Julie's in the same class."

"What if she isn't?"

"I don't know. If she isn't, she isn't, I guess. But I know she at least listens to the songs."

"What do you mean?"

"When I walked her back to her friends after our second dance, I told her not to forget who'd be taking her home, and she said she'd save the last dance for me. She has to listen to the songs to come back with that response."

"Where're you going after the dance?"

"I still don't completely trust Jake. Before he has the chance to entertain any other ideas, I'm going to suggest we go to Pork Chop John's first and then take a ride to the Donnabelle and then back up The Hill to Julie's in Centerville. After that, he can do whatever he wants."

"Do you want to meet somewhere after you take Julie home?"

"I don't think so. Not tonight. I told my mother I'd be home by one-thirty. I think I'll just have Jake take me home."

"Well, I'll be thinking of you sitting in the back seat with Julie. I watched you dance with her. You looked like you were in paradise."

"I felt like it, too," I said as Paul stood up out of his desk.

"I'm going to see if I can get a dance with Patty. I'll see you after the dance. Are you going to wait until the end to dance with Julie again?"

"No. I'll ask her again, but I don't have to worry tonight. I don't care who she dances with because I'll be with her after the dance. Good luck with Patty. I'll see you later."

"Later," he said as he walked toward the girls gathered across the dance floor in front, and to the right, of the stage.

The rest of the dance proved to be anti-climactic. I danced with Julie several more times and watched other guys dance with her as well. Whenever I danced with her, I could smell the Faberge' that seemed to live in the purple bow, and when the Everly Brothers sang 'Devoted to You,' I just wanted to dance with Julie Shaw. I listened to the song to let the magic work and hoped she did the same.

When I didn't dance with her, I sat in an empty desk and thought about my conversations with Jake and Paul. I didn't live in any dream world because I knew better. You can't live in a dream world after you've touched death at the age of five or six. A world that obviously includes death has to suggest that life, the time spent before death, just might be meaningless. In the face of that suggestion I think we need the dream world to show us how to live. Life would be pretty bleak without that world, even if we lived on the West Side. Macbeth realized that discovery, and I can understand the story's truth. I think we're surrounded by actual and potential Macbeths. But it seems to me that if we believe in the dream world, and listen to it carefully, we won't conclude that life is meaningless—unless we, for some reason, reject our belief and choose Macbeth's path.

These thoughts take me back to the Garden of Eden story. If that story isn't historical fact, the nature of life has nothing to do with sin. If the Garden of Eden story isn't historical fact, my dad died simply because death is real and a natural part of life. If life can be so monstrous, I can see why we need the dream world. Without it, the real world of experience would be absolutely brutal and worthless. But if this experiential world reflects natural life just as it's supposed to be, we need the dream world to show us how to live in it. My dad didn't die because Adam and Eve ate a forbidden apple. The Garden of Eden never existed in the first place. But that's okay because it just means that religion properly belongs to the dream world. And once you accept that fact, you can see the crucifix reflected in the songs which then means you can see the Light of the World reflected in them as well. Christ, as the Light of the World, is nailed to the cross, and he certainly lived a sacrificial life in service to the love celebrated in the songs. So, maybe love, and the subsequent service to it, represents the Light of the World.

Jake's right. Julie isn't the Light of the World, but a sacrificial life lived in service to love certainly is. If that's the case, why can't anyone who lives in its service represent the Light of the World? The more people choose to live that service, that obedience, the brighter the light. I don't know, but I actually feel better now that I realize the Garden of Eden story isn't a record of historical fact. I feel free, and I understand the purple bow better now, too. When you know the truth about the Garden of Eden story, you know it's okay to be crazy. In fact, you have to be crazy. You're supposed to be crazy, to prevent life from becoming "a tale told by an idiot full of sound and fury signifying nothing." If Macbeth had listened to, and obeyed, the dream world, he wouldn't have been so attached to the palace.

I have to admit that I feel strange talking like this, but don't you see the difference if the Garden of Eden story isn't a record of historical fact? We can be crazy. We're supposed to be crazy. We have to be crazy to avoid Macbeth's path. Shakespeare didn't want us to walk that path, but he could only illuminate it to help us recognize its dangers. But anyone who stays crazy never will walk that path, and Shakespeare himself was crazy because he didn't believe Macbeth. I know Chaucer was crazy because in 'The Canterbury Tales' he celebrated life just as we experience it. We created baseball just as Chaucer created his pilgrimage which means that baseball celebrates natural life as well. Anyone can be crazy, but not everyone can write like Shakespeare and Chaucer. Brother Kelley's crazy; my mother's crazy; and my dad was crazy. And I suppose I was amongst the craziest when 'Bouncing Billy' Venture announced that it was time for everyone "to find his favorite girl and snuggle up a little bit to The Spaniels and 'Goodnight, Sweetheart.'"

I smiled when I heard Billy's announcement because I knew I didn't have to say goodnight just yet. Not wanting to extend the hours of the dance, I walked to the girls' side of the dance floor and found Julie. I didn't have to ask her to dance this time because she remembered the promise she made after our second dance together.

"I told you I'd save the last dance for you," she said, offering me her left hand as her eyes sparkled behind her long, dark lashes.

"That's right," I said, taking her left hand in my right hand. "And I bet you didn't forget who'd be taking you home, either," I added as my eyes met hers and as my heart jumped to my throat once again.

We both laughed as I walked her out to the dance floor for the last dance. We danced as we had earlier, but this time I knew I didn't have to give her up to anyone else when the song ended. The Spaniels sang of having to go, but it wasn't three o'clock in the morning yet. In fact, it wasn't even one o'clock. The time was only approaching midnight as I put my arm around her waist and felt her arm around my right shoulder once again. I held her close and could feel her body move with mine. We danced by Jake and Lori, but I was too enchanted with Julie and the fragrance of the purple bow to pay much attention to him and his raised eyebrows. With The Spaniels' last goodnight the dance ended, and I stood still on the dance floor for a minute before I finally removed my right arm from around Julie's waist and met her left hand with my right hand as she took her left arm from around my right shoulder. The lights brightened the study hall, and Julie and I followed the rest of the couples as we walked toward the exit near the coat rooms waiting at the head of the Idaho Street stairwell.

"I'll get my jacket, and I'll meet you back here by the banister," I said as we left the dance hall and walked out into the school's main hallway.

"Okay, Dan. I'll find my coat and meet you here as soon as I can."

"Okay," I said, letting go of her hand and watching her walk into the girls' coat room. Finally, I turned and walked across the hall to find my jacket.

"Are you ready?" Paul asked just as I walked through the doorway.

"As ready as I'll ever be," I answered as I searched through a pile of jackets. "As Buddy Holly says, there'll be no 'hesitiatin' tonight."

"I know he says that, but what does he mean?"

"To me it means I'm going to kiss her goodnight if it kills me."

"I wish I could witness this, because knowing you, it probably will," he said, laughing.

"You should talk. You're not exactly the accomplished lover yourself, you know."

"Maybe not, but I don't have your entertainment value. Nobody's as crazy as you are. Remember?"

"I remember," I answered, finding my jacket. "Here we go, and I promise I won't hesitate," I concluded with a smile as I walked toward the doorway.

"See you tomorrow," Paul said as I walked into the hall and saw Julie standing next to the banister at the top of the stairs.

"Hi," I said, walking up to her.

"Hi," she replied, smiling.

"What time do you have to be home?" I asked as I helped her with her coat.

"My mother said that I should be home by one o'clock," she answered, putting her arms through her coat sleeves.

"That'll give us some time to stop at Pork Chop John's and maybe take a ride out to the Donnabelle to see what's going on," I said as we started down the stairs.

"That sounds like fun. Are we going with Jake and Lori?" she asked when we reached the door at the bottom.

"Yes," I answered, pushing the door open and holding it for her. I followed her out the door and held it open for the couple walking behind us. "His car is just around the corner," I added, letting go of the door as a steady stream of couples and singles walked down the stairs. "Shall we go?"

"Sure," she answered, smiling. "I'm ready."

"So am I," I said as we walked together toward Jake's Impala waiting for us around the corner on the Mercury Street side of the school.

"Hi, Dan. Hi, Julie," Lori said as we reached the car.

"Hi," Jake said, standing next to Lori on the driver's side. "Do you want to get in on this side or on the other side, Julie?" he asked.

"Hi, Lori," Julie said. "I'll get in on the passenger side, with Dan," she answered, looking at me.

"Yes, I can handle it, Jake," I said as I felt my heart start to pound again. "How are you, Lori?" I asked, opening the door for Julie.

"Fine, Dan," she answered, sliding onto the front seat just past the steering wheel. "I'm glad you and Julie are coming with us."

"Thanks," I said as I followed Julie into the back seat.

"Are you two in now?" Jake asked, shaking his head as he slid onto the front seat next to Lori.

"I think so," I answered.

"Then why don't you close the back door?" he asked, still shaking his head.

"Sorry about that, Jake. I guess I forgot," I answered, pulling the door shut. "How's that?"

"Just perfect. Where would you like to go?" he asked, turning around and smiling at me.

"Julie has to be home at one, and I thought we could go to Pork Chop John's first and then drive down to the Donnabelle to see what's going on and then we could head up The Hill to take her home."

"Sounds like a fool-proof plan to me," Jake said with a laugh. "I could use a pork chop," he added as he backed the Impala out of the parking space and headed it east across Mercury Street toward Pork Chop John's.

XXXVII

❧

I sat in the back seat, resting my hands on my knees, as Jake drove across Mercury. Lori sat snuggled close to him in the front seat, but he never drove with his arm around her. Instead, he kept both hands on the steering wheel, as if he didn't notice her presence, and drove the car as would someone completely in control of the situation. Julie sat comfortably next to me, but no one would mistake us for a steady couple. At least she didn't slide all the way across the seat to sit next to the door on the other side. I enjoyed the comfort of knowing that, if nothing else, she created the impression that she honestly wanted to go home with me. My heart pounded, as I knew it would, when Jake stopped for the red light at the corner of Mercury and Montana Street. He turned to look into the back seat and shook his head as I sat there, with my hands on my knees, taking in the fragrance of Julie's perfume and basking in the glow of the purple bow neatly pinned to her hair just above her right temple.

"Are you alive back there, Buddy?" he asked as the light turned green, allowing him to drive through the intersection.

"What?" I asked in return.

"I asked if you were alive back there. You look like you're in a trance or something."

"I'm alive, Jake. Just keep your eyes on the road so we can keep it that way. Lori, take care of the guy driving the car, will you?"

"I will, Dan," she answered with a laugh as she moved a little closer to Jake.

"What are you trying to do? Push me out the door?"

"Take it easy, Jake," I said. "Just keep your mind on your driving and on Lori."

"Why did you call Dan, Buddy, Jake?" Julie asked as I saw Pork Chop John's identifying sign come into view on the right hand side of the street.

"Because Buddy Holly's his hero. Didn't you know that?"

"I think I knew it. He talks about him when he calls me, but I've never heard anyone refer to Dan as Buddy."

"Only Jake does. But there was only one Buddy Holly, and his songs will never die."

"Why not?" Julie asked as Jake pulled into a parking space about one half block west of Pork Chop John's.

"Because he sings the truth," Jake answered, stopping the car. "We all know that."

"Jake's right," I said, "even if he doesn't believe what he says. Buddy Holly sings the truth and the truth never dies."

"The truth is," Jake said, "we've arrived at Pork Chop John's. Who's going to get the sandwiches?"

"I will," I answered. "Does everyone want a pork chop and a coke?"

"That's fine with me," Lori answered.

"Me, too," Julie said.

"That's okay," Jake said. "But leave out the onions this time," he added with a grin.

"Anyone want onions?" I asked, opening the door and staring at Jake.

"Not for me, Dan," Lori answered.

"Me either, Dan," Julie said.

"Okay. Four pork chops and four cokes comin' up," I said as I stepped out of the car, shut the back door, and walked in the spring moonlight toward Pork Chop John's.

My watch read 12:10 when I got out of the car, and people—young and old alike—were crowded onto Mercury Street in front of the Uptown landmark. But I caught the smell of the pork chops sizzling in the deep fat fryers before I noticed any gathering crowd. As I followed its allure east on Mercury, I remembered the smell of Uncle Tim's coffee at Naranche Stadium almost nine years ago. I remember the smile that crossed his face when his friend passed him the brandy, and I must have worn a similar smile as I walked across Mercury Street. Enchanted moments make you smile.

I could tell the Friday fast had ended because no crowd had gathered in front of John's earlier in the evening when Jake and I drove up The Hill on our way to the dance. Among other things, Butte is a city of food with a significant portion of its identity tied up in its supper clubs, restaurants and drive-ins, but Pork Chop John's remains in a class by itself—especially after midnight on a Saturday morning following the conclusion of the Friday fast. People crowded in front of John's sliding window at least five deep and had spilled out onto the sidewalk when I reached the doorway and shouted my order over the heads of the assembled multitudes. The people waiting in line for their pork chops didn't stand as solemnly as did those who stood in line to receive the Blessed Sacrament, but I'm convinced that the pork chop—as a sacred object in its own right—is every bit as blessed and sacramental as the consecrated Host.

My order came up, and I responded to the requests of the cook and reached for the pork chops and cokes as she passed them back to me over the heads of the believers standing in front. The line had grown since we pulled up, and I couldn't help thinking that George wouldn't have any trouble living on the West Side if he owned Pork Chop John's. I smiled at that thought as I carried our order back to Jake's Impala.

"Did you have to fight your way through the crowd?" Jake asked as I opened the back door and sat down next to Julie.

"I like that crowd. I could stand out there and watch and smell the pork chops forever. Couldn't you, Julie?"

"I don't know, Dan. I guess I've never thought about it before."

"That's okay, Julie. Not many other people have, either," Jake said as I passed the pork chops around.

"I have to admit they smell pretty good," Lori said as she accepted her sandwich. "I've just never paid too much attention to them."

"Don't tell me you're going crazy, too," Jake groaned as he took a bite of his sandwich. "It's just a sandwich that smells good and tastes good. What else is there to say?"

"Jake," I said, "you're impossible. Let's drive down The Hill to the Donnabelle to see what's going on. Okay?"

"It's okay with me if we don't mind eating our pork chops as we go."

"I'm fine," Lori said.

Me, too," Julie added.

"Okay," Jake said. "Lori, open the glove compartment and set the cokes on the door."

"We're all set," she said, complying with Jake's direction.

"I'll even turn on some music for you," he said as he pulled the Impala onto Mercury Street and drove toward Arizona where he would turn right and head down The Hill to Front Street and then to Harrison Avenue that stretched out onto The Flat and toward the Donnabelle Drive-in.

I felt calmer now as we drove down The Hill with the gallus frame lights receding behind us. Heading south, I couldn't see the empty darkness of the Pit. Jake and Lori didn't pay much attention to Julie and me in the back seat, and none of us had much time to talk as we ate our pork chops and sipped our cokes. Besides, as long as the pork chop and the coke kept me occupied, I didn't have to think of what to do with my arms and hands. I was thankful for the food and drink as we headed south to Utah where Arizona Street veered off to the left. We bounced softly over the railroad tracks that served the Utah Street warehouses, blessed ourselves as we passed St. Joe's, and continued down The Hill until we stopped for the red light at the intersection of Utah and Front Street.

"Enjoying the music and the pork chops back there?" Jake asked, breaking the silence and glancing into the rear view mirror.

"Yes," I answered. "I appreciate your concern."

"I thought I'd check as long as I had the chance. I want my passengers to enjoy themselves."

"Don't worry about us, Jake. Just drive the car and pay attention to Lori."

"Thanks, Dan," Lori said, snuggling up to Jake. "Thanks for reminding him."

"He didn't have to remind me. I didn't forget," Jake said as the light turned green, allowing him to turn left onto Front Street and head toward Harrison Avenue.

I finished my pork chop as Jake drove under the Northern Pacific Railroad viaduct onto Harrison and The Flat that now unfolded before us. Holding my coke in my right hand, I quietly reveled in the enchanted dream world of Julie Shaw and the purple bow, reinforced by musical groups such as The Shirelles, The Crests and The Teddy Bears and their renditions of songs like 'Soldier Boy,' 'Sixteen Candles,' and 'To Know Him is to Love Him.' The melodies of love lived in Jake's Impala, thanks to the magic of KXLF radio that played the current, and past, rock n' roll hits. As we continued south on Harrison, we drove past the ten-year-old Civic Center and near-by Silver Bow Creek with its copper-colored water and reinforced, concrete banks built by the WPA during the depression. We drove by pre-World War II apartment buildings—known as flats in Butte—where newlyweds of my mother and dad's generation began their married life, and past Safeway supermarkets that are making the neighborhood grocery stores, and delivery boys, obsolete. Continuing south on Harrison, we passed the fledgling Dairy Queen—featuring its soft ice cream—whose lines sometimes surpass those identified with Pork Chop John's, and drove by expansive used car lots encircling new car dealerships recently relocated from Uptown. Then, nearing the end of our southward journey, we drove past legendary night spots and supper clubs—like the White Swan, the Nite Owl, and the Red Rooster—that help celebrate Butte's just as legendary hospitality and vitality. Finally, and with little fanfare, we arrived at the Donnabelle. The drive-in stood as a symbol of freedom and mobility made possible by the automobile that replaced the street car, the defining image of Butte's storied past as related by my mother and Uncle Tim.

If you pay attention and stop to think about what you observe, driving down Harrison Avenue provides anyone with a journey through the passage of time. Butte's "Miracle Mile" reflects both the old and the new, and Mining City residents always talk of the city itself expanding and even moving off The Hill and onto The Flat to make way for the Berkeley Pit. It seems nothing can stop the Pit, and if it succeeds in eating Uptown Butte, the city will be forced to move south. And if such a move occurs, nothing that supported life on The Hill will remain to do the same on The Flat. No wonder Brother Kelley's worried, and no wonder he encourages us to think. Then if you respond to his encouragement and especially think about the dream world of religion and baseball—reinforced and supported by the songs of The Shirelles, The Crests, The Teddy Bears and of Elvis

Presley, Ricky Nelson, and Buddy Holly—you discover that its essence never changes. That dream world sings the same, constant song no matter how much time goes by. And as long as we have to live in a world with time, I'm going to listen to the dream world, regardless of any opposition I may encounter. Even Pork Chop John's can burn down, but the dream world is indestructible. It houses monuments to eternity, like gallus frames and the crucifix, that celebrate the mystery of love and our capacity to live in service to it. I don't think we can live without the dream world and its promise.

Once we pulled into the Donnabelle, I could feel my heart begin to pound. I knew we would have to turn around and start our return journey up The Hill to Centerville and Julie's house. I also remembered that I told Paul I was going to kiss Julie goodnight if it killed me. I had to start thinking about taking her home now that we had reached our southern destination. All of us had finished our pork chops and cokes by now, and someone had to throw the wrappers and empty cups in the garbage can before we started back up The Hill. I had to find a way to position my left arm around Julie for the trip, and I realized that if I got out of the car to dump the pork chop wrappers and empty coke cups in the garbage can, I would have my chance. When I returned to the car, I could slide my left arm along the back of the seat and then around Julie's shoulders, instead of placing it on my left leg as I did when we left Central and started our journey down The Hill to the Donnabelle. Someone had to get rid of the garbage, and I didn't hesitate to volunteer.

"Are we all done with our cokes?" I asked as we sat in the Donnabelle's parking area with the Impala pointed east toward Harrison Avenue.

"I think so," Lori answered as she applied some soft, red lipstick to her lips, fluffed her auburn-colored, Doris Day bangs, and smiled with her sparkling hazel eyes.

"I'm through," Jake said. "What's the big deal?"

"I just thought I'd throw the cups and the pork chop wrappers in the garbage can," I answered.

"I should have known," Jake groaned, recognizing my motivation and handing me his and Lori's garbage.

"Are you through, Julie?" I asked, moving to open the back door.

"Yes, Dan. I'm through," she answered, handing me her empty cup with the pork chop wrapper stuffed inside.

"Thanks. I'll just dump these in the garbage can and be right back," I said, opening the back door and stepping outside. "Don't go away," I added before I closed the door.

"Come on, Buddy, just dump the garbage and get back in the car," Jake complained as I closed the back door.

I walked over to the garbage can, knowing all the time that I couldn't hesitate once I disposed of the garbage. Still, I had to act as naturally as possible. I dumped the cups and the wrappers in the garbage and walked back to the car. I could see Jake watching me as I walked around the front of the Impala to the back seat. I opened the door, stepped inside, slid my left arm along the top of the seat and sat down next to Julie. I was ready, now, for the trip up The Hill toward the beckoning gallus frame lights and Julie's house in Centerville—below the Walkerville crest and just west of North Main Street and the Mountain Con mine.

"Are you ready now, Buddy?" Jake asked as I settled into the back seat.

"I'm ready," I answered as my heart pounded in my throat as well as in my chest. "Are you ready, Julie?"

"Yes, Dan. We'd better head up The Hill. I don't want to be late."

"Okay," I said. "We'd better go, Jake. Julie has to be home by one o'clock."

"Well, let's not be 'hesitatin,'" he said, smiling, as he put the Impala in gear, turned left onto Harrison Avenue, and headed north toward The Hill.

If you study The Hill driving north on Harrison, you can recognize the battle between the forces of light and darkness, and from the looks of things, the force of light is losing. The Pit has been operating for seven years now, and it just keeps growing as it eats into the gallus frames' territory. Now I understand the importance of the dream world. No open pit mine can swallow up that light. Maybe the lights of The Hill will be extinguished someday and maybe no one can prevent it. But if we can explore the past in the "ugliest city in the continental United States," as Brother Kelley says, we can discover the permanent Light of the World that always has burned brightly within the boundaries of "The Richest Hill on Earth." With that discovery we can learn that the light can shine anywhere, thereby spreading the riches, which means that life doesn't have to be a "tale told by an idiot full of sound and fury signifying nothing," even if the space explorers don't find any next world in their travels. I think monuments to eternity populate our world right here and now, only we don't realize it because we've never had to look. I know I'm just 17, but I can study The Hill and know it's time to start.

I know something else for sure. The Crests' 16 candles might make a lovely light, but it's not as bright as that which filled the Impala's back seat as Jake guided it up The Hill. Whenever I looked into Julie's eyes, I could see the light that the Pit and its darkness never could threaten. The light of her eyes set my heart in motion, and as we climbed The Hill and closed in on the Mountain Con gallus frame that identified Centerville, I could feel it jump to my throat. We stopped for the red light at the intersection of Granite Street and North Main, just two blocks north of the center of Uptown Butte at the corner of Park and Main, and by this time I had managed to move my left arm off the back of the seat so that my left hand rested gently on Julie's left shoulder. Jake glanced into the rear view mirror and groaned as he saw me tighten my arm around Julie while she responded by inching closer to me. The light turned green, and he turned right up North Main toward the Mountain Con and Centerville.

North Main is a steep grade, but Jake's Impala moved easily up The Hill past the Federal Building and St. Mary's Church. With my right hand I reached for Julie's that was resting on her right knee, and we didn't say anything to each other while I held her hand in mine. She laid her head on my left shoulder as Jake coaxed the Impala further up The Hill past the Steward mine and finally past the Mountain Con's black, iron gallus frame toward Center Street where he turned left and searched for Missoula Avenue. The Impala seemed out of place amidst the natural, steep hills and clustered frame houses of Centerville with their black or dull orange or murky yellow slag heaps serving as playgrounds and even, in some cases, as front yards. It belonged to the wide streets and right-angled intersections of The Flat. I was holding Julie's right hand in mine and had my left arm secured around her shoulders, while she rested her head gently on my left shoulder, when Jake finally maneuvered the Impala through the bumps and narrow turns of Missoula Avenue and announced that we had arrived at Julie's house.

I looked up and noticed that he had managed to stop the car in a perfect spot. I couldn't hide on Julie's front porch or in the shadow of the back door. But I was going to kiss her goodnight, and I didn't care who'd be watching or what anyone would say.

"I guess you're right, Jake," I said as I let go of Julie's right hand and reached for the back door handle.

"Thank you for the ride, Jake," Julie said as I opened the back door. "I had a nice time. Goodnight, Lori. I'll see you in school Monday."

"Goodnight, Julie. I'm glad you could come with us. I had a nice time, too."

"Goodnight, Jake," Julie said as I stepped out of the car and helped her out of the back seat.

"Goodnight, Julie. I'll see you again sometime. Take care of Buddy."

"Real funny, Jake," I said, catching the smile that crossed his face. "I'll be back in a minute," I added, closing the back door.

I held Julie's left hand in my right hand and walked around the back of the car, through the gate and along the sidewalk leading to her back door. I knew Jake was watching every move I made and my heart had jumped to my throat once again. But I knew there was no room for "hesitatin'" tonight. I held Julie's hand as we reached the steps attached to her back door. She stopped, turned and looked directly at me with eyes brighter than any light from any 16 candles anywhere.

"Thanks for taking me home, Dan," she said. "I had a wonderful time. That was the best pork chop sandwich I've ever had, but most of all I enjoyed being with you."

"You're welcome, Julie. I had a great time, too," I said, shuffling my feet and reaching for her other hand.

"Maybe we can do this again sometime," she said.

"I'd like that," I said, moving a couple of steps closer to her.

"Be sure to keep calling on the phone because I like talking to you better than I do anyone else. You always make me laugh."

"Don't worry. I'll keep calling," I said as I placed my left hand on her waist.

"Well, I'd better go in now, but before I do, I'd like to give you something."

Then she reached up with both hands, unfastened the bobby pin holding the purple bow in her hair and handed it to me as my heart pounded in my throat. I accepted the bow and carefully placed it in my left shirt pocket. I moved closer to her and put my arms around her waist as she put her arms around my neck. Our eyes met, and she smiled as she looked up at me. My heart still pounded in my throat, and I could feel the closeness of her body as our arms tightened around each other. She tilted her head back. I moved forward, kissed her and felt her hand resting on the back of my neck. I would have held her and kissed her forever, but she had to be in by one o'clock.

"Goodnight, Julie," I said finally, looking into her eyes.

"Goodnight, Dan," she replied, taking her arms from around my neck. "Be sure to call," she added as she turned, slipped out of my arms, walked up the back door steps and disappeared into the house.

I stood at the bottom step for a minute and then turned and walked as tall and as proud as I could back down the sidewalk and through the gate toward Jake's Impala still idling in front of Julie's house. I walked around the front of the car this time, stopping to smile at Jake as I walked past the windshield. Then I walked around the passenger side to the back seat, opened the door, sat down calmly and closed the door. As I caught the fragrance of the purple bow, now resting securely in my left shirt pocket, I placed my hands comfortably on my knees and announced: "Take me home, Jake."

Jake groaned once again, put the Impala in gear and headed toward North Main Street where he would turn right and head south down The Hill toward The Flat.

The End